P9-CMP-691

THE PREVALENCE OF WITCHES

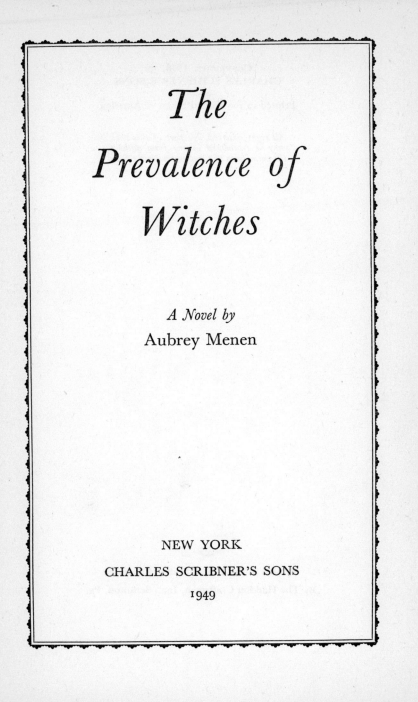

The
Prevalence of
Witches

A Novel by
Aubrey Menen

NEW YORK

CHARLES SCRIBNER'S SONS

1949

Copyright, 1948, by
CHARLES SCRIBNER'S SONS

Printed in the United States of America

*All rights reserved. No part of this book
may be reproduced in any form without
the permission of Charles Scribner's Sons*

 1

Printed in the United States of America
By The Haddon Craftsmen, Inc., Scranton, Pa.

For

PHILIP DALLAS

THE PREVALENCE OF WITCHES

CHAPTER ONE

I HAD come to Limbo because I had always wanted to possess a country of my own. I did not want a large country that would be bound to get me into trouble with other large countries, but one quite small, and preferably round. There was a time when I almost entered the Church in order to become a bishop and have a cathedral of my own: or, to be precise, not so much a cathedral as a cathedral close. The word 'close' gets my meaning very well. Someone whom I met in another part of India, not very far from Limbo, once told me that he often wished he had the courage to pitch a tent in the corner of his room and retire into it when he grew cross with the world. For me, a tent would be rather too small: the Federated States of Limbo were rather too big. They were six hundred and fifty miles of clumsy hills and jungle: not tangled jungle but the sort where the trees grow straight and the only confusion comes from clumps of bamboos that spread out at the top like shaving brushes. But I thought it would do. On the map it was as beautifully round as it was blank. For a thousand years the inhabitants had shot at everybody who came into it with arrows and their aim was usually adequate to their purpose of keeping people out; where the bowmen failed to get home, the mosquitos did not. Once a year one Englishman visits Limbo, surrounded by clouds of insecticide through which can just be discovered the Union Jack. During this visit, Limbo is a part of the British Empire in India. When the Englishman has gone, the various Chiefs of Limbo, sighing with relief, take off their trousers and go hunting again with their bows and arrows, the mosquitos come cautiously out to bury their dead, and Limbo is safe for odd persons like me who are determined to live in a country of our own, even if it kills us.

When I first arrived at the central village I could tell by the smell of insecticide and the flag that had been run up on a rather bent flagstaff that the English King of the place had got there before us. His friends called him Catullus: the name had nothing to do with the Roman poet; it simply fitted Catullus' Roman face. I do not suppose that any Roman ever looked like those busts which they have left behind them, with the smooth segments of eggs instead of eyes, but Catullus did, most especially when he was doing his Civil Service job of being an itinerant King of the Federated States. When he was being your friend, it was different. The stone face remained, very obvious and bold about the nose and lips, but the expression changed. It was as though a schoolboy had reached up and drawn two mischievous eyes on the blank egg-segments, and had been caught just before he could draw in the saucy moustaches that obviously went with them. When he was being your friend you could not understand how he could bear to be an official king.

Catullus loved a good hard talk as other people loved a strenuous game of tennis. He was a bad talker if the conversation became anything but a sport. He talked very rapidly, and he himself delighted in telling you how he had begun to do this. When he was five years old (he would say) he suddenly began talking with the persistence of a character in a play by Bernard Shaw, only very much quicker. He gabbled about his parents' house from the time he got up to the time when his distracted listeners finally put him to bed. The doctors said it would stop, but it did not. They taught him to read in the hope that books would provide them with intervals of silence. He took to reading with glee, reading aloud the passages that annoyed or amused him and launching into a one-sided conversation with imaginary authors. They took him to the Opera in the hope that he would develop a taste for music. He was entranced, but only by the long recitations that he found in Wagner. He altered his technique so that by the age of seven he not only was never silent, but now he sang, in a falsetto voice, the monologues that he previously spoke. Frantic, his parents hit upon the device of engaging one of those tutors who undertake to remove impediments of the speech. This man set him at reading aloud long passages from Buckle's *History of Civilization*, not to improve his diction, but in the hope that he would discover the glimmerings of a hesitation in the boy's speech which he could encourage. But in vain. Catullus talked his way through school and through Oxford, where his conversation gave rise to a sort of Trappist dining club. Undergraduates of his own generation would invite Catullus to a sherry party, and when he had gone, steal off in a body to an obscure eating-house and dine, lengthily and well, in a ritual silence. Any diner who broke it, even to speak to the waiter, was penalized by having to pay for the next sherry party and, moreover, was excluded from the blessed relief of the subsequent dinner. It was inevitable that with so much practice he should become a good talker, when among the more taciturn generation that followed the Great War he found people willing to listen to him; with that, he expanded, and became brilliant. But even at the age of fifty, as he was now, his conversation, though of surpassing interest, was still dictated, as it were, to an invisible stenographer who had set herself to break the world's record in her profession.

"I *hated* ceremonial at first," he said as we sat on his veranda. "But Bay you know Bay you must know Bay you must meet him he's coming here I believe at least I invited him in a letter and he wrote back at first saying that he was in no mood to consider it because the only pig in England who could both spell words of four letters and walk on a tight rope simultaneously had died and he was disconsolate that's Bay he made the greatest friend of life of a don whom he found sitting under a table reading one of his books on those grounds alone because he sat under a table reading a book and Bay could ask him to parties and say casually I read such a good book yesterday Charles I would like your opinion on it I've left it underneath the table in the hope that you'd run through it while you're here Bay put me on the right lines about ceremonial."

One listened to Catullus with both hands full of commas and full-stops, and one scattered them into the flood as it poured over you. I shall do that here, with the warning that the punctuation is all mine.

"Bay was the first man to point out that 'God Save the King' was a good tune provided it was sung rather slowly, like German lieder. His theory was that it had been deliberately ruined as a part of the anti-monarchical feeling against the Hanoverians. When Queen Victoria came to the throne what had been a political demonstration became the accepted method of singing the anthem because she had no ear for anything but Moody and Sankey hymn tunes. After that, whenever a band strikes up 'God Save the King' and I have to stand at the salute as the Crown Representative, I hum, quietly and to myself, variations in the manner of the masters. It gets me through the rest of the ceremony, and once, when the recent war had just begun, it helped my career in the Civil Service. It was a particularly dreary ceremony and the band was very bad. Fortunately I had hit upon a magnificent orchestration, done in a bold, block-like way that owed a good deal to Sibelius. Towards the end I brought up the clarinets really well, and I was so pleased I stopped humming and positively sang. Of course I was embarrassed, but not for long. The entire audience, including a Ruling Prince who was anxious to be made an honorary Lieutenant-Colonel, took my singing as an outbreak of patriotic fervour, and sang the whole anthem through at the tops of their voices. The Resident, who was presiding, was so moved he recommended me for a decoration. Have a benzedrine."

I started up in a guilty fashion.

"But Catullus, I wasn't asleep."

"No, but you will be at the Durbar, and if you fall asleep the Chiefs will be offended. And you mustn't think because you are in the middle of the jungle you can turn up in any old clothes. You must dress formally. What are you going to wear?" he asked turning to me. "I am mentioning you in my speech as our new Officer of Education. You must put up a show. I suggest bathing drawers, as a gesture to the local costume, an M.A.'s hood and gown to symbolize education, and two retainers following behind, one bearing crossed birchrods to symbolize Discipline, the other a pile of leather-bound presentation sets of the works of Oliver Wendell Holmes to symbolize the Rewards of Scholarship."

It was time to go if I was to get to the Durbar. I said goodbye and walked the quarter-mile back to my own bungalow. I discovered that the jungle has its own manners. The road down which I walked was visible to Catullus along its entire length. One said goodbye and turned on one's heel abruptly as though one had quarrelled, and so did one's host, busying himself about artificial business so as not to make it necessary to turn round and smile continuously as one walked down the long road. When I got to my own house I heard Catullus' voice drifting down the wind in a long-drawn, jungle hail, such as the aboriginals use to keep in touch when they are hunting. "Don't for-get the benz-ed-rine!"

The Durbar Hall had been built overnight of bamboo and matting. The aboriginals squatted, a thousand of them, all around it and on half of the floor inside. In front of them was a raised platform made up of tables. On that was yet another table and a swivel chair such as is used at office desks. To bring a touch of state to this chair somebody had thrown across it a tablecloth of Victorian red plush, with rows of small pendulous balls around its edges. The occupant of the throne had been provided with two bottles of ink, one red and one black, both as they came from the makers and still with their labels, a gavel in the shape of an iron-headed jackhammer, a rocker such as is used for blotting signatures, and an empty gin bottle with water and no glass. From end to end of the bamboo hut hung paper chains of various colors, diversified with the small silver bells that are hung on Christmas trees. At one end of the hall these paper chains ended in a bunch around a poster that must have been put up during the war which had been finished a year and a half before. It showed a British soldier facing up to an enormous and shadowy German, with the legend "It won't be long now." At the other end the streamers made loyal loops around full-length portraits of the King and Queen, flanking a colored center-piece of Prince Albert and Queen Victoria boating on the Lake of Windsor, the small craft filled to the point of danger with young Princes and Princesses of the Blood, the whole illustrating the legend underneath "A Happy Family." Underneath this and behind the throne was a row of seats for officials, each bearing a neatly printed label of the names of officials who had held office five years ago.

I was conducted to my seat by a servant dressed in white and scarlet. He saluted and showed me a chair marked *Miss Thelma Macey* on which I sat. I turned to the man sitting next to me and said, "I hope Miss Thelma Macey will not turn up at the last moment." He turned a pale grey face to me glittering with a pair of rather skittish American spectacles.

"You're the new Education Officer."

"Yes. You must be the American missionary." I had heard that there was one, from Virginia, and this man's accent fitted.

"I am."

"I was saying, I hope Miss Thelma Macey does not turn up now."

"I agree with you," he said. "She has been dead ten years."

"Oh! I'm sorry," I said rather foolishly.

"Not that there aren't quite a few people out there who wouldn't be in the least surprised if she *did* come back," said the missionary, nodding his head at the squatting Limbodians. "Dead witches do."

"Was Miss Macey a witch?"

"She *said* she was."

"Really? Tell me, Mr. . . . er . . . "

"Small is the name," he said, shaking hands with me. It was a diffident handshake, part of his whole nervous manner. But his expression was pleasant; he seemed willing to be friendly but almost certain that nobody would like him.

"Have you seen a witch yet?" he asked me.

"No. I should like to."

"Don't do anything in a hurry about witches. Things go wrong. Things get back at you."

"You take witches very seriously, Mr. Small?"

"One does, in Limbo. Limbo's witch-country."

"How can I see one?"

"Just ask. Say to any village headman 'I want to see a witch.' But be careful to add 'any time at your convenience.' The Limbodians are polite people and if they think you're in a hurry they'll just put up any old witch so as not to disappoint you. Maybe just a witch-trainee."

"So they train them?"

"There's a regular five-year course, with examinations every so often. For the final examination she has to kill a member of her own family by saying spells."

"Who holds the examination?"

"A sort of board of other witches."

"At midnight, I suppose, on a bare mountain?" I said.

"Dear me, no. In broad daylight. Everybody knows who's a witch and who isn't. The thing is to discover *which* witch is doing them dirt. That is done by the witch-doctor."

"How very interesting. Can I also see a witch-doctor?"

"Why, surely," said the Reverend Small obligingly, "there's one standing over there." He pointed to a Limbodian who was leaning against one of the small tree-trunks that held up the roof of the Durbar Hall. He was well over five feet, tall for an aboriginal, and he wore no clothes save a turban and a bag in his crotch. He was an old man: just now he had his chin sunk on his bare chest and he seemed to be watching his belly with interest. As he breathed in, it grew round and smooth, and became an even, polished dark brown. As he breathed out it collapsed suddenly into a network of grey wrinkles.

"He's down here at the central village on a professional visit. There's been sickness and witch-trouble and he's here to pick out the witch."

"When he does I shall ask to see her."

"Yes, but do be careful. Well, of course, you being an official of the Administration you will naturally be careful, but when I did it I was only a silly missionary, and I caused a lot of trouble."

"I should very much like to hear about it."

"Would you?" said Small gratefully. "Well, it was this way. I asked the headman to bring me a witch and he said, 'Yes; when?' So me being fresh out from home I said 'Right now.' And about ten hours later they brought one."

"Very prompt," I said.

"Well," said Small, "the word 'now' in Limbo is a pretty large word. When one Limbodian says to another he wants a thing done 'now,' he means he wants it done while the thing is still in his mind. What he's really saying is 'Do it before I get drunk and forget all about it.' It's quite a good measure of time, really, since every Limbodian gets drunk every evening. So they brought me a witch just about sundown, which they took to be just before my heavy drinking time."

The witch had done her best, Small explained, but they hadn't been able to get hold of a fully trained one,

not at that short notice. She had said some spells for blast-
ing crops, and then some more that they use when digging
up dead bodies. She was rather shy about saying the dig-
ing-dead-body spell, but the headman insisted on it. Small
had said that he didn't want to embarrass the woman and
she need not say anything she would rather not.

"But the headman wouldn't hear of it," said Small. "He
pointed out that as a missionary I had certain spells which
I always said when burying people. He thought that no
doubt they were very good spells so far as they went, but
since I had the chance I may as well complete my training
and learn the spells for digging them up again. So he
made her say them, which she did in a sing-song voice.
That got us on to the topic of killing people, and the
headman told the witch to show me how she did that.
Well, this led to quite a little scene, because she said she
didn't know the spell, and the headman said she did, and
she said if she did she wouldn't say it. Then the headman got really annoyed and said that she was letting down
the village and if he'd have known she was going to behave
so badly he'd never have brought her to see the missionary.
She said she was right down sorry to be rude but it was a
professional secret; so there it was. The headman told her
not to be a silly woman and that missionaries were as much
in the business as she was, if not more so since I'd probably been longer at it. He was an obstinate man when he
was crossed. She saw his point after a while and agreed to
say the killer-spell if he, as a layman, would cover up his
ears. Well, he did, and she reeled off a lot of names and
then gave a happy little chuckle. That was the end of the
performance and they both went home."

That night it had been very hot and Small had been
struggling with the bad dreams that always come when
you first sleep inside a mosquito-net. One of them was
filled with horrible shrieks and cries of pain, coming from
nowhere. Small woke up sweating, still hearing the shrieks.
Then he was out of bed and scrambling into his clothes

because he had realized the shrieks were real ones, and coming from the village. When he got there he found the witch hanging by her heels from a tree branch and two villagers beating her with bamboo sticks.

"You can imagine how I felt," said Small. "Here was I getting a poor woman a beating just because of my curiosity. I was entirely in the wrong, so of course, being human, I made out it was everybody else's fault. They told me that the headman had gone down with some sickness as soon as he left me, but I said that was no excuse for beating a poor old woman. So I told them to take her down. They said they wouldn't, because she was a wicked witch. I went up to her, and upside down as she was, I asked her, 'Are you a witch?' She was crying, and do you know, just to show you how heartless one can be—at least I can—all I could think about was how funny it was to see her crying upside down with the tears running into her hair. I said 'Look, are you a witch?' She said 'No.' I asked her three times, to make it sound ritualistic and each time she said 'No.' I made them cut her down, and I took her home and made some tea. She drank it out of the saucer and asked for more."

What with the heat, his bad dreams and the worse things he saw on waking, Small was in low spirits. He kept on apologizing to the woman for getting her into trouble. She neither blamed him nor consoled him but merely went on drinking tea out of her saucer. In the end Small was so contrite that he offered her houseroom so that she could live in safety from the villagers. She stopped her tea-drinking long enough to say that it was a good idea. Small told her that the very next day he would call the villagers together and speak sternly to them. He would tell them that all the spells that she had told him were just a lot of childish nonsense.

"They know that already," she told him.

Small asked her what she meant.

"They know it's nonsense because they fixed it all up themselves. They couldn't get a witch, not a real one. The only real witch they could get is Gangabai, who has been dead two years, and she only comes back in wet weather. So they asked me, seeing that I was a friend of Gangabai's when we were girls. I didn't know any spells, but they didn't want me to disappoint you. So I made them up. It was all nonsense."

Small was relieved and delighted, and his heart warmed towards the unfortunate woman. He said that it was most unfair for the villagers to make her pretend to be a witch and then beat her as though she were a real one.

She thought that it *was* most unfair.

Small said that if he ever heard any man in the village accuse her of witchcraft, why, missionary or not, he'd give him a beating just to see how he liked it.

She thought that it would be a good lesson to them if he did.

Small by this time thought she was one of the most friendly souls he had ever met, and he found it so easy talking to her that he was even telling her about Christianity. "A thing," added Small to me in extenuation, "I hardly ever talk about in private conversation." She still remained agreeable. Small told her that he thought she had a Christian soul, particularly since she had seen that witchcraft was all nonsense. She crowned his happiness by raising no objection when Small suggested she should become a convert.

"It was my first job as a missionary and I was very moved," said Small to me. "She was not only the first heathen I had convinced of Christianity, but I really think she was the first person I had ever convinced of anything in my life. I never was a very persuasive man. I felt I had to do something to mark the occasion. I might have gone down on my knees and prayed, of course, but it might have looked a bit vainglorious, and in any case I was shy.

So I made some more tea. I think it was a good choice. Praying would have been a bit one-sided anyway, and tea sort of brought her into the celebration."

He had poured out two cups, then, remembering his manners, poured the tea into the saucers. They sat sipping for a while, until Small thought of the sick head-man who was the cause of the beating. Small said that first thing in the morning he would go down and see him. Perhaps he could give him something to make him better.

"Oh, don't worry about that fool," said the woman. "He'll be all right by tomorrow evening."

Small asked how she could be so sure.

"It was one of Gangabai's curses that I used," she said simply. "One I remembered her telling me. She said they always got better by next evening."

Small put down his saucer very carefully, without spilling a drop, he remembers, and waited for the woman to go on.

"Yes," she said, "after all I was doing my best. Then that big good-for-nothing headman started insulting me and making me look silly in front of you, thinking he could talk to me as he pleased because I wasn't a witch, so I thought I would teach him a lesson, just like you said all of them ought to be taught a lesson to treat one with respect. So I tried hard to remember what Gangabai had told me, and all of a sudden I remembered that spell. It isn't a very bad one but," she said, screwing up her face with glee at the thought, "Ooooo! What a horrible belly-ache I gave him!"

He looked thoughtfully round the Durbar Hall and then again at me.

"I've never made another convert," he said. "I don't really think I've got the courage. So you have to be careful." He glanced toward the door. "Anyway, I think it's almost time for the ceremony to begin and it's certainly time I stopped chattering. But you know you shouldn't listen to me. I'm only a missionary. What you want to do is to get to know the Chiefs. Those people out there in front," he said, pointing.

ii

The Chiefs sat on bentwood chairs facing the platform but on the ground level. Each was dressed in white garments that the Administration had starched the day before, giving each Chief a pair of tight trousers and a jacket. Each Chief had his name clearly marked in washable ink on the collar, together with a drawing of a tiger or a dog or, in one case, a woman eight months gone with child, these being the Chief's personal symbols, celebrating some incident famous in their careers. This was done so that when the trousers and jacket were handed back to the Government warehouse (as they had to be at the end of the ceremony) they could be stored till next year on the proper shelf. The Chiefs could not read their names since none of them was literate, but they could recognize the symbols and that reassured them: they were very particular about getting their own coat and trousers each year, and not another Chief's.

On the floor around each ruler sat his courtiers, about thirty to each Chief. These were all men of dashing appearance, given to rolling their eyes in a threatening manner and spitting with decision. They wore no clothes save the usual modesty bag, with the exception of the chief courtier or prime minister, who in some cases wore a shirt. The courtiers who were in the inner confidence of the Chief each wore a broad red ribbon, eight inches wide, that ran over one bare shoulder down to the opposite bare thigh. About where it crossed the stomach it carried a heavy brass plaque, as big as a dentist's shingle, on which was engraved the name of his royal master. Occasionally, to attract the attention of onlookers, one of the courtiers would dribble slowly on the plate and polish it with the palm of his hand. Nobody in any court entourage could count with safety beyond ten: but each of the courtiers knew exactly what fraction of the Chief's annual income was their hereditary due. One of their reasons for coming to the Durbar was to see that they got it. The money itself was in big white bags, closed with a string round the neck and a seal, which now stood in rows on the table. From time to time a courtier would hitch up his brass plate, walk over to the bags and feel them critically. The sound of "God Save the King" drifted in from the outside, played, as far as I could judge the orchestration, on a police bugle, side drums and a sort of bagpipes. I am sure of the bagpipes because they took rather long to fill with wind, and so started late, finishing solo about a minute after the rest of the orchestra had stopped. This had inspired Catullus to a pastiche of Debussy; as he proceeded to the throne I could hear his faint, nostalgic humming, varying the dying theme of the bagpipes. He was dressed in his official uniform of a cocked hat with white feathers, a blue jacket and trousers, all laced with gold leaves. His costume evaded being too archaic or too military, and for all its gold, its magnificence was sombre. It would have done exactly for the Chief Fireman to the Widow of Windsor.

A clerk moved among the Chiefs urging them to get up. They did so, but only when Catullus was almost past the chairs on which they were sitting. They got up and sat down again in one quick movement, each of them doing something to show his subjects that the fact that he got up when the Englishman was passing was quite coincidental and had nothing to do with paying homage. One yawned and stretched his arms as though he had sat too long. Another peered over his shoulder and ignominiously scratched his buttocks, searching for a bug. Another belched. Another craned his neck in order to study the decorations. The Chief with the oldest lineage of them all, a boy of ten, neither stood up or sat down, but ingeniously used his shortness to slide forward on the seat of his chair so that his feet touched the ground, and nobody could say whether he was standing up or sitting down.

Catullus, progressing through this political demonstration, gave me the odd feeling that I had gone deaf. To judge by his smiles and duckings of the head, he was passing through a hall ringing with loyal shouts. In fact the Limbodians, for the first time since I had arrived, made no noise of any sort. Catullus smoothed down the tablecloth on the chair and seated himself with imperial slowness. In the unnatural silence a clerk cleared his throat and, bowing to Catullus, began, "Your Honor . . ."

A volley of rifle shots rang through the Hall. The clerk swayed on his feet and went grey in the face. I stood up in alarm and looked towards Catullus, fearful lest one of the shots had found its mark. Catullus was every inch a great man meeting death fearlessly in the pursuit of his duties. His chin was up, his lips formed a regretful smile, as though he were already forgiving his misguided assassin, his hands gripped the sides of his chair, holding himself upright against the inevitable moment when he should slump to the floor. The tableau was held for so long that an interested spectator would have had time to consult his catalogue and identify the figures.

Then the clerk said, "I am sorry, Your Honor, we had arranged that when Your Honor stepped out of Your Honor's motor-car a volley should be fired in Your Honor's honor. That was Your Honor's volley. It was a little late, but the men are not quite used to the guns."

To confirm this statement, a single shot sounded from the courtyard, from a guard who had presumably fumbled his first attempt but nevertheless was determined not to be thought lacking in zeal. The tableau moved again. I sat down. Catullus blew his nose, and began to give the clerk a furious dressing-down in whispers. The premier Chief tucked his feet up in the seat of the chair and began giggling. Somebody outside bawled abuse at the guard of honor. The missionary turned to me and said:

"Now I wonder if I would have flung myself forward and saved his life if somebody had really been shooting at him?" He examined the profile of Catullus and the braid on his collar with great care.

"No," he said at length, with satisfied decision. "I would *not* have done so."

By now the proceedings were under way. Catullus was asked by the clerk to honor the Durbar by giving them the honor of hearing His Honor's speech. Catullus got up and propped a page of typescript against his hat. He disentangled one of the fluffy balls of the tablecloth that covered the chair from a particularly plastic piece of braid on his cuff and began to speak. In contrast to his conversation, his official diction was slow and dignified, with the tiny little surprises of inflection and vowel-sonorities that actors use when imitating Abraham Lincoln on the field of Gettysburg. He spoke in English of Saxon simplicity, so that all could follow him, as indeed they would have done had anybody but the three of us behind him and the clerk understood a word of English. The gestures, the voice, the pauses swept us away. Surveying the year to come he mentioned that an Education Officer had been appointed, at which the missionary nudged me hard two or three times.

"We expect . . ." said Catullus, "that he . . . will do much . . . to improve . . ." Catullus paused even more heavily and gazed for a moment on the faces in front of him, "to improve . . . education." Catullus left time for applause, but there was none. In the silence he turned to me, and in a whisper as theatrical as the wink which accompanied it he said:

"*A lapidary phrase.*"

By the time I had recovered from my astonishment, he had begun his peroration. His speech had to be short, but he threw into his oratory all the feeling and the artifice of a man who has now to bring to an end the greatest speech of his parliamentary life.

"Rinderpest . . ." he said, "is rampant. I appeal to you . . . Chiefs . . . and subjects . . . to bury your dead cows . . . not to eat them."

He sat down. The clerk got to his feet and thanked His Honor with tears in his eyes.

Then the Chiefs were summoned one by one to get their money. When the clerk called out a Chief's name, the ruler in question instantly plunged into conversation with his neighbor, or pretended to be asleep, or yawned and rolled his eyes to show that the proceedings had no interest for him. By these means the clerk was forced to read out the name again. Then the Chief would knit his brows and look at the clerk sceptically, with the expression of a man who doubts whether he could have heard correctly. The clerk would nod and smile and do everything but point (nobody points in Limbo, it is very rude to do so). When the clerk had made it quite clear that he had in fact called the Chief's name, the ruler would slowly rise from his chair and walk towards the dais. Meanwhile he would throw amused and embarrassed glances left and right at his followers in the manner of a member of an audience called, against his will, to assist a conjuror. Each Chief would then trip over the dais, conveying by this that never in his life had he been forced to go up to meet a man seated higher than himself. When, with unnecessary stumblings, he finally arrived on Catullus' level, he thrust out one hand at Catullus' belly so that it should be he and not the official who appeared to be offering to shake hands, while the other hand groped at one of the bags in an attempt to take it for himself and thus avoid the indignity of being given it.

Catullus, his stone Roman face weathering gradually into a bazaar-opener's smile, usually managed to get his hand on the bag first. He then lifted it, thrust it into the Chief's groping fingers, gave his other hand another shake and immediately washed his face clear of all expression. The Chief would then turn his back on Catullus, wait for a moment on the edge of the dais for the ground to rise up and save him the dishonor of having to step down, then finally got down with a nervous skip and made his way quickly back to his seat. Once there, he seated himself abruptly, and threw the bag of money down on the floor. Neither he nor any of his followers gave it another glance.

The distribution done, the clerk went out and came back with garlands of flowers, squeezing them together with his moist hands. One of these garlands he put round the neck of Catullus, who now so resembled a bust that his arms and torso looked like the work of an incompetent restorer. The clerk then moved over to the Chiefs and began to give each one of them a garland, but since they preserved their air of complete detachment from the ceremony, he was forced to lasso the strings of flowers over their heads. The moment he had done this they each took off their garland and threw it on the floor beside the money-bags.

The clerk next asked Catullus if he could have His Honor's permission to have the honor to declare the proceedings closed. Catullus bent his head graciously forward and, surprisingly, bent it back again, although there was doubtless, as a result, a serious crack in the neck hidden by the garland. The clerk declared the Durbar over, and Catullus got up and walked the length of the Hall to the exit, marvellously balancing his stone head on his stone shoulders. He walked into the open and disappeared. We heard the sound of his car driving away, and we began to move towards the door ourselves. To do courtesy to the Chiefs, we hung back and allowed them to go first, which they did very slowly. Some five minutes after Catullus had driven away we heard a fusillade of rifle shots. The clerk, sweating from his exertions, smiled weakly at us. "The farewell salute," he said, his hands still full of garlands for persons whom he had forgotten to decorate, "a little late."

iii

As we left the Durbar Hall the missionary asked me if I would like to see the witch's stone. I said that I would and he took me some little distance outside the village. Then he showed me a smooth black stone about two feet high with a garland of withered flowers flung round its top.

"It marks the spot where the greatest witch of Limbo is buried," said Small. "Or perhaps I should say the second greatest."

"Who was the first?"

"Well, maybe that place should be reserved for Thelma Macey."

"Oh yes. You mentioned her in the Durbar Hall. Her name sounds English."

"American. She was my predecessor."

"A missionary?"

"One of the best."

The stone was towards one end of a clearing, and I looked around the open space.

"There seem to be the ruins of a sort of shrine here," I said.

"It's Thelma's church," he said. "Poor Thelma." He sat on a stone and looked up at me. I saw that he wanted to be asked to explain himself, so I sat down and said:

"Well, what about her?"

"She was a remarkable person," said Small. "She was the first white woman ever to come to Limbo, and she had her difficulties. But she got along all right, except that she had no church and the Mission said they couldn't afford to build one. So Thelma Macey set herself a program. She split up her life into three-year periods. Two years she'd spend working here, doing good and spreading the Gospel. Then back she'd go to the States to raise money to build a church. The Mission paid her

passage both ways, but that was all they would do. But
Thelma had a way of making money out of everything.
Not for herself, mind you, but for her church. She lived
for that church. She used to get jobs as a stewardess or
a nurse-companion on the boats that took her to and
from the U.S.A., and save the passage money. Every cent
she saved she entered in her account books and then put
it away in the bank. When she got home she would
start organizing bazaars and lecture tours and everything
she could think of to raise money: and she was a woman
with plenty of ideas in that direction. It all went down
in her account books. It took a long time getting the
money and she was a long time without her church. But
she got so that her account books were almost as good a
thing to her as an actual stone-and-mortar church. She
loved figures, and she'd spend hours looking at her sums,
as happy as a woman could be."

Small looked thoughtfully at the witch's gravestone for
a while and then went on.

"One day she was adding up what she'd got and what
she'd made by investing it, and it all totaled up to enough
to begin the church. Not enough to finish it, but enough
to begin. By that time the Limbodians had got around
to liking her, and when she talked to them about her
church they promised to build it for her. She drew them
plans and pictures and she gave them an idea of where she
wanted it built. Then she left for the U.S.A. on her last
trip to raise cash. She worked as though she was inspired,
and got the cash and a little to spare. She got a boat for
Limbo once more, though she was so happy she felt she
could have walked across the Atlantic Ocean on her two
feet. When she got here she found that the Limbodians
had prepared a surprise. They'd built her church for her.
It wasn't all that an architect could have desired, maybe,
but it was everything that Miss Macey wanted. It
wasn't exactly where she had thought of it being built. It
was here where we are sitting, but that suited Miss Macey

too. The Limbodians had spent all her money and wanted some more. She gave it to them, with both hands, every dollar she had. She would have given them her eye-teeth if they'd mentioned that they wanted them.

"She didn't belong to my Church. Ours is pretty austere, but hers was even more so. They didn't have Baptism or Christening, but something they called Submission. To be a member of their Church all you had to do was to go to a certain number of services and there you were. The Limbodians came in their hundreds and kept on coming, so Thelma made more converts than any other missionary her Church had ever sent out. She felt they were genuine too. There was no altar in her church—that sort of thing wasn't approved of—but there was a sort of platform at one end for the preacher. Every time Thelma Macey came into her church she found the platform covered with touching little gifts. Rice, fruit, sometimes pieces of the women's silver jewelry, and always plenty of garlands.

"She swept and garnished her church every day. If a teak board warped she worried about it all night until she could get it put right. She even became quite a good carpenter herself. Then one day she found that white ants had got into the platform. There was nothing to do but to pull the thing down and build it with fresh wood. She didn't wait to get help. She just got a crowbar and began to pull it to bits herself.

"When she had got about half the top of the platform up, she found this."

Small put his hand on the witch's gravestone.

"It didn't take her long to see what had happened. The Limbodians had cheated her: they had used her money to build a handsome shrine for their premier witch. That was the meaning of the gifts which she found each day on the platform, and the flowers which she had thought such a charming tribute to her church. She sat down and swore. She'd never sworn in her life, and she was not very good at it. She put every word she said in her diary, as a sort of penance. I've read it, and she repeats herself. But there's no mistaking her feelings.

"Then she went back home and took out her account books. She brooded over them for a long while, and when she closed them she knew just what she had to do. She made up her mind that the Limbodians should pay back every cent of the money. Then she would build another church. It was no good just rooting up this old stone. A witch was buried here and it would be witch's ground for evermore. She had to get a brand new church, and for that she wanted her money back on this one.

"There was one way to do that, and she took it without a moment's doubt. She pulled down the platform so that this stone would show plainly. She made it all neat and tidy and then called the Limbodians together. When she had got as many in the church as it could hold she talked to them. She didn't say a word about their trickery: she did not accuse them of anything. She said that it was about time she told them the truth. She had had a long talk with the dead witch, who had thanked her for raising the money to build her a shrine. In return, the dead woman had passed on to Thelma all her powers of evil. In a word, Thelma Macey was setting up in business as a witch.

"She went about it with the same energy as she had brought to getting the money for the church. She had learned a good deal about it from her work in Limbo, and what she didn't know she invented. She threatened to curse the crops, and the Limbodians had to buy her off with tithes. She muttered spells whenever she heard of an impending wedding and could only be mollified by presents of hard cash. She took responsibility for every stomach-ache and cold in the nose in the village, and it all meant payment to her in cash or in kind. The kind she used to take once a week outside Limbo and sell in a local market. Whatever she earned went down in her account books.

"The Limbodians thought it was all right and proper

and took it with good grace. Witches hand on their powers to their favorites, and Thelma Macey, especially whenever she thought of the money she had lost, had a look which anyone who had seen a witch would recognize as a first-class evil eye. So they paid up and considered themselves lucky to have the chance to do so. On the whole they thought her a fairly tolerant sort of witch: there were no epidemics and no man-eating tigers while she held sway, but only the usual run of small misfortunes.

"The misfortunes may have been small but there were plenty of them, and soon Thelma Macey had got all her money back. She checked it up in her account books one evening, drew a red line under the totals, and wrote the whole story in a letter back to her Church in the U.S.A. She was frank about what she'd done, although she didn't put it as plainly as I have. She said that she had gone through all the ceremonies that a witch is supposed to do and she said it had not been very easy. Once or twice she had had to drink strong liquor with witch-doctors, as custom demanded, and it had made her pretty sick. But now it was over. She enclosed a cheque for the money and asked permission to pull down the abomination of a church that she already had, and build a new one on a new site. When she finished telling of what she had done, she added that she felt she had labored not unworthily in the vineyard of the Lord, though maybe at a peculiar job. She signed her name and felt satisfied.

"While she waited for the reply (and it took weeks) she did not go to the church and she gave up being a witch. Then the letter came. It was from the head of her Church. It did not say a word about her having been a witch. It did not mention the stone in the church. It just said that they had held a meeting and sought guidance. As she well knew, it was strictly against the fundamental principles of their Church to touch strong liquor. They were waging a bitter war against the demon of alcohol in the States and they felt that one weak member

of their community would bring into discredit the whole
glorious fight. They were sorry she had fallen by the way-
side. In other words, she was fired. They thanked her for
the money."

Small paused and took off his spectacles. He peered
at the witch's stone for a little and then said,

"It broke her heart. As I said, she's been dead a good
few years now. Dead," said the Reverend Small, "and,
I sincerely trust, in heaven."

CHAPTER TWO

I WENT back to the wooden bungalow which had been given me as my house. It stood on the shoulder of a hill: higher up was the bungalow in which Catullus lived, and to make a place for the houses, half a mile of the long hilltop had been cleared of all but a few of its trees. Even so, it seemed that the jungle came almost to my doorstep, because small shrubs and clumps of six-foot grass had crept out from the forest and grown in my compound in the few months since my house had been built.

Three hours after the Durbar I was sitting on my veranda looking at the sunset, when I saw Catullus coming down the hill. He had changed his gold and blue uniform for a very old shirt, a pair of shorts, and huge walking boots. In his hand he carried a staff of patriarchal length. On his head he wore a smart pork-pie hat from some obviously good London hatters. He was singing a soprano solo from *Die Walküre* in a falsetto voice.

"It looks so like the cyclorama in *The Ring*," he said, poking his staff at the sunset. "Come for a walk and see the Chiefs sitting under trees and counting out their money and everybody going to spend it at the Government pub and putting it back in our pockets come along."

"Can you go among the Chiefs dressed like that?" I asked as he came to the veranda.

"It's perfectly proper. It's in the fundamental rules governing the conduct of Civil Servants; it's all right as long as I'm walking for exercise. Why? Do you think I ought to have gold braid down the side of my shorts?"

"The staff no doubt lends the necessary dignity."

"It's not a staff, it's a whippy stick. Everybody who knows how to live in the jungle carries a whippy stick."

"What for?"

"To break the backs of snakes."

"Have you ever broken the back of a snake?"

"Never. Whenever I see one I run like hell. But if you're going to be accepted here you'll have to carry a whippy stick. It's like swinging a tennis racket in the suburbs of London on a Saturday afternoon. You must do the proper thing. Nobody realizes that the frontier Englishman is a petty bourgeois. Do you know that Limbo has got no hospital, no proper schools, no clinics, no telephone, no post-office and no shops. But it has got a club and a tennis court and a silver tournament cup which was last competed for ten years ago when two Englishmen and their wives and families were sent here as a punishment for some minor wickedness in the Civil Service. One of the daughters died of malignant malaria soon after she won the cup. The other Englishman expressed his perfectly genuine grief by saying that her death put an end to their mixed doubles, and the first Englishman understood. The official report on the possibility of anti-malaria measures here says 'Paragraph 2 The area surrounding the village may best be described as being suitable terrain for an eighteen-hole golf course.' That was just after three workmen had dropped dead building the bungalow you're living in from the worst sort of malaria of them all—cerebral. Come along, come for a walk."

We walked down the hill and came to a great tree whose trunk writhed with creepers, thick as small trees themselves, and twisted as no real tree-trunk could be unless it grew at the bottom of the ocean. Such trees are meeting-places for the Limbodians, not so much, I think, for the shade they give, but because they are the only big things in the land, much bigger than any stone monument and ten times bigger than any house. There are many such trees, and the Limbodians choose between them: once chosen, they never change their tree. With the ribbed trunks rising forty feet in the air before the branches

begin, the intricate vaulting of the limbs, and the crowds
that gather around the base, they remind one of the pillars
that held up the roof of the old cathedral of St. Paul's in
London, round which merchants would gather each day to
discuss their business, each group to its own pillar. There,
as in Limbo, there was worship going on, and but little
notice was taken of it. Here, from time to time a woman
or an old man would put some rice or flowers before a
round stone that was entangled in the roots, distinguished
from the other stones only by a brilliant smear of red lead.
This was the dwelling of the spirit of the place or the spirit
of the tree. But there was more than that. The dead were
there, interfering in the conversation, listening to gossip,
ears alert for scandal about themselves, saving up malice
to strike when the living are at their weakest. The Limbodians believe that the dead like walking about under
trees, and one should be careful. It would be wiser, perhaps, to avoid trees altogether. The Limbodians have
considered that, but decided against it. If you were to
avoid all the places where you find the dead, you would be
dead yourself, or as good as dead. Better, they think, trust
to your luck and keep a sharp lookout for witches.

There were thirty people under this tree, sitting and
standing, all men and mostly naked. In the middle of
them sat an old man. As we came nearer I recognized
him as one of the Chiefs at the Durbar, and he must have
recognized Catullus, but he gave no sign that he did. We
stopped a few yards away, and although some of the
courtiers looked at us, none got up and none came forward.

"They don't know who you are. You need that gold
stripe on your shorts," I said to Catullus.

"They know quite well who I am, but technically I am
now in the anteroom of his audience chamber and he has
a perfect right not to admit me. The only way I can
retaliate is to cut down the tree," Catullus explained with
great enjoyment. "You see, the land belongs to the

Chiefs, but the trees, being teak and worth a good deal of money, belong to the Administration. That's me. I often wonder what sort of meanly wicked men made these treaties for England with their quibbles and tricks. We got an uncomfortably large slice of our Empire not by being good soldiers but by being quick at languages. First we sent the missionaries to make grammars and translations of the Bible, then we sent the Civil Servants to use the grammars to write out treaties. The Americans got the Red Indians drunk on gin: we got *our* Indians fuddled with words. That is why there are so many lawyers in India, because for a century we quibbled away a piece of land here and quibbled away a piece of land there till the whole country collapsed about the Indians' ears in ruins and we ran among them, squeaking with delight, gobbling up the bits. Good evening!" he said, smiling at the Chief.

The Chief rose, and his courtiers grouped themselves in a half-moon around him. All there was to see was an old man, thirty aboriginals with oiled rags around their private parts, a tree, and stone-littered earth; but with that single grouping the Limbodians had made an audience-hall and put us on our best behavior. This was their art, the only one they had. They did not draw pictures, or only a very few set-pieces required for certain festivals; they could not carve in wood or stone; they neither wrote nor read; their music was so much banging and blowing, enough to keep a rhythm and no more. But in the subtle art of making patterns out of their daily life they excelled. Here was rigidity of form, here the treasuring of classic models, here the scope for genuis in inventing new ones. They could not bear to find themselves a mere crowd, and their dislike of the Durbar came not only from the homage that they were supposed to do to a foreign ruler, but from its slackness, its lack of dignity, its casual organization. When many Limbodians found themselves together, they were not happy until they had marked a center by building a fire, and then had sorted themselves out into circles and begun to dance. Here, under the tree, they arranged themselves around the Chief, each man in his place, according to the amount of money he had been allowed to take from the bag that the Chief received at the Durbar.

Catullus had begun a conversation with the brass-badged first courtier, and thinking it might be about official business I walked away around the back of the tree. There, seated on a stone, was a small boy. I recognized him as one that I had played with that morning and I went up to him. The boy turned away his head. He was wrapped about in a white shawl, leaving only his face showing, and he was trembling violently. I put my hand on the boy's forehead and found that he had developed a high fever: yet this morning he had been full of health. One of the courtiers, who had followed me, said that the boy was the Chief's younger son, and that they were all distressed because they were afraid it was the swift fever and no one could be sure what would happen. He went up to the boy and wrapped the shawl more closely about him, but he did not smile or try to encourage him as we do with a child that is sick. He, too, felt the boy's forehead, and when he had done so he repeated, so that the boy could hear, "If it is the swift fever, nobody can tell what will happen to him by tomorrow."

I asked if they had taken him to a doctor. Yes, they had, the courtier said, but not a good one. They had been able to get only the local magician, who knew noth-ing about the witches in the boy's village. He had done his best, and had diagnosed three possible evil spirits that might have been called up by a witch, provided there had been a death recently in their village. A new grave was essential for the witch to keep vigil by during one night: that is, if she were so malicious as to want to induce the swift fever in the boy and not an ordinary one. There had been no recent death, but then (and the man raised his right hand in a cautionary gesture) they had been away two days, walking to the Durbar. Somebody might have died while they were away. They were going back early to-morrow morning, and a man had been sent ahead to warn their own local magician to be ready. Everything that could be done had been done. But if there was a new grave when they got back—well, then there would be a second one very soon.

I do not know why, but I always expect primitive people to be halting in their speech and to say only very simple things. When conversations with Limbodians did not turn out that way I was disconcerted. It is a foolish belief, like the one that Orientals are always grave and courteous, when of course, as anybody knows who has travelled, they are often ill-mannered and always excitable. Everybody who has lived among primitive people for any length of time discovers their talk to be small in its vocabulary but, inside their few words, intricate in meaning, stilted, often formal and always full of egotism. There is almost no small talk. If an aboriginal asks a question it is because he wants an answer; if he makes an observation it is not to entertain you but to impress you with how much he knows. I do not say that this makes up all their conversation. Occasionally one will decide to idle away an hour. But then he always does it by telling a story.

The courtier's precise description of what seemed to me lunacy left me feeling uncomfortable and with nothing to say in reply. This was the witchcraft of broad daylight that the missionary had told me about, magic taken as much for granted as we take medicine. I was not yet used to it, and smiling rather feebly at the boy, I walked back to Catullus. He caught sight of me as I came round the tree and beckoned to me where he was talking with the Chief.

"This is the Education Officer," he said; "he is going to build you schools. Will you send your children to school? Your own children?" The Chief pointed to his

ear out of which grew a tuft of grey hair. He said that
he was deaf. A courtier with a red band and brass badge
shouted at him, repeating Catullus' question. The Chief
made no sign in answer.

"I shall teach them very many useful things," I said.
"I shall reach them to read and write, and how to count
money and how to use a saw and hammer." I nodded to
the courtier to shout all this into the old man's ear, but
the Chief stopped him.

"The sons of Chiefs do not need to use their hands,"
he said.

I agreed.

"No. But they should know how things are made, so
that they will not be cheated by outsiders that they bring
in to work for them."

He had grown quite deaf again and my deep argument
had to be relayed to him in more shouting.

"I do not want them to learn how to use their hands,"
he said again, when the shouting had finished.

"But he does not want them to be cheated," I said to
the courtier. I spoke quietly, but the Chief's hearing was
instantly restored.

"No, I do not want them to be cheated," he said, showing his brown teeth in a grin.

"Then what do you want them taught?" Catullus
shouted.

The old man continued to grin for a while, nodding his
head to show that he had heard and did not need the question repeated.

"English," he said, "to be able to deal with you."

Then they were all laughing. Catullus said something,
but the man with the badge took no notice of him and
did not relay his question. The Chief turned his head
from side to side, looking straight into each courtier's face
to see if they were laughing at his wit. Then, satisfied that
he was properly appreciated, he went stone deaf again,
and would hear nothing that was said to him. This way he

brought the audience to an end, and when Catullus and I turned to go it was quite clear that we had been dismissed from his presence.

We walked away and Catullus cut around him with his staff at the tops of the long grass. When we were out of the Chief's hearing, he burst out with delight: "What a wicked, wicked, *wicked* old man! He's my pet Chief. I call him George III. He has the same bigoted stupidity, the same skill to make himself a king. He regards his subjects as unruly scoundrels, just as the Hanoverians regarded the British. That's the secret of ruling, and he's got it. His mind spins dynastic intrigue around heirs-apparent and heirs-presumptive to thrones that are no more than an upturned box in a mud hut. Just like the Hanoverians he hates his eldest son and has slowly de-bauched him with drink and women until he is no more than an idiot. He cannot read or write, like the majority of all the kings of history, yet he can remember the genealogies of every Chief of Limbo for a hundred and fifty years back. He arranges diplomatic marriages be-tween ruling families whose only possessions are a yearly cut from the money-bags I give them: and if his plans are spoiled he employs witches to destroy whoever has stood in his path. This bare-behinded monarch is a lesson. Nonsense like his, his quarrels and intrigues over what royal woman lies under what royal man, made up most of history until George Washington, very much against his every instinct, showed that history could be run on lines other than those of the stud-farm."

I told him of the sick boy and asked if anything could be done.

"I dare not interfere," he said. "The boy might die."

"He'll die if you don't."

He stopped and a peculiar expression crossed his face. There was irritation in it, but above all an urgent, vexed sympathy. It was the expression of someone who had warned a favorite child not to climb a tree, and now hurried to help him as he lay in pain at the foot of it after a heavy fall.

"A hospital," he said, "a hospital might help, because the wicked old man might send him there of his own accord. I think he is too clever to believe in witch-doctors, provided he does not have to admit it to my face. A hospital with a quiet back entrance."

He cut again with his stick at the grass about him.

"But we haven't got a hospital. For sixty years we've been chuckling busily over our bargain as we cut down their trees, and we've had no time to build one. No. Let the boy go back to his village. The witch-doctor will throw rice in a winnowing fan, and tell his father the names of the evil persons who are bringing about his son's death; that is, if he can pronounce their English names."

Suddenly his eyes looked mischief again and he cast around for something, anything that he could talk about, searching for farce as a distressed man looks for alcohol. Very quickly he found it.

"Look there," he said, pointing to the village street of round grass huts. "Somebody's built a tiny hut beside that big one. I wonder what it's for?" He trotted off down the earth road to find out.

The small hut was built exactly like the larger one: round walls of plaited bamboo, a tiny mud doorstep too small to put one's whole foot upon, and a round grass roof rising to a point. In all it was four feet high.

"It's a kennel. I'm sure it's a kennel. Or a chicken-run," Catullus said as he bent over it. "How charming, how sweet, how utterly ridiculous."

He bent down to peer into the small doorway. There was a giggle from inside and three small boys, quite naked, crawled out one after the other and, shrieking with laughter, fled down the road. Catullus straightened himself, delighted.

"It's a brothel," he said, with immense satisfaction. "Isn't that interesting? Imagine one of these little huts in every school playground in England and America, and you will get some measure of how remarkable these people are. 'Jones, where is Smith major,' " he said, imitating a schoolmaster. He changed his already high voice easily to the treble, " 'In the hut, sir, with Brown minimus. Shall I call him, sir?' 'Good Lord, no, boy, I wouldn't think of such a thing.' These people have no sense of sin at all. They can't have, because evil is due, wholly and all the time, to witches, and it is plainly absurd to blame a man for being the victim of a witch. They go further: witches are busy people and do not concern themselves with trivial things we call vice. Death and disease, ruin and madness are the things they deal in. These and catastrophes like them are what the Limbodians call evil. Small sins, the sins that concern our schoolmasters and parents and divorce judges, our priests and Sunday journalists, do not measure up to the vast wickedness of witches. They are too small to be noticed. With us, our eyes fixed on little sins, we do not notice the big ones, so that those who commit them are not hung up by the heels and beaten within an inch of their life, but made statesmen, tycoons and archbishops. We look up and adore them while they rain disasters down upon our silly faces. What shall we do now?" he asked breathlessly. "I know, we shall go and see the prison." He cantered off down the road towards it, singing in a falsetto voice. Then he noticed that I was not too happy at his project, and he burst out with a flood of advice. "But you must *always* see prisons if you want to understand any country. I always make them the first thing I see. It is very intelligent to be interested in prisons. It tells you everything about a people at a glance."

"You mean the criminals are a sort of cross-section," I said, half running beside him to keep up with his trotting walk.

"But no, no, *no*," he said; "you don't go to see the criminals, you go to see the jailers. Prisons are vicious

places. Always study the vices of a people, not its virtues.
Virtues are always the same wherever you go. Has anybody thought of any new virtues since the Greeks? No.
Not even the absurd Christians who made a virtue out of
being eaten by lions. Socrates had already made great
play with drinking the hemlock. Origen might have
thought he had invented a new virtue in castrating himself
so that he would have no lustful thoughts, but Socrates was
again before him with his much-advertised night with
Alcibiades, and he made his point in a much less disgusting
manner. But wickedness . . . ! When have people stopped
inventing new wickedness? Only once, you are about to
say, about the time of the division of the Roman Empire,
and you would be quite right, quite right. A good point, a
very good point."

I said it was his point, not mine. I hadn't said a word.

"Well, whoever made it," Catullus sped on, "it was a
good point, but it does not go far enough. The Romans
had exhausted their pagan ingenuity and New Rome in
Constantinople was pretty much as filthy with the same
sort of filth as Old Rome. Then along came St. Augustine
and practically invented the Manichees, and in a couple of
books gave the world a whole list of new wickedness
which it spent a thousand years in stamping out. And, of
course, no sooner had St. Augustine invented the Manichees than lots of people started being Manichees. I
learned all that from Bay. Bay is a Manichee. Do you
know Bay? You must. He comes to stay with me tomorrow.
He is officially a Manichee. It says so on his diplomatic
passport. He will tell you all about it. No, study vices,
not virtues."

We had arrived at the only stone building in the village,
a long, grey place with one story. Catullus jabbed his staff
in the direction of the building.

"I collect prisons," he said, "like John Howard the
Quaker. Everybody thinks he wanted to abolish prisons
and that's why he went visiting them. Nonsense. He was

a good man and so was bored, inexpressibly bored, with goodness. But wickedness gave him vast entertainment. Do you remember the zest with which he described that poor devil of a Quaker? The Quaker was only a lad, and they put him in a hole in the wall big enough to lie down in but fourteen feet from the ground. He had to climb up and down on an old slippery rope. The longer he stayed in the cell, the weaker he got, as his jailers very well knew he would. One day, of course, he slipped but did not fall very heavily. For the next few days he climbed in an agony of fear. Then he really did slip and fell and broke his neck. That's the essence of any prison. That's what a prison's for: not to break your neck (that's too swift) but to break your spirit. Each day you're let out of your cell and given a little freedom, a very little freedom, *if* you can hang on to your rope—that's your sanity. But the cell they put you back into is not meant to keep you sane. It weakens your mind and your spirit little by little, till one day you slip and your guts have gone. You agree with everybody that you're a criminal. I suspect that when that happens you become a bore to your jailers, and they give you remission marks to get rid of you. Prisons are inescapably wicked places. You've got the people who run them and the people who approve of them in a corner. You can say to them, 'This that you are doing, or paying warders to do instead of you, is cruel, horribly cruel, in a measured-out, thoughtful way. Right!' " The warder of the prison and the chief policeman came out as they saw Catullus approach, and now stood in front of him, bowing respectfully. As Catullus said, 'Right!' he jabbed his stick at one of them. "You can stick a pin through their bellies and examine them at your leisure. 'It's cruel, cruel,' you can say to them, 'and you know it. Now let's see you wriggle off your pin.' Good evening," he said to the bowing officials, who had not understood a word he had said.

They let us into the prison. It was made up of four rooms, side by side, with a veranda running the length of

the building. Two of the rooms had doors and were the
jailers' quarters. Two had bars instead of doors and were
the cells. There were no prisoners. In one, stacked behind
the bars, were the chairs and decorations that had been
used for the afternoon's Durbar. Catullus sent the two
men away and sat on the floor of the veranda, his back
propped against the iron grill of one of the cells. I sat
down beside him, tired from the walk.

"Wriggle off your pin," he repeated, half to himself.

"Who?" I asked. "Those two unfortunate jailers?
They're probably proud of having a Government job, and
that's all there is to it, for them."

"No. Everybody who sends people here. The delators,
the spies, the witnesses for the prosecution, the magistrate.
These are the ones I like to see twisting sense and decency
in order to get off the pin." He spoke with a deliberation
and quietness rare in him.

I looked around one of the cells. "It's not so very
inferior to one of the Limbodian huts," I said. "When it
rains, I should think it was better, except for the bars."

"Except for the bars," said Catullus, "and the carefully
spread-out pleasure of everybody who's put you behind
them. Except for the voices of the warders talking about
going for a walk down the road and sleeping with their
wives, and what their children said this morning. Except
for the memory of the magistrate, who, just when you've
at last eased the tightness of your throat enough to let you
have your say, looked at his watch and adjourned the
Court for lunch."

"Who is the magistrate here?" I asked.

Catullus pushed his stick carefully through the bars and
fed an invisible animal with a bun.

"I am," he said.

He waited for me to say something, and when I did
not, fidgeted.

"You look at me," he said, "as though I were some
new Alva come to ravage Limbo with fire and sword. I

sometimes think of him when I want to remember the population figures. Alva personally ordered the execution of eighteen thousand Dutch and Flemish Protestants, almost exactly the entire population of these Federated States. No, I don't *think* I'm that sort of magistrate," he said, conveying by his tone that he had an open mind about it. "But of course I might be if I believed in anything. I find that a most important principle. You must observe it, since you are now a Civil Servant. When you find you have power to punish a man, do so if you must, but believe in nothing while you are doing it. When I sit on the bench I try to do that. I try to believe that nothing is certain except that imprisonment hurts, with a living pain in the body and the mind, and that hanging is death by torture. I am very frightened when I think of what I might do if I believed in justice."

"You quoted Alva," I said, having just remembered who he was, "but the Spanish Catholics sent him to the Netherlands to be a persecutor. Surely you can punish a man without persecuting him."

"You can," agreed Catullus, "but the choice between the two does not lie in your hands. It rests with the prisoner. If he agrees with you that he has done wrong, then you can punish him. But if he does not agree, then what you do to him will be persecution. At least, that is what the prisoner will say."

"Naturally he will. But does it matter what the prisoner will say?"

"The Duke of Alva said he was punishing criminals when he roasted Flemish Protestants to death over slow fires. The Protestants said he was a blood-soaked persecutor. The Duke of Alva said it didn't matter what the Protestants said, and put a couple of cities to the sword to show that he meant it. But the Protestants were right and Alva was wrong. It was a persecution."

"Yes," I agreed, "but we no longer punish people for their opinions. Not if we're civilized."

"By being civilized we mean," said Catullus patiently, "that there is a certain list of things about which we permit a man to have an opinion different from ours. Usually they are things which we have ceased to care about: for instance, the worship of God. But in the important things we say, like Alva, that no sane and respectable man can ever think differently from ourselves, and if he does we jail him, or flog him, or hang him."

"But, Catullus, there *are* things which everybody, or practically everybody, thinks are wrong."

"Exactly what Alva's master, King Philip of Spain, thought," said Catullus, nodding his head. "The Netherlands refused to accept the Inquisition, so he wrote a letter condemning the whole three millions of them to death. Practically everybody, from the Pope downwards, agreed with him."

"But it is nonsense," I said, "to judge every sentence you give from the bench by what it would have looked like in the sixteenth century."

"Probably," agreed Catullus. "But in that case it must be equal nonsense to judge everything that the Duke of Alva did by what it would look like in the twentieth century."

"Now you put it to me," I said, "it is."

"So what the Duke of Alva did was all right so long as you were the Duke, and what the Protestants did was all right so long as you were a Protestant. The incidental question of who burned whom depends on who has the best aim with an arquebus."

"What is an arquebus?"

"A gun," said Catullus.

"I see. So you base your sentences on the moral principle that you hold the arquebus and the Limbodians don't?"

"I try to," Catullus said.

"Of course I'm new to Limbo," I said, "but——"

"But you're shocked. Why? Would you have me tell

you that I act on the belief that eighteen thousand naked savages are in solemn agreement with my code of ethics?"

"No," I said, "that wouldn't be sense."

"It would be blazing nonsense," Catullus assured me.

"Limbo," I said, "seems to make nonsense of a lot of things."

"That," said Catullus, "is because they have a different sense of right and wrong: or rather, no sense of wrong at all because they think that evil is all due to witches. You will find it very confusing at first."

"Just to help me over the first hurdles," I said, "tell me how you, with all your powers of punishment here, guard against becoming a Duke of Alva?"

"I carefully arrange to have an insufficiency of arque-buses," said Catullus.

As he said this, a Limbodian came running round the side of the building with two officials running after him. When he saw Catullus he stopped and began to raise his hand in the dignified greeting of Limbo, but one of the officials, coming up, grasped his wrist and twisted it behind his back. The other official came up on the other side and hit the man a painful box on the ears. Immediately he saw this, Catullus jumped to his feet and ran over to the wrestling group. He raised his stick and beat the official furiously over the shoulders, the stick whipping through the air and bouncing off the man's body. With a sudden shout of pain the official ran, while the other officer, whom I judged to be a warder, seeing what had happened to his friend, let go the newcomer's wrist and brought himself sharply to the salute.

"This man wants to speak to Your Honor, Your Honor," he said. "I told him Your Honor was busy, but he would not listen."

The man that Catullus had struck reappeared, hesitantly, from behind the corner of the building.

Catullus looked at him, and then at the stick in his hand. "I've never struck a man before in my life," he said to me. Then he threw the stick on the ground. He stared at the man who had beaten the prisoner, and his face slowly reddened with anger. The Limbodian who had been the cause of the trouble coughed to attract his attention. Catullus shifted his stare, and brought his mind away from the official with an effort that showed on his face.

At length he spoke to the warder.

"Bring the man who wants to speak to me inside," he said.

CHAPTER THREE

W HEN you go into any office of any functionary of
the Indian Government you can tell the importance
of the man who sits there by the size of his desk. It is carefully regulated in feet and inches: and if, as rarely happens,
the functionary gets up off his seat, you can make quite
certain by seeing whether he sits on a cushion. Only
important people are allowed to have a cushion. There was
one on the seat of the desk-chair in the office into which
we now filed, Catullus first, then the official, then the man
who had asked for an audience, and lastly myself.

Catullus sat on the cushion and the official ran forward
in consternation. He asked Catullus to get up, which he
did. The official took the cushion and beat it with his hands
till the office was filled with dust. He put it back and invited
Catullus to sit again. As Catullus lowered himself, the
official managed one last shake of the cushion, deftly
inserting his hand under Catullus' rump, and extricating
it before Catullus actually sat on it. Then the official
pushed aside the yellowed and filthy papers on the desk,
found a memorandum pad and pencil and put them in front
of his master. Nothing could be done properly in government unless one took notes, made a file, and passed it on
for others to make notes: nothing was real, not even the
man who stood now in front of the desk with sweat on his
bare body, licking his lips, unless it was described in one
of the dirty, crumpled bundles of paper that lay in confusion
to the right and left of the desk, like midden heaps.

Catullus picked up the pencil. He spoke to the man.
"What is the name of the village of which you are the
headman?"

I noticed for the first time that the man wore a red
turban, the sign of the headman's rank. The man licked

his lips again but they were still too dry for him to answer. Instead, he looked slowly round the room, his eyes dodging across our faces but staring at the cupboards and shelves and the piles of papers on the desk. I wondered what he was thinking. Later, when he was in prison, I went to see him, and he told me.

ii

He felt cold at first, although he was used to wearing no clothes. Rather, first he felt how hot it must be for all of us, particularly the officials, to be so overdressed. Then, after he had been beaten and seen the other official beaten in turn, he remembered that we were all important people and knew what we were doing, so he felt naked, and therefore cold. Besides, he had never been inside a stone building before and the air felt strange about his belly and loins. He tried to find words to say what he had come to say, but the piles of papers frightened him. He made up his mind that every word in every sheet of paper had something to do with him: the files on the shelves were all about him, the files on the desk discussed what he had done in the past. The room itself was designed and built just to hear his story. He had not thought that there would be so much trouble taken over him. He was not frightened, but embarrassed; he could not imagine that a man so delicate that he could not sit on a bare wooden chair would have the nervous strength to listen to the sort of story he had come to tell. He had noticed how the cushion had been placed for Catullus to sit upon, and a theory formed in his head. All of us—Catullus, the official and myself—dressed so heavily because our skins were stripped from us and we were raw underneath, as our reddish complexions showed very clearly. The story he had come to tell would have been quickly understood by his villagers, thick-skinned, rough and naked as they were. But to tell it to these people as he had intended, plainly, 'I did this and I did that,' would be bad manners. He made up his mind to soften it. Not to tell lies (which he could not do, for the Limbodians do not tell lies as everyone knows), but to make it something that might have happened to these dressed and sensitive people, an act that one of their friends might well have done. He gave the name of his village, and set his imagination at work to see all the villagers in coats and shirts and trousers and himself with so sensitive a backside that to sit on an uncushioned seat would be intolerable agony. "Our village has a witch," he began; "she is not one of the ordinary dirty witches that you meet anywhere. She is a very clever woman and always wears as many clothes as she can. She keeps the top half of her body covered even in the hottest weather." He was immensely pleased with this beginning, and paused to admire the way he could adapt himself to any company.

"What is her name?" Catullus asked him.

"Gangabai."

"Have you brought her with you?"

"Oh no."

"Where is she?"

"That is not easy to say."

"Has she run away?"

"Oh no, not *run* away."

"Very well, has she gone away?"

"No, in a sense, and then, yes, in a sense," said the headman.

"Which? Yes or no?" asked Catullus.

"Both. She has been dead three years."

"Please begin again, and at the beginning of your story," said Catullus.

"Our village has a witch called Gangabai," said the headman politely.

"*Has?* You mean your village *had* a witch," Catullus corrected him.

"You are quite right," said the headman. "Our village

had a witch and she died and now our village *has* a witch."

"Another witch?"

"The same witch," said the headman, gravely shaking his head.

Catulus leaned back in his chair.

"Perhaps you had better tell me the story in your own words."

The headman agreed, but he privately told himself that he had no intention of doing so. It would be much too gross for these delicate (and, he was beginning to suspect, not very keen-witted) persons. He had to make the whole thing sound whimsical and gay, although it had really been very far from that. He wished these people could face the crude facts of living, but it was so clear that they could not. He took a deep breath, and in a careless fashion said:

"We were all laughing and joking and playing games with one another in the cool of a very pleasant evening when my young son fell down on the ground with a horrible pain in his guts. My son is a very clever boy with very nice manners and he costs me a great deal of money every year when I buy him a shirt and trousers and jacket and shoes and things to wear round his neck, and I am sending him to school when he is old enough. So we said among ourselves, laughing and joking, 'Gangabai has done this,' so we asked her." He stopped because he saw that Catullus wanted to speak.

"How did you ask her?" said Catullus.

The headman laughed and spread his hands in an easy gesture.

"Only in a game, because we were spending a pleasant evening; we were full of fun and everybody was laughing. We took her to . . . to . . . the village Durbar Hall."

Catullus spoke again.

"You took her to a tree and hung her up?"

"You cannot ask witches questions as you would ask your own wife," said the headman, and cast around in his head for some way of making it plain to these sensitive people. Already he could see that the man he was talking to was getting hurt, in spite of all his efforts.

"When you ask a witch," he said, " 'Is there any water left in the well?' or 'Do you find the weather very hot?' that is not an important question, because it's the sort of question you can ask any woman and you are asking the witch not as a witch but as a woman. So it does not matter how you ask her. But when you ask her an important question like, 'Did you cast a spell to make my son sick?' she will not answer unless you hang her upside down. When you come to the Durbar," he ended, in a sudden illumination, "you wear gold and all the rest of us do not wear gold. When we examine a witch, she is upside down and all the rest of us are the right way up."

"Then you did beat her?" The headman could not tell from Catullus' voice whether he thought that this would be a proper thing to do or whether it would be too harsh for him to understand. This was difficult: no doubt, in the end, he must say what happened exactly as it did happen. There were no two ways about that. No Limbodian told lies, as everyone knew, because there was always a witch or a magician who could talk to the dead and find out the truth in no time. But he did not want to hurt these people's feelings, and it would be gross ill-manners to do so, since they were listening so politely to him. Then he remembered the scene outside the office when the official had been thrashed, and he sighed with relief.

"Oh yes," he said, "we beat her and beat her and beat her and beat her." He watched for the smile of understanding from Catullus, but it did not seem to be coming. "We all of us beat her," he said, then, taking care to be accurate, "at least, two of us beat her at a time, while the others watched . . ." He looked again for the friendly understanding, but it still was not there. Then, to make it sound more sensitive and dressed and like what these better-off people did, he added, "laughing and joking."

"Did you kill her?" There could be no doubt that this question was not friendly, in fact it was asked in a manner which the headman considered a little rude. But it was not so much the rudeness which struck him, as the extraordinary foolishness of asking such a thing. It was the idle question of a village child who does not care whether it makes sense so long as he can pester you into an answer. Pehaps these people were so sensitive only because they were so young. He considered for a moment whether they might live to enormous ages, and that these were really still children, in their reckoning. Possibly, because no one but a child flipped serious words like 'kill' so lightly into their talk.

He answered as he would have answered his own son.

"What is the use of killing a witch? You do not get rid of her from the village by making her dead. All she does (so to speak) is to cross the road and go and live with her friends. Once she's settled down to being dead she likes it better than being alive. So she says to herself, 'My, it's good to be dead,' and rubs her hands and gets down to some even worse mischief."

"Then why does she trouble to stay alive at all? Why doesn't she kill herself and be done with it? Why?"

This time the question was so exactly that of a child that the headman smiled down at Catullus, waggled his finger and said:

"You must not ask so many questions."

The official who had been leaning against the wall leapt at him, shouting abuse. He seized his arm and shook him violently. He stuck his face under the nose of the headman and bawled threats at him. He gave him a push that sent him staggering back two or three paces. The official turned to Catullus and, wringing his hands, babbled an apology in a single breath so that it sounded like one long servile word of a hundred syllables. Then Catullus hammered on the desk, and there was quiet again.

The headman put his red turban straight, and spoke slowly and firmly, as one should when telling a delicate truth to one's children.

"A witch is not only a witch, she is also a woman. Women like men: they like men to go to bed with them. The witch likes men to go to bed with her. But they cannot go to bed with her when she is dead. Dead men do not bother about women because they are too busy with their evil tricks, like a man who is busy hunting does not think about women until he gets home. The dead never get home. So the witch stays alive because she is still a vain woman who thinks she is pretty like all women, and wants to prove it by having lovers. There, now you know."

"Thank you. Now I know. Then you never kill witches?"

"Kill?" said the headman. "No. Sometimes if we beat a witch very much she gets annoyed and says to herself, 'I shall die and go and do these people some really low and evil tricks and that will teach them who I am.' So she stops screaming all of a sudden and there she is hanging dead. Or," said the headman, carefully and precisely, marking his point with a thin, raised finger, "she is not there but somewhere else."

"Somewhere else? Please explain."

Well, the headman thought, if they wanted him to talk as though he were sitting under a tree in the evening with all night before him, then he would talk, but in his own way. He could not have these interruptions and he could not have these questions. He was a good talker, if he were left to talk in his own fashion, and all the village knew that he did not like interruptions. The very best way to stop them was to tell a tale, and that was what he meant to do now. He would tell the truth, but in the way of a story.

"I remember," he began, scratching himself underneath

his ribs (that would show them that it was going to be a story: everybody in the village knew the sign)—"I remember that some time after Gangabai made my son sick she began to be very bad, and gave us all a great deal of trouble. So one day, when we had no less than three men sick in the village from her witchcraft, we decided to argue with her once more and make her put them all to rights again. But you were visiting the village . . ." The headman paused a little and looked at Catullus, his eyes twinkling a little as he saw him lean forward with interest. It was just these personal touches that had made him famous for his stories in the village. Not everybody had got his memory for the sort of details that made a story sound like a story and not one of those dull rhymes about devils that other people told. "You were there on a visit, living in the house on the hill for just one night, and we did not want to wake you from your sleep. So we could not beat the witch, and we could not leave her to go on working her mischief. Have I already said that three men were sick? We could not have any more go down, not with you there. So what did we do?" He paused again. He scratched his ribs on the other side, not really for effect, but to show his satisfaction. Now it was he, the headman without any clothes, that was asking the questions, and all because he was telling a story. Indeed, how like children they were! "So *what* did we do?"

"Go on," said Catullus. "Tell me what you did. I remember that I did sleep in the bungalow above your village one night. Go on."

"We took her to the little lake that is at the bottom of the hill on which you were sleeping. We were very quiet. So was the witch because we had tied a cloth around her mouth. Then we waded into the water until it was up to our thighs. Two of the strongest and tallest of us took up the witch in our arms, and put her head beneath the water. We were careful to hold her upside down, as I have explained to you before. That is very necessary, even although this was not a regular and proper argument.

After a while, we pulled out her head and asked her if she would take off the spells and make the men well. She made no sign, so we dipped her again. We dipped her several times, and then the strong men got tired and left her head under quite a while; they were quite out of breath with holding her, because she was a heavy witch. You see what I mean? She had become heavy because she had so much wickedness in her. Then she decided to die. When we pulled her up and asked her the usual question, she was all blue and swollen, like the picture of devils. I thought that maybe she had exchanged faces with the devil underneath the water. Not because it meant anything special, but just because it would give us an unpleasant surprise.

"The two strong men threw her body on to the bank and said, 'That's the end of her.' As I said, they were young men, and they knew no better. The discussion had come to nothing, the witch had not taken off the spells, so we were all very angry and tired. We took her body to where we could bury it and be sure no other witch would dig it up without our seeing her. As we left the pond a dog started howling. I picked up a stone and threw it at the dog because I did not want the noise to wake you. I hit the dog and it ran off, not down the path like any other dog, but straight into the jungle; it did not look where it went, but often ran into trees—straight into them as though it was blind. Each time it hit a tree the dog fell over. Then it would get up again and run forward, straight, until it hit another tree. It had stopped howling. We were all very quiet because of you. We could hear the sound of the dog's skull hitting the trees. Somebody whispered that it must be the witch's dog. I did not want to let them all start talking, because then there would be no stopping them, and you would have had no sleep that night. I told him not to be a fool. The witch had no dog. I was right. But *I* was the fool. The next morning you left. The dog was back again. It ran barking beside your car for a long while. You stopped the car, and were very

angry. You told your driver to throw stones at it and send
it away."

"I remember," said Catullus.

"It went away. But it came back later. We were all
sitting under the tree, talking about you and the witch
and what had happened the night before. The two strong
men were standing up, and they were making us all laugh
very much by showing how they had held up the witch
and dipped her head in the water. They had got hold of a
boy who was wriggling and laughing as they held him
upside down, showing how they had done it. The rest of
us were sitting on the ground, or rolling on it, because we
were laughing so much. Then the dog came running down
the road, straight, as it had run the night before, only
there were no trees to stop it. It came up to the two young
men who were standing up and dashed its head against
their legs. Then it bit them both, hard, sinking its teeth
deep. They shouted and dropped the boy. The dog threw
up its head and turned on the boy. It seemed that it was
going to bite him too, but it did not. At the last moment it
ran away, straight, into the jungle, cracking its head
against a tree, and leaving white foam from its mouth on
the grasses.

"The two men were very ill that evening, much more
ill than they should have been. Most of us guessed what
had happened, but we were quite certain when we tried
to give them water to drink. They struggled and fought
and screamed as though the water had been a snake we
were holding to their lips. Some of us went out to chase
the dog and kill it. I told them it was no use, but everybody was very angry by now and they wanted to kill
something. That is very silly, as I have explained, like
quarrelling when you are drunk. But they wanted to do
it. We found the dog, and we chased it to where we could
stone it. It was easy to drive the dog in the way we wanted
him to go because he never turned or bent round as he ran.
Except once, and that was when we had got him near the

pool. There was a small pool, no bigger than a man could jump across, on the path that led to the big pool; it was a dip in the ground and it had got filled with water from the women's pots slopping over as they walked back from drawing water out of the pond. The dog came to it, and then ran away from it to the right, screaming. Not howling, but screaming, in the way a monkey does when you have broken its leg with a lucky shot. Then we knew it was the witch.

"As we ran after the dog, I tried to tell them what had happened. The witch had grown frightened of the water as we dipped her and dipped her again into it. She had seen the demon underneath, and had she called to it for help in the right words he might have made it all right and comfortable for her. But she could not say the right words because of the cloth that we had tied across her mouth. And then the terrible thing had happened, the really terrible thing for the witch. The demon had not known that she was evil. The demon had not recognized her because she could not say the right words. So he behaved as he would have done when anybody else fell into his pond, any ordinary person drowning. He had laughed at her, each time her head came dipping down; he had made frightening faces, and jeered at her, and told her secrets that make the blood stand still. Then it had happened, as it often happens when one is frightened by a demon: her face took on his look and color, and none of her spells could put it right because she could not speak. It is no use thinking spells, you must speak them out loud. She must have known what had happened. Maybe she saw her face in the pool as they dipped her downwards, or maybe she felt the change. Whatever way she knew, she was certain that her looks had gone and no man would ever sleep with her again.

"So then she died, angry, and plotting great mischief. As she died, she left the body that the strong men were holding and went into the body of the dog. She must have sat there, thinking mischief, and watching the men lift her body in and out of the water; she must have sat there as a dog, watching until the men found out that she was dead.

"I tried to tell them all this as I ran beside the men who were chasing the dog, but I do not think they understood. It is not everybody who can understand witches. One of the men made a screaming noise just like the sound the dog had made when it saw the pool, and he threw a stone. It hit the dog and it stumbled. The other men laughed and then they were all making the screaming noise, or barking, or laughing. They threw more stones, and the dog fell down. I do not know if the dog was still screaming, because all the men were making the same noise as they stoned it, and they sounded just like dogs. I shouted to them that it was no use killing the dog because it was a witch, but they could not hear me. They were very stupid. One man was howling with his mouth pouted out just like a dog, and picking up huge stones that were too heavy to throw far: because he was afraid of the dog he would not go close enough to hit him with such big stones, so he howled and laughed and threw them one after the other, yards short of the dog. That was the sort of fools they were. But enough stones hit the dog to kill it and soon it was lying quite still. When the men were sure it was dead they got sticks and poles from the jungle and pushed the dog about. Then they began pushing it towards the pool, until it was on the edge. I ran up and told them not to put the dead dog in the pool, but as I was talking one man gave the body a push with his stick and it fell in and sank. They all said that that was the end of the witch. All but me.

"What happened after that you must have got written down in those papers. One by one we fell sick, and many of us died, more than had ever died before in a month. Then everybody was sick but me and my family. It was so strange, everybody being sick but the people in my hut,

that they would have taken my wife to the tree as a witch,
if they had not been too ill to do it. But I used no magic.
It was not needed, because I knew who was causing the
sickness and I could guard against it. I told the doctor—
your doctor that you sent to look after us—I told him,
and he said that I was right."

The headman hesitated, trying to find the best words
with which to finish his story. As he did so he saw the
official bend forward and talk to Catullus. He heard him
say, "Your Honor, it is not right that this idiot should
waste Your Honor's time with his lying stories, and it is
not proper that he should say that his honor the doctor is
a believer in witchcraft. It is not proper, Your Honor."

The headman moved forward to the desk, spread his
hands in appeal, and raised his eyebrows in the way he
always did when he was coming to the end of what he had
to say.

"But what, then, *did* the doctor say? Surely you must
have it in the papers there on the shelves and on your
table. Did I not ask him if the sickness came from the water
in the pool? He said, 'Yes. It did.' And I asked him, 'Was
it not because I and my family did not drink the water, that
we were well?' He said, 'Yes. It was.' Then I told him I
knew that the sickness came from the pool and I had made
my family get its water from a spring high in the hills,
and a whole morning each day went in bringing it. And
the doctor said that I was a very wise man. A very wise
man. The rest of the village could have been wise too but
they would not listen to me. I told them that I knew that
the pool was bewitched, and that the woman was not dead,
and the dog was not dead, but all the evil had gone into
the pool. But they did not listen to me and could not be
bothered to go to the spring in the hill. So many of them died
and all fell sick because they drank water from the pool, as
the doctor said, straight out of the pool where they had
tried to kill the witch. But I knew, and you know now,

there's no use in trying to kill witches because," he raised a thin finger to mark his point, "you cannot do it."

The official who had tried to stop him before now leaned over the desk and spoke softly and quickly to Catullus. The headman could not follow what he said. He never could understand this smooth way that these people had of talking among themselves. His own voice was hard and plain and loud, as became a man who had nothing to speak but the truth. When his children mumbled he would say to them, "You must be ashamed of what you are saying or else you would say it so that your father can hear." But these people talked so gently when they chose that it was like the touch of a kitten's paw on your ear.

"Perhaps you have something more to say?" Catullus was speaking now, and looking at him.

The headman shrugged his shoulders and pushed his red turban askew to show that what was coming was in no sense to his credit, but was calculated to make him look rather a fool.

"Yes. I have made myself out to be very clever, but that is not the truth. I was very proud when the doctor agreed with me and said that I had been wise and beaten the witch. It was not sick, my son was not sick, my wife was very healthy. Yes," said the headman, giving his turban an even more comic and self-deprecatory tilt, "very healthy. I was so full of my victory that I began to tell the villagers that witches were clever but there were certain people who were cleverer still, certain persons of importance who were not so very far away from the village, and you might pick them out by their red turbans." He laughed broadly, laughing separately into the faces of each of his listeners in turn as good manners required, so that they might all know that a good joke was pending and not miss it when it came.

"I was a very happy man indeed except for one thing. That was my wife's cooking. She was very beautiful.

She was also a very good cook. But just about the time that I am telling you, she began to be a very bad cook. She used to hurry over the meal and take no trouble to grind the spices. She always wanted to go out by herself. I thought that perhaps I had been thinking so much about how clever I was with witches that I had not paid enough attention to her. So I bought her eight large silver rings to wear on her toes. She wore them, but she did not seem pleased. One day I was talking about this under the tree in the evening to some of my friends, and a young man interrupted me. That never happens. Nobody interrupts me when I talk under the tree because I am the headman. I saw that he was not trying to be rude, but he wanted to stop me talking about my wife. I was angry at first and did not know what to say. Then I saw an old man who has always been very fond of me. He was looking at me and was very sad. I knew from that why they did not want me to talk about my wife.

"I got up and went to my house. It was dark by now and of course my wife would be at home. But she was not. I went and looked in the woman's place behind the screen in the hut, but I could not find her. I called her. I walked down the road, calling her, and nobody answered me. But somebody laughed. It was dark and I could not see who it was that laughed, but I knew what that person meant. I got a torch and lit it at the fire. I went off the road along a jungle path. It was on the way to the spring in the hill from which we got our water when the pond was full of evil. Soon I found my wife. She was lying on the ground with no clothes on and in her arms was a tall young man.

"I could not see his face because he was kissing my wife. But his body was bare and I could see that he was much stronger and taller than anybody in my village. I was just about to ask him his name when I heard the howling of a dog, close by, in the bushes. Then I knew who he was. I did not trouble to ask his name because he would only have told me a lie. Demons always tell lies when you ask them their names, and of course he was a demon. The dog was howling at me in triumph, and I knew who the dog was. It was the witch that they had tried to kill. I called myself a fool for thinking that I could ever get the better of a witch. All the time that I had gone around saying how clever I was and how I knew how to handle witches, she had been busy at her mischief. Every day that my wife had gone to get water she had met this handsome demon, as the witch had meant she should. No doubt he was a demon which the evil woman had bound to her service. Not that she would have found it hard to get a demon to do the sort of mischief she had planned. They like that sort of mischief; they like it even more than we do. So the witch had made herself a dog again and watched my wife lie down again and again in the jungle and give her body to the demon. And now the witch was sitting in the bushes howling with triumph at me.

"The demon moved a little as he heard the dog howl and I picked up a stone to defend myself in case he should turn and rend me with his claws. I called out loudly, 'I know what you are. You are a demon sent to plague me by the old witch who became a dog! Turn round and let me see your face!' "

The headman shouted these words loudly, as he had shouted them in the jungle. He stood with his arm flung back as though holding a stone.

" 'Turn round and let me see your face!' I shouted."

The headman brought his arm quickly forward as a man might do when striking with a heavy stone. The official edged forward, his hands out to seize him should he move a step. The headman's empty hand beat the air low in front of him, while his eyes watched it curiously. The the headman moved his gaze to something at his feet. He spoke quietly for the first time.

"The demon turned his face to me. It was very horrible. There were no eyes and there was no nose, but only red and a great deal of blood."

The headman made the gesture of throwing a stone on the ground. He looked in each of the faces that were watching him, in turn, and laughed so that they could see that something very humorous was coming, as courtesy demanded it should.

"The old witch had beaten me, you see," he said, frankly and smiling. "She had made me try to kill a demon. I should have been wiser, but she knew that I loved my wife."

Nobody moved in the small room. The headman, his story told, modestly gazed at the piles of papers.

Catullus picked up the pencil that had been placed before him and wrote something. He spoke once to the official, who rustled among the files and pushed out a paper. Catullus read it, and then spoke to the headman.

"You are charged with murder," he said, "and you must now go to prison until you are tried. You must not say anything more."

The headman said, "So I have come here to ask you to do something about the witches. I have come myself because I have done my best, but it is not good enough. And now you must do something to stop them."

There was no answer. The official moved towards him and took him by the arm. He felt himself pushed toward the door. Then the official was making him walk quickly along a corridor. He twisted in the official's grip, broke loose, and ran back to the room with the desk. He saw Catullus standing beside it, turning over some papers. He shouted, "But you must do something about the witches. You have not told me that you would do something about the witches and I have walked all the way here and told you all that I have told you because you must do something about the witches."

The room was suddenly filled with men in uniform

with leather belts and brass plates on them. Someone hit him, and another seized him around the neck. He began shouting again, but he could not get his breath. He felt an arm round his throat and it grew tight so that the blood began to pound in his ears. He felt himself being dragged away, his heels beating the floor.

He began screaming. "The witch! The witch! I have done nothing. It is the witch. The witch that made me do it. Don't you understand? It was the witch. I have done nothing wrong!"

The men around him began shouting as well. He felt them let go of him and he fell heavily on his back. He lifted his head, and pain began eating at all his muscles. He saw that they had put him in a cage. He screamed once more, "The witch!" and the men outside echoed him. "Witch, witch, witch," they jeered and copied his scream. "Witch, witch witch! You must do something about the witch." One of the men outside the cage had contrived to mimic his voice exactly, his loud voice that he always used because he always told the truth.

CHAPTER FOUR

"**H**OW do you like Limbo? Has it astonished you?"
Bayard Leavis had been in Limbo no more than two
hours, but already I had learned that it spoiled his conversation to answer his questions. They were merely a
courteous way of announcing that Bay had made up his
mind to talk on such and such a subject. For instance:
now, he was clearly determined to talk of the reaction of
a cultivated man to a savage country.

"It is a mark of genius not to astonish but to be astonished. Thus Diaghileff, when he made his celebrated
remark to Jean Cocteau, 'Jean, étonne-moi,' proved himself neatly to be the greater man."

Catullus, Bay and I had come to the end of a pleasant
dinner. Catullus pushed the port decanter to Bay, who
poured himself a glass, having first delicately whisked out
the enormous beetle that had set in his glass for the last ten
minutes. He pushed the decanter to me, and went on,
talking now to the beetle that was trying out its legs on
the tablecloth.

"Or Chateaubriand, for instance, who refused *not* to be
astonished when he went to America, at that time considered by all Frenchmen to be solely inhabited by splendid
savages. Chateaubriand was a man of some determination. He arrived in America firmly believing that there
was a direct road from Albany to the North Pole. Deterred
from putting his theory to the test, he was not to be
deterred from being astonished. He went due South, convinced that he would find the Perfect Woman. So he did.
She was a savage from Florida, and Chateaubriand wrote
a book about her. Then he went North again, to find
solitude. Again he succeeded, finding what he was seek-
ing in the forests around the Niagara Falls. And then

one day while he was walking he heard sounds of music
and voices. At first he hesitated to break his loneliness
by meeting other human beings, but next he determined
that he would do so, for the sounds must come from a
party of Red Indians celebrating their savage rites, free
from the trammels and corruptions of civilization. No
doubt, though I have no authority for saying so, he thought
that he would discover the Perfect Man, and so find a
sequel for his last book. He pushed through the under-
growth, and what do you think he found?"

Neither Catullus, nor I, nor the beetle knew.

"He found a party of Red Indians dancing in a circle,
learning the latest ballroom steps from an immigrant
French dancing master."

The beetle discovered how to use its legs and went and
sat in the butter. Nobody took any notice of it, because
when one dines in the jungle it is etiquette to pretend that
the jungle is not there. We had no electric light, but the
patent oil lamp had been hung by the carefully trained
servants in such a position as to suggest modern indirect
lighting. The meal had been one of four courses, although
three of them necessarily had something to do with chicken,
that being the only food that was available. The port had
been brought by Bay as a present, and he had carried it
successfully across five river fords; both he and the port
had fallen into the sixth. Dinner was now over and the
servant was apologetically laying napkins at each of our
places. The unfortunate man had previously forgotten
them and was suffering the miseries of a bishop who had
tripped over his crozier while dedicating a church. The
ceremonial of the English dinner was none of our choosing.
One observes it, in the jungle, to please the inhabitants,
with whom it takes the place of the cinema. Or rather of
the ballet, because they stand outside in the compound,
invisible in the shadows, watching every move; and any
omission of the classic steps in the performance will be
widely discussed and generally disapproved.

Bay was giving me my first experience of this side of jungle life and I was liking it very much. He had arrived, after a hundred-mile drive in a truck, dressed in a black felt hat, collar and tie, and a light summer lounge suit. Down to his thighs he was admirably dressed, in a loose, genial way, for some such function as a strawberry-tea on the lawn of an Oxford college. Below his thighs his trousers were a mass of mud where he had fallen in the river. I had a lesson in jungle manners when Catullus greeted him and brought him on to the veranda for a whiskey and soda, without a glance at his sodden legs. Catullus chatted easily and at length, talking to Bay as though he were a torso floating in air. I learned that it is not polite to talk of difficulties in Limbo, and indeed, if one did, one would talk of nothing else.

As for Bay, I have a difficulty in describing him, in that I can never remember the face of a person who is of great and penetrating intelligence. I no more see their faces when they talk to me than I see the face, say, of Joseph Addison when I read a number of *The Spectator*. For all I know or care their faces may be made up of the odds and ends from a printer's outfit, like the decorations of Victorian books. When, as now, I make an effort to remember what Bay looked like, I rather imagine that something of the sort is very near the truth, at least for him. He had a very casual face, square, I recall, and the features were formal. A nose? Yes, he had a nose; eyes, most certainly, and a pair of horn-rimmed spectacles; a mouth like any other mouth and a chin that had nothing to do with his character. When he began speaking you realized what a lot of woman-ish fuss was made over faces and good looks, and how much time the world had wasted in going after them.

He was, I suppose, thirty-five, but his age was neces-sarily uncertain. To judge from the depth of his reading, if he was anything approaching the age he looked, he must have begun his studies at the moment of his con-ception. He spoke carefully, flattening his A sounds, previously constructing his sentences in his head, in the manner which, at school, I always thought must be natural to a German, because the German must put his verb at the end of everything he has to say. He was not the sort of talker that one could imagine rapping out orders in front of a burning building; not, at least, unless he had been informed well in advance what sort of building was one fire and just how far the conflagration had progressed. But his conversation was not studied: only the conversation of fools is studied, and that is why they mostly rely on funny stories. He spoke always with a sense of the importance of speaking, as though a cataclysm had destroyed every printing-press in the world, and conversation was all that we had left. Suppose such a thing to happen; then, if a hundred men like Bay survived it, so would civilization.

After dinner we moved out into the compound that surrounded the bungalow. It appeared to be an enormous, unlit ballroom, with a circle of black walls that in the daytime was the edge of the jungle, and a domed roof of translucent slate grey, pierced here and there, in the manner of ballrooms, with imitation stars. The moon must have been up, but we could not see it because of the height of the trees. A servant hung a lantern on one of the small gallows put around the house for that purpose. For a moment it gave a hard yellow light, and then it fell steadily into a dim amber glow as myriads of flying ants clustered on the globe and forced the light to shine through their packed brown bodies. We sat in chairs with long arms on which we put our legs, and the servant brought us drinks, each covered with a little piece of muslin held down by colored beads to trap the insects.

Catullus said, "Bay, I want to know what you think about witches. There is a man in jail here for what appears to be murder. But he denies all responsibility and puts it down to evil women. What do you think?"

Bay sank very low in his chair and said, "Nobody has

yet traced out the connection between women and ruin, but it is there. Most certainly it is there. It was two women, for instance, who were responsible for the collapse of the Roman Empire."

Bay raised himself two inches and said, "It is a most interesting story, and I must now tell it you. The woman's name was Honoria, and she was the sister of the Emperor Valentinian. For many years the Roman Empire had been rocked with disputes as to the succession to the purple, but on this occasion the Administration had a plan to put a stop to them. Should the unfortunate Honoria have a son, a faction would be sure to gather round him, and the Emperior go the way of so many of his predecessors: that, too often, was the Cloaca Maxima, down which the Romans had developed a taste for throwing the bodies of usurped Caesars. The plan was extremely simple, and it was to declare Honoria a permanent and official virgin. This they did, giving her a title at the same time. She was called Augusta, to mark the fact that she was a State-approved virgin. We do not know whether her position irked Honoria, or whether her title tempted her Chamberlain. Whatever the reason, her Chamberlain very soon rendered the title a polite fiction, which not even the Roman civil service could maintain when, as shortly happened, Honoria became pregnant. I imagine that the unhappy woman was something less than tactful about the whole matter, since the people of that time were experts at explaining such things away. They had only recently been breaking one another's heads over a similar question concerning the Virgin Mary, and, as we all know, a compromise was possible in that case. But apparently they were not in two minds about Honoria, and she was packed off to a convent. There she stayed for fourteen years, surrounded all day and every day by women who were real and official virgins. The poor woman's anguish may well be imagined, but scarcely the means she adopted for putting an end to it. Taunted daily with having had a husband, and yet having none at all, she determined to get herself one. Since by stooping low and embracing her Chamberlain she had not got herself very far, she made up her mind this time to aim as high as she could. So she wrote a letter offering to marry Attila, the Hun. You must imagine this lonely woman, walled up in a convent, and having to manage all the delicate arrangements of a marriage and a proposal by herself, and what was worse, by letter. Yet she did not show any of the signs of hysteria which might have been pardoned to such a woman in such a state. She was entirely practical and she even remembered that she should have a dowry. Therefore, enclosing a ring in her letter to the Hun as an earnest of good faith, she also offered him half the Roman Empire. Attila was at the time master of an uncomfortably large part of the hitherto civilized world, but he was not a man of sensibility. He cold-shouldered the heroic spinster and filed away her letter and her ring in case it should come in useful at a later date.

"It did. In due course Attila made his way to Rome, leaving a desert of burning villages and massacred populations behind him to mark his marriage progress, and, appearing beneath the walls of the city, demanded his lawful and pledged wife. The delight of Honoria was frantic. At last, after a weary lifetime of chastity, only more galling because it was not technically complete, a husband was demanding her hand. And such a husband! The Pope Leo himself had gone out to meet him and turn his wrath, accompanied by all his ecclesiastics in their most gorgeous vestments, together with the ghostly figures of Saints Peter and Paul on either side of him to see fair play for the Church. Honoria's persecutors were now her suitors. Embassies went to and from the Senate and the tent of Attila, endeavoring to soften the harsh terms of her dowry. But her husband was firm, and the bride, no doubt, radiant.

"But not even the ruin of an Empire could bring Honoria

happiness. Suddenly Attila fell in love with a pretty little thing that had taken his fancy, forgot Honoria, packed his tents, and went back to his palace on the Danube. There is reason to suppose that in his last interview with Honoria, Attila was accurate, ungallant, and definite. He did not want to marry an old woman.

"It was one of the unwisest actions of his career. So happy was he on his bridal night with the chit thus cruelly substituted for Honoria that he broke a blood vessel, choked, and was found dead next morning by his weeping bride."

A giant moth had made its way past the lampguard and put out the light. But it did not matter, because now the moon was up, and the ballroom, still with its black sides, now had a silver roof. Somewhere among the trees the armed guard who protected us each night from panthers (for there were no thieves in Limbo) coughed and shifted his feet.

"She was a witch," said Catullus.

"Plainly," Bay agreed.

"She cast a spell on Attila, just as the headman said they did, when they could not find a lover." Catullus poured us each another drink. "I wish I could do something for that man. He insists that I do something about the witches. Perhaps I could institute a cadre of official virgins for Limbo."

"It did Rome very little good," I said, "if Bay did not make the whole story up."

"The story may have been made up," said Bay, "but if so, then it is not I who should get the credit but Edward Gibbon, in whose entertaining book I found it."

"It failed in Rome because the scheme was bungled," Catullus went on. "Adapted by a man of my administrative experience the plan has possibilities. I would not, as they did, create one single post for one official and permanent virgin. I would create a whole series of posts, with definite scales of pay. The scale is most important.

The original experiment failed largely because the woman in question saw no prospect of advancement or improvement in her official post. It is a mistake which we Civil Servants are always making. For my official virgins in Limbo I would suggest an attractive starting salary, and a clear provision for an increase of pay after each year of Government service. There should be, of course, from the point of view of sound budgeting, a limit, after which retirement and pension would be the usual thing. But loyal service would be rewarded, and each official virgin should have an annual increment. Naturally, after every five years there would be the usual efficiency bar, which the lady in question would have to pass to the Government's satisfaction before she got her rise."

Bay tinkled his muslin cover on the side of the glass.

"The scheme is excellent," he said, "and may even rid Limbo of its witches for ever. What you have to do is to choose all the ill-favored women who do not look likely to get themselves lovers. From these select the clever ones and there you are. You will have trapped all your future witches. To these, make your offer of Government employment, stressing the social honor which it will imply. If you have chosen the really intelligent women, they will accept at once. No woman of brains wants to spend her life worrying about her lack of beauty, but every woman of brains who is not attractive knows that that is exactly what she will be condemned for the rest of her life to do. Your cadre of permanent and official virgins provides her with a dignified method of getting rid of the worry and she will gladly accept it. Deny her this way out and she will become a witch, whether she is in London or in Limbo. I do not mean that she will buy herself a broomstick and a black cat, but she will become a witch in the sense that she will do mischief, and a great many people, like your man in jail, will find themselves doing mischief too, and, quite rightly, not feeling in the least responsible for it. But it is not an entire solution, and you should be in possession of all the facts about the wickedness of witches before you begin. I must now tell you of the second woman."

He paused to sip again at his drink. The jungle had fallen quite silent, as it often does in Limbo, unlike the howling forests of the story books. The guard in the darkness coughed again, and Catullus with genuine irritation called to him to be quiet.

"Her name was Eudoxia," said Bay, "and she was the wife of the same Emperor Valentinian who had been so cautious over his sister. But he was killed by Maximus, who forced Eudoxia into his bed. Note that in Eudoxia we have the beautiful witch, a rare type, but, as you will see, even more dangerous: the woman who rates her beauty higher than an Empire, and will destroy her country to gain a tribute to it. Eudoxia did not like Maximus. We do not know why, but perhaps she felt that she was made his bedmate for reasons which, however important in the history of dynasties, had nothing to do with her good looks. It is incredible (but it is true) that Eudoxia, instead of performing those trivial but effective acts of coldness which would have secured her nightly rest, preferred to write to the barbarian king Genseric to come to her aid and take her as his bride. No doubt Honoria's story had egged her on. The rivalry of witches is a very terrible thing. Attila had been a dangerous choice for a knight-errant, but with the aid of the Pope and Saints Peter and Paul civilization had been saved. Genseric was a Vandal, and this time the two Saints did not appear, preferring to let history have its head without divine interference. Genseric came at the head of an army, entered Rome and pillaged it from end to end. He stripped the temples of their golden roofs, he loaded his ships with the statues of Greece, he roasted oxen over bonfires made from the manuscripts of great libraries. He even stripped Eudoxia of her jewels. He put her in the foremost ship and sailed for Carthage, the better half of history lying hugger-

mugger in the boats behind him. Eudoxia had got her
lover, the witch had this time triumphed, and Europe
went down into darkness for a thousand years."

"Then you do believe that there are witches?" said
Catullus.

"Without doubt."

"That poor man in the prison." Catullus got up as he
spoke, clearly ill at ease. "He might go down into darkness because of one too."

"Will they hang him?" I asked.

"I don't know. I don't think so. It is not in my hands.
I have asked for a judge to come and try the case." He
fiddled with the lamp in a nervous fashion, trying to
make it light again. "But ten years' jail for a jungle man
is worse than any hanging," he said, and shook himself as
though it had turned cold.

Bay looked up at him. "Catullus, I am sorry I have been
talking nonsense."

Catullus laughed but did not look very happy. He and
I together gave Bay the details of the case. Bay listened
carefully, asked a question or two and then fell silent. At
length he said, "We must form a defense committee. We
three, who all believe in witches."

Catullus sat down and began talking excitedly and
quickly as he had done before the incident at the prison.
"Good. I was hoping you would say that, Bay. Only you
can do it. I was hoping very much you would believe in
witches. I thought you would. How can we defend him?
What line shall we take? You studied law, didn't you? Of
course you did. You studied everything. How can we
defend him?"

Bay said, "I shall appear myself as his defending lawyer.
Can that be arranged? There is no Bar association here in
Limbo, is there?"

"None," said Catullus. "It is arranged that you appear,
here and now."

Bay sank deeper into his chair and thought once more.

Away in the jungle a bird began to make a loud jeering noise, like a drunken man trying to start a fight. The man who was in the jungle guarding us from panthers began to snore, but Catullus was too absorbed and excited to notice him.

"I shall begin my defense with the first chapter of Genesis," said Bay. "I shall use it to prove that the idea of the wicked woman is fundamental to all morality. Eve was, of course, the prototype of all witches. In its original form the story must have said so very clearly, but unfortunately it has come down to us only in the vocabulary of what appears to me to be an old man with a remarkably libidinous mind. Then I shall go on to quote the Fathers of the Church, all of whom firmly believed in witches. I shall wind up with St. Thomas Aquinas, and in case the learned Judge should feel that my style was a little heavy, I shall crack a joke. I shall say that St. Thomas Aquinas, when he died, had his head cut off (as in fact he did), and reverent monks boiled it in water in order to preserve it. That," he said turning to me, "will lighten the trial a little, don't you think? It is very important not to be too solemn."

I said that I thought it depended on the Judge.

"The Judge," Bay continued, "will be a Church of England man, no doubt, and when I have reduced him to listening to me with respect by my quotations from the Fathers, I shall show my hand. I am *not* a Church of England man. I am a Manichee." He took his legs down from the arm of the chair as Catullus got the lamp to light, and I could see his face, beaming with enthusiasm.

"A Manichee always gets the better of a Church of England man, and I shall flatten the Judge when I reveal my true beliefs. We Manichees would have got the better of the Catholic Church if we had had one man, one single man with a good prose style, to answer the Bishop of Hippo."

"What do Manichees believe?" I asked him.

"That there is an equal amount of good and an equal

amount of evil in the world," he answered, "and that the forces of one are as strong as the forces of the other."

"Couldn't you write the pamphlet yourself and put paid to the Bishop of wherever it is?"

"I could. But the answer will sound labored and too long considered. A pamphlet should be hot off the press before the one it answers has had time to cool. The Bishop of Hippo's other name," he said, as a kindly afterthought to me, "was St. Augustine."

"The Judge's name," Catullus interrupted, "is Mr. Justice Chandra Bose and he is a Hindu."

"Better and better. We shall play upon his orthodoxy," said Bay. Then he stood up with excitement. "I have it! Tell me, Catullus, is there not a clause in the constitution of whatever it is that governs Limbo and all India that no law is valid if it interferes with a man's religious belief?"

Catullus thought for a moment. "There is no clause, but it is a principle which is never broken. As a Civil Servant I may do nothing contrary to a man's religion."

"Then you certainly can't hang him for believing in it," said Bay. "What we have to do is to prove beyond doubt that this man believes in witches, and that everything he did, even the murder that you say he committed, was done in accordance with that belief. If we can prove that, the most that he can get is a couple of years in jail, and we can fight that through every court in the land even if he gets it. Now, do we know what he believes?"

Catullus turned to me. "We don't, but you can find out. Tomorrow you start your school. Ask the parents questions. Ask the children questions. Officially these people are Hindus, but that is no more than official laziness. They are nothing of the sort. But *what* they are, nobody knows because nobody has asked. You must ask and ask and ask, and put everything you find out down in writing."

Bay raised his glass and said, "To our success, and damnation to the wiles of witches."

We drank, and then decided that we should go to bed and sleep so as to be fresh for planning further moves in our defense the next day.

I said good-night, and Catullus and Bay walked away toward their veranda, and I towards my house down the hill.

As Bay reached the balcony, I heard him stop and say, in a voice that rang across the jungle,

"*The worst of men does not injure another because, abstractedly, he would do him mischief, but in order to get rid of some pressure of evil* . . . mark that, Catullus . . . *some pressure of evil upon himself.*"

I heard Catullus say, "Who said that, Bay?"

And then Bay's voice, growing fainter as they went inside the house, "Leigh Hunt. It is in his most interesting, if rather prejudiced, Treatise on Devils. The argument is faulty, but the examples are well chosen. I must now tell you the story of the devil that . . ."

But what the devil did I could not hear, because Bay's voice was drowned by the bird that, once again, was drunkenly trying to start a fight.

CHAPTER FIVE

I BEGAN my research early next morning. I chose a village some eight miles away, and drove there in a truck. I chose it both because it was close at hand and because it had the only school in Limbo. I had been a little disappointed when I heard of the school: I thought that nobody but myself had ever tried to educate the inhabitants. This school spoiled my clean sheet. But it had been set up by the missionary that I had met at the Durbar, and he assured me that in no sense would it interfere with my work. He said that nobody had ever been known to learn anything at it in the twelve months of its existence. A gathering of middle-aged American women, somewhere in Virginia, had met on a hot afternoon and heard his missionary lecture on Limbo. He was appealing for funds for a harmonium for his church, but he had rambled a little, no doubt because of the heat, and let slip that nobody in Limbo could read or write. Partly to get home as quickly as possible out of the stifling lecture-room, and partly through human kindness, the Chairwoman had insisted on taking a collection for starting a school. So he had come back and started one, regretting that Sunday service in his church still must needs rely for its music on the same young (and by no means obliging) man who was the only person in Limbo who could play the mouth organ. The missionary, coming out to meet my truck as it passed his little house, begged me to use my official powers to close the school, as he was sure I would want to do as soon as I had seen it.

We drove for seven miles through the jungle, and then the scenery changed abruptly. I felt that the jungle must, in this part, have been submitted to an artillery bombardment. The trees had no branches and no leaves: they were

tall sticks stuck upright in the ground, quite dead. Around
their roots the earth had been thrown up by what I took
to be the explosion of the shells. Some trees had caught
fire, and burned down to the ground, leaving wide patches
of grey ash. We drove half a mile through this desolate
belt before I could gather from my Mohammedan clerk,
who was riding with me, why this should be.

The Limbodians fed largely on a crude rice-like crop,
he told me, and this was how they grew it. When the
season for sowing crops came round, a man would gather
his sons and daughters and his wife about him, and such
of his relatives with whom he had not quarrelled, and
they would go for a walk in the jungle. When the head of
a family came to a place which was to his liking, he sat
down. The rest of his family sat down beside him. The
head of the family then said, "We shall clear the ground
from that tree to this tree, and we shall all of us sow it
with seed." The members of his family then set up a
clamor, asking the man if he were mad, or drunk, or joking, because no family had ever been known to be able to
clear and sow such a vast stretch of land. They would then
suggest an area about half the size. The head of the family
would consider this proposition carefully on the grounds
that he loved his family dearly, and, as everybody knew,
he was a slave to their wishes. Nobody could ever say that
he drove them to sickness and premature old age by working them too hard in the fields. Certainly no. He therefore, of his own accord, and from the goodness of his heart,
divided the half area they had suggested for tilling in half
once again, and handsomely contented himself with that.
The whole family would then walk in procession round this
area, to make quite sure that they all understood. They
usually followed the head of the family, who, from time to
time, would veer slightly inwards towards the center of
the plot, thus lessening it a little more. When the narrowed
circuit was completed they would sit down again, and
congratulate one another on their zeal for hard work, and

consider how they would all, this year at least, have so much grain that they could sell it for an enormous profit in the market.

They then sent the smaller boys of the family climbing up the trees to the very tops, from which, each year, a certain percentage of the boys fell off. It was remarkable, said the clerk, how steady the percentage was, as you could see from the annual report. Statistics in Limbo were sparse, particularly since there were no medical services. But under the heading "The Year's Health" there was always one entry, and one entry only, and that was the number of boys who fell off trees. This was due to the fact that the Administration paid compensation for such accidents, in order to encourage agriculture. Such boys as did not fall off worked their way down the tree, loping off its branches. These branches, falling on the ground below, were gathered by the rest of the family and spread over the marked-out area. They were then burned, and the ash allowed to sink into the soil. A day or two later the family worked over this with pointed sticks, and when it was sufficiently broken up, sowed seed. Exhausted by this labor the whole family then retired to the village and celebrated their unparalleled industry by getting themselves drunk.

From now on the crop was left to the demons of field, tree, sun and rain. The Limbodians made a great point of not interfering with the demons since such presumptuous meddling would only irritate them, and cause them to down their airy tools and leave the place altogether. The family would therefore stay in its huts, avoiding all mention of work, and impressing the demons with their entire trust in spiritual help by doing nothing at all but hold a party every evening. When the rainy season was nearing its end, the crop appeared, and was gathered, with much junketing and more drinking, all in honor of the demons. As a result of the original family discussion about the size of the land to be worked, there was never enough to feed the family for more than two or three months. It was then necessary to borrow from neighbors lucky enough to have more obliging demons who had provided them with a surplus. When this failed, the family went hunting squirrels and lizards in the jungle, shooting them with their bows and arrows. When sowing time came round again the next year, the same procedure would be adopted, except for this difference: a slightly smaller plot of land would be selected, in order not to discourage the demons, and there would be still heavier drinking in their honor, in the hope that the spiritual powers, in appreciation, would, this year at least, give them enough to eat, and something over to sell in the market. They were always quite confident that it would happen.

I thanked the clerk very much for his information, and put it all down in a notebook.

By this time we had reached the village. It was scattered about a sort of rolling parkland, free from trees for half a mile round, and then hemmed in by a ring of lopped and burned-down forest. The school was well situated on the highest and breeziest part of the parkland. It was a long, low hut, with projecting eaves, the walls made of plaited strips of bamboo and the roof of whole branches of trees, the leaves left on them to wither and provide shade and protection from the rain. This was the manner of building all the huts in Limbo, but the school had this difference: that one half of the roof had fallen down. The clerk assured me that in this case the school-teacher would move into the roofed half and not think of replacing the fallen portion until the rains. However, during the rains it was even more dangerous to go climbing trees to cut down branches. It would therefore be left till more suitable weather. When this came, however, there would be little purpose in roofing the school, since most of the time was spent in the open air, owing to the heat. My clerk therefore gave it as his opinion that the school would stay unroofed for a considerable time, unless I gave express orders, and twice the cost in cash, for it to be done. He was quite certain that these tactics would succeed, because the school-teacher would spend the money on drink, and be so ashamed that she would see that a roof was built for my next visit, in order that I should not ask questions.

The truck stopped, and I climbed the small rise to the hut. The school-teacher came out to greet me. I had formed a clear picture of what the school-teacher would be like from the clerk's story. I was therefore astonished to be met by a middle-aged lady, dressed in the best Indian fashion, and saying, "How do you do, sir," in very good English.

The clerk introduced her as Mrs. Joseph.

"Joseph?" I asked.

"Yes. I am a Christian. I come from such-and-such a place" (and she named a town beyond, but not far beyond, the borders of Limbo), "I went to the Christian school, and now I am here. Please come into the schoolroom."

I bent my head and went into the hut. The furniture of the schoolroom was very simple. There was one desk, and a chair to go with it. A number of slates stood on the floor, leaning against the bamboo walls. The walls themselves were decorated with large colored pictures. Two were of Biblical scenes: one was of a large St. Bernard dog, a barrel of brandy tied to its collar, gazing somewhat dismayed into a prospect of snow and ice, and the other was a picture of a woman in a bathing costume holding up a bottle of non-alcoholic drink, plainly labelled with the name of its American manufacturer. The middle of the floor of the schoolroom had been built up with stones and clay into a fireplace. A charcoal fire was, at the moment of my inspection, just bringing a bowl of curry to the boil.

Mrs. Joseph noticed this and, apologizing with a pleasant ease of manner, squatted on the floor and attended to her cooking for some minutes. When the curry was to her satisfaction, which she decided only after many trials of it by dipping her finger into the pot and licking it clean, she smiled at me, wiped her hands carefully on her dress, and stood up.

"Mrs. Joseph," I said, "I suppose today is a holiday?"

"Oh no." I felt that she was a little hurt. "I *never* give the children holidays. The Reverend Father at my school always said that education was the most important thing in life and you must not waste precious time in giving holidays. No, I never give my children any holidays except the proper ones and they are a long way off." She gazed out of the door, into a vista of laborious days in the classroom, until the blessed relief of the vacation.

"Then, Mrs. Joseph, the children are all playing truant?"

"They are very good children," she almost snapped at me, "and to play truant is the wickedest thing a child can do. The Reverend Father always told us that at my school. No child in this village could be as wicked as that."

"Then why are there no children in your classroom?"

"It's because of the parents. They won't send them to school." She raised her hands in a wide gesture. "I tell them that they should send their children, but they come and argue with me."

I looked round the schoolroom and at the fireplace in the middle of it. "I should imagine, Mrs. Joseph, that they get the better of the argument."

"Oh yes," she said simply. "I never answer them back. A lady should never argue. The Reverend Father told us that."

"Do no children ever come to school?"

"Oh yes, some do," she said. "When they are naughty their parents send them here for the day instead of beating them."

"Do they come back next day?"

She assumed a motherly expression. "No," she said. "It would be cruel to punish them again the next day. The mothers and fathers here are very fond of their children."

I sat down at the desk in the hope that it would give me a little dignity for what I was about to say.

"Mrs. Joseph, would it surprise you if I told you now that I mean to close this school, in my capacity as Education Officer for Limbo, and that I have the Reverend Small's agreement in doing so?"

She pursed her lips and gazed shrewdly into her boiling pot of curry. "No," she said at last. "It would not surprise me. It's that organ of his again."

"Harmonium," I corrected her.

"He tried it once before. He wrote back to America that I was not doing any teaching and that he was going to close the school. I heard all about it from one of the Mission girls, and how he wanted the money for an organ." She stirred her curry again. "So *I* wrote a letter back to the kind American ladies, too."

"Good heavens! Did you tell them about the harmonium?"

"Oh no!" she said. "The Reverend Father Small is a good and kind man. How could I be so wicked as to do that?"

"Then what *did* you do?"

"I wrote to them about the jungle, and the tigers, and the panthers, and the snakes."

"Nothing, I take it, about the school?"

"No," she said with simplicity. "The Reverend Father Small had done that, and I could not write as good a letter as he could."

"Did you say nothing else, except about the tigers and the snakes?"

"No. Except at the end I asked the kind American ladies to pray for me."

She lowered her head submissively and kept her eyes on the ground.

"Well? What happened?"

"They wrote lots of letters back to me. They were very kind letters, and some of them sent me presents, like chains with crosses on them, and frocks and oh! such a lot of things. Then they wrote to the Reverend Father and said that he must keep the school going whatever happened and he must take a picture of me. So he did. I have got it here."

She lifted the top of the desk at which I was sitting and, moving aside a pair of old shoes and some untouched textbooks, took out a small photograph, torn at the edges with handling. It showed Mrs. Joseph, seated against a tree, extending her arms round a number of small and naked children. A boy somewhat older than the rest of the children was seated on the ground a little to her left, and had clearly been told to look into Mrs. Joseph's face. He had his head flung back in violent adoration. Mrs. Joseph had apparently dropped a little to the right as the camera operated, bending even more tenderly over a small girl in the crook of her arm. The boy's ardent gaze thus fell rather too high, and he had the appearance of earnestly trying to ascertain the exact position of the noonday sun. Across the bottom of the photograph, in a heavy, childish hand, Mrs. Joseph had written a religious and humble presentation of her love. The picture, I assumed, had been one of many intended for America, but which, at the last moment, she had kept back for herself.

"This one is rather old," she said. "The kind American ladies have the best ones. They must look very nice. One lady wrote to me that she keeps it in her bedroom, with flowers all round it."

"Did they pray for you?" I asked, giving her the picture.

"Oh yes. They prayed every week that my self . . . self . . ." she stumbled and looked embarrassed.

"Your self-sacrifice?" I suggested.

"Yes. My self-sacrifice should be rewarded, and that children should one day come and learn at the school."

"They did not pray very successfully," I said. "Have you a piece of paper?"

She opened the desk again and found some paper underneath the old shoes. I took it and began to write.

"This," I said as I wrote, "is an order to close this school. As for the kind American ladies, I shall write to them and tell them that unfortunately their prayers have not been answered, and that they are wasting their money."

"Oh, but, sir, their prayers *were* answered." She clasped her hands in front of her and tears began to fill her eyes. "Oh yes, sir. The very day I got the letter a little boy walked straight into the school and sat down, and there he was, my first pupil!"

"Really. Then I shall go and congratulate his parents for being the only sensible people in the village. What is their name?"

"I do not know, sir."

"Did you never ask him?"

"Yes, sir."

"Well?"

"He didn't know, sir. You see, the poor little thing was an orphan, and he'd walked here through the jungle."

"What did you do with him."

"Sir, I adopted him. I have not very much money, but the wages the good Reverend Father Small pays me help, so I can keep him. I do not really like children at all. That is why I became a convert, because I wanted to become a nun. But I love my little boy. I do not know where he would go without me, or what he would do. This is his dinner cooking now. He will be home soon, and I must get it ready. Excuse me, sir, if you please, sir." She sat down slowly by the cooking-pot, and tears ran down her face.

I tore up the paper I was writing. I did not like to throw it on the floor, so I lifted the lid of the desk. Then I saw the photograph of the woman who did not like children, and decided I would be wiser to wait for the little orphan to come home, and satisfy myself that he existed before I let the school continue. Then I thought again, and made up my mind that I would not wait. I felt a little sorry for the Reverend Small because he would not get his harmonium, but I felt that my decision showed balance and maturity, the sort of compromise with facts that I had been told was expected of a man working in the jungle. I went outside the hut.

I heard a loud murmur as from many voices and I looked about me. I was surrounded on three sides by the men of the village. They were greeting me, but not with any enthusiasm. I answered their greeting, and waited to see why they had come. Nobody seemed willing to speak, and they stood quite still for some moments, brown shoulder to brown shoulder, and bare thighs pressing against one another to form a living hedge around me. In the front row were mostly old men, with faces sunken about the mouth and tiny chins on which grew white down instead of beards. Behind them were the younger men, broad-nosed and with fine eyes, their hair hanging in oiled masses almost down to their shoulders. A few of the older men were dressed in sleeveless waistcoats above the cloth wound through their crotches, but most were naked. A man in a red turban moved forward a little, and I knew enough of Limbo by now to judge him to be the headman of the village.

The headman cleared his throat and said, "Your Honor, we have been talking to your clerk."

I looked round for the young Mohammedan that he had named, and found him hiding himself in an embarrassed fashion behind the back row of villagers.

"Your Honor, he tells us that you are closing the school."

I saw at once that the clerk, in the maner of clerks, had been boasting of my authority while I had been talking to the school-teacher, in order to magnify his own.

"It is possible," I said. "Well?"

The brown hedge swayed and there was indignant

exclamations. The headman, although he controlled his voice as became one official speaking to another, was also deeply disturbed.

"Sir, you cannot do that!"

"Why? It is not a good school."

"Your Honor, it is a very bad school."

"And none of you sends his children there."

The headman regarded this as a witty remark and repeated it to the encircling brown hedge. Some of the villagers laughed.

"Of course not," he said, turning back to me. "None of us would think of sending his children there. Why should we? That woman does not know anything, and if she does (because she ought to, since she was sent to school herself) she is much too lazy to teach our children."

"Well, then," I said, "why should you mind my closing the school?"

"But Your Honor," said the headman, deeply serious again, "the poor woman has her living to earn. You cannot take her living away from her!"

There was a loud noise of approval from all the villagers. The clerk saw the exhausted expression on my face, and hastily broke through the ring, and brought the chair from the schoolroom. Very gratefully, I sat down.

"You do not want to send your children to the school," I said very deliberately, "*and* you do not want the school closed. You think the school-teacher a bad woman *and* you do not want her to lose her job. Please, headman, I am quite new to Limbo. Please tell me if I have got it right?"

"Quite right," he said promptly. "Except that she is not altogether a bad woman. No. We could have far worse. And if you send her away, we shall certainly get far worse."

"But you say she is too lazy to teach. Who could be a worse school-teacher than that?"

A young man spoke from the second row. "But she knows she is a lazy woman and she does not make trouble when we do not send our children to school. The next woman will make a great noise and we shall have to argue a great deal with her and maybe hit her a little." The brown hedge gave this statement general approval.

"Very well." I remembered the necessity for tact and adaptability when working in the jungle, though I felt that my stock of both was running low. "If I keep on your teacher will you send your children to the school?"

The headman eyed me for a moment distrustfully. "How can you ask us to do that when you have already said she was a bad teacher?"

The villagers regarded this as a shrewd point, well struck home, and it was received with an approving "Ah" from everybody.

I felt that if I were to recover my prestige I should change the line of the argument. It seemed to be the right time to begin my work as a member of the Defense Committee.

"But she is a Christian: and you are not Christians. Are you?"

"What is a Christian?"

"I mean she has a different . . ." I lost the word, and the clerk supplied it in the Limbodian language— ". . . belief."

The headman put his legs apart comfortably and folded his arms. He looked up at the sky, then at the villagers, and then at me before he spoke. "I have had many talks with the woman," he said. "She believes two things: that when a man sleeps with another man's wife, and when a man drinks liquor, both are the work of the devil. She says so. It's all due to the devil, she says. And so do we. So I think perhaps we are Christians. These things are certainly the work of devils, as indeed what is not? What is not?" he said, with a rhetorical flourish of his voice to the surrounding crowd. "Yes," facing me again, "maybe we are Christians."

"But not everything comes from the devils. Some

things come from God, at least that is what Christians think."

"What things?"

I thought of what things, but they seemed very vague. Grace was one of the few that I could remember, but I did not feel equal to entering upon a description of grace, nor was I very sure that I knew much about it. *All good things around us* was another phrase that came into my head, but looking over the heads of the crowd at the jungle on the horizon, I felt that the words fitted better into the scenery of the North Temperate zone than there. An impatient cough from the headman brought me back to Limbo. I fell back on an official line. "I shall consider leaving your school-teacher with you. But I am opening a bigger and better school for your children. Will you send some of them there?"

Incredulous smiles broke out like flowers round the brown hedge. "But what for?" asked one of the oldest men among them.

"To learn to read."

"We have got nothing to read."

"I shall send you books so that your children can read them."

The headman said, "Thank you for your gift," and raised his hands in salute as one must do whenever anyone offers you something in Limbo. But then he dropped his hands and said with a touch of impatience, "Is not that like the man who gave a village a tiger and then gave the village a gun to shoot it with?"

A roar of approval at this quip came from his listeners. "We have no books and so we do not need to read. Why should you go to the trouble of sending us books and then go to even more trouble to teach our children to read them?"

"What about writing and arithmetic?" I said, with less calm than I could have wished. "You have money, at least, and you want to know how to add it up. At least your children will want to know."

The headman swivelled on his heels and faced the crowd. "Is there anybody here," he asked in the politest of voices, "who has more money than he knows how to count?"

The villagers slapped their thighs, beat one another over the back, and some of the older men sat down on the ground, overcome by the violence of their laughter.

"Listen," I said, and I got up to show that this was going to be my last attempt. "Listen. I want you to give me your children to take away and I will give them free food, I will give them free clothes, and I will give them a free house. Now, will you send them?"

The laughter stopped. The headman unfolded his arms, screwed up his eyes and searched my face.

"Free food?" he asked.

"Yes."

"Free clothes?"

"Quite free."

Suddenly an old man in the front row shouted, "Well, what is all the talk about? You can have our children and the parents too!"

The meeting broke up. Cheering and laughing, the men made a dash for the truck and climbed aboard. And as they did so, I saw that behind them, all during the conference, had been a row of women, and behind them again, well out of my view, a row of little boys. The women now surrounded me, pushing their boys forward and demanding that I take them in the truck. Everybody was shouting at once, and I had to bellow to make myself heard. I tried to distinguish between the boys, and thought sadly of the intelligence tests which I had planned to choose them out. All I could do now was to shout, "I'll take that one and that one and that one," pointing to identically naked, grinning, and dirty small boys. The women said "Yes, we understand," and cuffed two or three children on the head to show it. But very soon I noticed that the spaces in the truck which the men left (and there were not many) were being filled by any boy who had the dexterity to scramble up and hang on to his place. When the truck seemed dangerously overloaded I shouted for my clerk and climbed in beside the driver. I gave the signal to start, which was greeted with a howling cheer from the men and boys in the back. As the truck moved off the women sprinted after it in a body, some of them managing to catch hold of the tailboard and climb in. Then I remembered something and stopped the truck. I got out and went round to the back. By this time they had all started singing, and one man was beating the metal top of the driving cab as though it were a drum.

"Luggage! The boys have got to bring their luggage!" Nobody could hear what I was saying. I caught hold of a boy who was sitting on the extreme edge of the tailboard. "You will have to stay a long time," I shouted in his ear. "You must bring your luggage with you." The singing grew much louder, but he heard me, and he nodded.

"Well, where is it?" I looked him up and down. He was dressed in a small turban and a loincloth, and there was no sign of a bundle or a box anywhere near him. Another man joined the impromptu drummer in hammering on the metal roof. "Where is your luggage?" I yelled.

The small boy opened his eyes in a frightened manner as he saw what must have been the desperate expression on my face. Then he slowly felt around in his turban and, unwinding something carefully from out of his long hair, produced a catapult.

"Here it is," he said. "I've got it all right," and he gave me a broad, kindly, and reassuring grin.

Just then the driver, catching the holiday mood of the singing villagers, started the lorry with a long and happy shout. I ran after it, and was hauled aboard by my clerk. who stopped singing long enough to apologize to my Honor for the trouble my Honor had been given.

CHAPTER SIX

THE next day I walked over to Catullus' bungalow
before breakfast to report on what I had discovered
about the religion of Limbo, so that Bay might use it in
preparing his speech for the defense. Both Bay and Catullus
agreed that I had not found out very much, and telling my
story in the rather chilly morning air of the hill-top I could
not find much in it to prove them wrong. We sat down to
breakfast. At first we did not talk very much. We all read
ten-days-old newspapers that had been delivered by a
runner and had been, of course, dropped in the river. The
ducking had in a way improved the news: report of war
and threats of war, political stratagems and coups were
inclined to disappear, after a legible start, into a grey blur,
as though the Press correspondents, after getting well
launched in their stories, had looked up and found themselves in Limbo and realized that this sort of disturbing
thing would not do at all. Bay finished some of the news
items aloud, filling in the gaps in the manner of *The Times*
leaders of about 1850.

Catullus listened to him for a while and then said to
me:

"You know, I like your idea of printing a special newspaper so that the boys can have something to read."

"It was not my idea, but the headman's. He suggested
books."

"Books might be difficult. But we could easily manage
a newspaper."

"But how?"

"We could reprint copies, day by day, of *The Times*
from the reign of Queen Victoria. Nobody in Limbo would
know the difference. Bay, what do you think would be a
good starting date?"

Bay considered for a moment. "Louis Napoleon," he said. "Modern journalism (and I imagine that you would want to give them as modern a newspaper as you could without corrupting them) began with Press photography. And whatever the books say the first really successful photographer was the Frenchman Disderi. Louis Napoleon was setting out at the head of his troops for his Italian campaign, leaving Paris with the most impressive martial pageantry, when, passing down a crowded and cheering boulevard, he caught sight of Disderi's photographer's shop. The extraordinary monarch dismounted (for I am sure he was riding a white horse), entered the shop, and demanded that Disderi take his portrait. The delighted photographer did his best, and that, in those early days of photography, took a very long time. While Disderi pulled blinds and wheeled his camera about, and fussed with imitation folio volumes for the great man to rest his hand upon, the entire army waited in the boulevard. Finally, the shutter was clicked, the King bowed out, and the whole absurd business of artificially inflated personalities which is the very meat of the modern newspaper was begun."

"Good," Catullus said. "We shall begin with copies of *The Times* published during the reign of Louis Napoleon and proceed steadily, day by day, through the subsequent issues. Your Limbodian boys," he went on, talking to me, "will be brought up in an exclusive atmosphere of Victorian politics, Victorian morality, and Victorian economics. They will do startlingly well at the examinations for the Indian Civil Service, and will rise to the top of the Administrative tree. There could be no sounder or more practical method of education. Talking of education, this is the first day of your new school, isn't it?"

"Yes. Much to my surprise the boys I brought in the truck and put to bed last night were still there at six o'clock this morning. At least, so the headmaster tells me in a note."

Catullus did not seem to hear me, but was still following in his mind's eye the daily issue of back numbers of *The Times*. "Yes, indeed," he said, "there are vast possibilities in education in Limbo. Vast and exciting." Then, recollecting himself, "Are you going down *yourself* to the school?"

"I thought I would."

"Oh, but it's not at all necessary. In fact, I do not think it would be quite in keeping with your dignity as a Government Officer. You do not have to teach. You merely have to organize the schools. No, take a rest. You look rather tired. Yesterday must have been most exhausting. Leave the school to the schoolmasters. One must learn to delegate authority. Leave them alone this morning to make what mess of it they choose. Go home and relax, and stroll down to the school at midday."

I was rather glad of this advice, and I took it.

The school was a new wooden building, very airy, with wide windows so that anyone approaching it was easily able to see the class of boys at work. As I came down the hill at twelve o'clock I was surprised to see that nobody appeared to be inside.

I went in and found the explanation. All the boys were sprawling on their bellies on the floor, or squatting in corners, drawing with thick black pencils on enormous sheets of paper. In the middle of them, and also on the floor, was Catullus, drawing as busily as any of them. Nobody noticed my entrance, and I stepped among the prone artists looking at their work. It was charming, full of the naïve animals and out-of-perspective humans that is the sign of a child's drawing when he is left free to express himself. I walked over to where Catullus was sketching, and looked at what he had done. It, too, was charming and, if anything, even more naïve and out of perspective than the drawings of the children.

He saw my shadow on his piece of paper and looked up with a guilty grin.

"I'm so sorry to come here without your permission," he said.

"Not at all. As the King of Limbo you can come and go as you please."

"Well, you see, it wasn't at all that I was *inspecting*, but I began thinking over your excellent scheme to reprint issues of *The Times* . . ." I nodded, and forebore, this time, to remind him that I had nothing to do with it. ". . . and I thought that although, of course, I would give you my fullest official backing, maybe I could not get it past Higher Authorities. I was so disappointed at having let down the boys that I thought I would come over and see if there was anything else I could do. And there was, indeed there was."

He clambered up and snatched a drawing from one of the elder boys. It was of a tiger, drawn in three triangles, and of a man shooting him with a bow and arrow, drawn in two triangles and several irregular circles. In its way, it was a masterpiece of simple, untrammelled drawing.

I said so.

"I'm so glad you agree," Catullus said. He patted the solemn, four-foot-high artist on his bare rear, and said, "Do you know, an hour ago this boy was the most shockingly bad artist that you've ever met? In fact, he wasn't an artist at all. Of course, part of the credit should go to the headmaster, because he really started it."

"By the way, where is the headmaster?"

"We tried to work together for a bit, but I don't think he grasped the full potentialities of what we were doing. He seemed to grow rather harassed, so I sent him home to rest. I knew you wouldn't mind. But he should have the credit for starting the whole thing. When I came in he said, 'Your Honor,'—you know how servile these low-paid officials are—'Your Honor, will you set the boys an examination?' Well, they had only been at school for a day, so what could I examine them in? I pointed this out to the headmaster and he said, 'Your Honor, examine them in drawing. All boys can draw.' Well, these boys couldn't, because I said, 'Now, boys, draw me a tiger,' and after about ten minutes this was the vulgar horror that one of them produced." He snatched up a piece of paper from the floor where he had been treading it underfoot, and showed it to me. It was a very neat, very literal drawing of a tiger seen from the side, such as one might meet reproduced in a child's alphabet book.

Catullus waved the drawing in the air. "I said, 'Is this how you *see* a tiger?' and the boy said 'Yes.' I said, 'But nonsense, boy, you can't possibly *see* a tiger like that!' and the boy answered me back, 'But doesn't it *look* like a tiger?' Of course it did, of course, but the silly boy had missed the whole point of primitive art. No drawing done by a real primitive ever looks like the thing that he's drawing. It mustn't. That's the whole basis of all that modern criticism which has done so much to show us the excellences of primitive art. And here was this slip of a boy saying 'Doesn't it look like a tiger?' "

"Which slip of a boy?" I said, because from Catullus' description I had taken rather a liking to him. Catullus pointed him out, and they grinned at each other amiably, like two boys who had planned a successful piece of mischief.

"Well," Catullus swept on, "I thought 'Here's a fine state of affairs. What will the Education Officer think? He's doing his very best to set up a school for primitive children, and what is he going to find? No primitive art. Not a line, not a squiggle, not a smudge of primitive art. Any sensitive man in his position would resign, and I wouldn't blame him if he did.' So I got down on my hands and knees and *showed* them how to do primitive art. I'm not bad at it, you know. I've several excellent books of reproductions at home, and I drew what I could remember of those, throwing in a little child art here and there, which I recalled from something I read about drawing by infants in London County Council Schools. The boys were lambs, and got down to it most obligingly. And just look at the result! In one hour we have enough primitive art to run a fair-sized exhibition." He stalked over and round the various drawings on the floor, from time to time picking one up to show me. "Just think," he ended, "one hour ago there was no primitive art in Limbo at all."

He observed my reaction.

"You need a good strong whiskey and soda," he said next. "Come up to my bungalow and I shall mix you one."

On my way up the hill he expanded his theme.

"The thing has possibilities. Suppose we take the most promising boys and set them down to manufacture primitive art in considerable quantities. The world market is insatiable. Of course, we shall not confine ourselves to drawing. We shall introduce modelling and wood-carving, and in one year I guarantee that our Limbodian boys will have every piece of that tiresome negro art down in the junk cellar. We shall sell at high prices, of course, and use the money to start a fund for the further art education of all Limbodian boys and girls. Limbo schools will rapidly become self-supporting, and completely independent of Government interference. As specimens of our art spread through the galleries of the world, a school of painters will rise, proud to acknowledge their debt to the simple but inspired minds of these primitive children. Why, one of our own boys might well be discovered, like Douanier Rousseau, and himself become the most admired artist of his time. There is no end to what we can do. All that we need in education here is new ideas."

ii

"There are no new ideas in education," said Bay when we were relaxing on the veranda with our drinks. "The last and final one was thought of by James I, who shut up a boy from the age of one in a cellar to see if he would talk Hebrew when he let him out ten years later. Modern educational theories are no more than timorous adaptions of the same bold idea. The most advanced teacher of the most advanced school believes nothing more profound than that the best way of teaching a boy is to leave him to his own devices. Exactly, you will note, the theory of King James. He, however, wisely confined himself to the hope that the boy would turn out to know just one single language, whereas modern educations absurdly expect the child to be proficient in a minimum of two, together with advanced mathematics, far from elementary science, the complete range of English literature, European history, and, of all the preposterous demands, expect him to turn himself into an expert athlete into the bargain. But perhaps I do advanced schools an injustice: in some, I am assured, the practice of kicking a football has been dropped in favor of the practice of kicking the master, a change which, in fairness, I admit is on the side of reason. No, do not be misled by books written by schoolmasters to ease their perpetually guilty consciences into asking the boys what they would like to do. A child quickly learns these days that if he is to survive in society until he has the muscular strength to defend himself he must as soon as possible become an accomplished liar. Ask him what he would like to do at school and he will be careful to tell you that he wants to study biology, when in fact he wants to play hookey in the woods. Either turn your boys out of your school and threaten them with a beating if they ever show their faces inside it again (which is the only humane thing to do) or decide that you have not the slightest idea what they want to do and care even less, and that you are sending them to school because you are an Education Officer and so there must be some education somewhere around the place. Do not deceive yourself that a good school is the first step in civilization. The

great ages of Europe, which produced world-encompass-
ing genius such as it would be rash indeed to say that we
could parallel today, were also the ages of the most
abominable schools and pervertedly brutal schoolmasters.
Erasmus, who liberated the mind of Europe, swore that
his lifelong rheumatism was due to kneeling so often on
a stone floor at school to be flogged. Are you proposing
to return to the school before lunch?"

I said I thought that I would not.

"You would not mind if I went to have a look at the
boys?"

"Well, no. Are you thinking of teaching them anything, like Catullus?"

"I don't think so. I would suggest, however, that you
teach them how to read by setting up large letters from
the alphabet as targets and inviting the boys to shoot at
them with their bows and arrows."

Catullus was enthusiastic. "But, Bay, it's a brilliant
suggestion. And it disproves your theory. It's a brand
new idea in education."

"On the contrary," Bay said, standing up and putting
on his black felt hat, "it was invented by Sir Thomas More
as a method of teaching his daughters Greek."

He went off down the hill towards the school.

iii

In the evening a servant came with a note from Catullus.
It was written on a sheet of paper embossed with the
Royal Arms, and began:

"We have forgotten the parents. I consider it v.
important that we should not do so. Essence of a successful
school is that it sets to rest gnawing suspicion in all
parents that their children might turn out cleverer than
themselves. N.B. Notoriously bad private schools in
England, but always with v. long waiting list. Have asked

all parents of prospective pupils from five surrounding villages to come to party in your compound this evening ten p.m. sharp. Supply plenty of liquor and charge it to Abstract Contingent Account Deposit VI Heading Educational facilities Yrs. C."

Shortly afterwards some men came and began cutting down a tree in my garden. I asked what they meant by doing such a thing and they said it was for the party. I wanted to know if I had to hang gifts on it, but they said, no, I just had to burn it. You could not have a party in Limbo without a fire, they said.

I went indoors and replied to Catullus. I wrote:

"Good, but be careful. Parents of boys already enrolled as pupils are having three meals a day out of the school canteen, and refusing to pay for them. They say that we can take the price out in forced labor from the boys on the roads. See you at the party."

I sent this off by my servant, and then watched the drink arrive. It had been sent by Catullus. It was liquor that was made from a local flower and tasted rather like gin and lime. It was brought to my bungalow in baskets, twelve bottles to a basket, and eight men carried it, one basket to each man. I signed receipts for it in my official capacity as Education Officer in Limbo, while the men who had been cutting down the tree now began to set it on fire.

It took them a long time to get it going, but by ten o'clock it was going a steady blaze, which still was not bright enough to eat into the shadow of the surrounding forest. The woodcutters had by this time gone away, and my servants had taken a basket of liquor off down the hill to warm themselves up for the party. I sat on my veranda, watching the fire and quite alone. Some bats, annoyed by the untimely glare, came wheeling and shrieking overhead, small angry pieces of the surrounding blackness that had torn themselves away to make a protest. Then everything became still again.

I mistook my first guest for an injured and enormous bat that was trailing a broken wing across the ground, he was so silent and so dark. He moved out of the forest and came just near enough for the fire to catch his features. I thought he appeared to be fitting on a face to the top of his black trunk to oblige me, in a manner dressing for the party. Then another came, equally without sound, and sat nearer the fire, reassuring me that he was human by coughing slightly and clearing his throat. Then a dozen villagers filed out of the trees, some of them women, the firelight sparkling from the metal rings round their necks and in their ears. The women sat away from the men, and nobody spoke. Next came some boys, solemnly, in double file, like a choir that some eccentric clergyman had suddenly stripped of their clothes as they left the vestry. Two men followed them carrying between them a huge drum. They put it on the ground and tested it, sending out a deep and threatening rumble that echoed back from the tree-trunks.

There was quiet again for a while, and then came a brassy, howling noise, pitched high, that lodged in my head and spun round between my ears. It was a physical hurt, and I got up, with my hands pressed to the side of my head, to see what it was. A man, seeing me, smiled, and held up a long instrument like a clarinet, which he had been trying out. About a hundred shadows had by this time disentangled themselves from the forest and sat down around the fire, turning themselves into my guests. I thought it time to begin the party.

I called for the drink, and my servants, reeling a little, brought up one of the baskets. A man from the group sitting round the fire got up and, coming over to me, grinned and made signs that he should take the bottle. I gave it him and he pulled at it, drinking about a quarter. He passed it to the first of the sitting figures, and that man also drank, watched closely by all the other guests. He was very unwillingly passing the bottle to the man next to him when I heard a high pitched voice in the trees behind me saying, "No, no, no, no, no, that's *not* the way at all."

Catullus and Bay appeared from behind my house, and Catullus, snatching bottles from the basket, began to hand them out to everybody within range. Bay called for another basket and set to work on that, and soon dozens of bottles were being opened and poured down the throats of the villagers. They came up and formed a crowd round the basket, waiting until they should each be given a bottle, and when they had got it, going back to the squatting place from which they came. The choirboys lined up and, still with the same earnest expression, got each of them his bottle and went away to drink.

The drummer began beating in a desultory fashion on his cowhide drum, until a large man with a very small loincloth and no other dress save blue tattoo marks took a bottle from a passing boy, and seizing the drummer by the hair, tilted back his head and poured the liquor into his mouth. The drummer gasped happily and spun away from the large man, treading out tight little circles with his feet and making his hands fly on the skin of his drum. This was the signal for the dance to begin.

The women first made a circle round the fire, and outside this circle the men made another. The boys, too few to make a complete ring, capered in groups on the very outside. The women began a shuffling dance, going round in one direction, the men, doing the same step, moved in a wavering circle in the other. From time to time a man would detach himself from the dances and do a cadenza on his own, beating his feet and snapping his fingers, wailing in a high, piercing fashion that seemed to me to express the depths of unhappiness. But this could not have been its proper meaning, for any particularly anguished wail brought an answering happy shout from the dancers, who laughed and clapped, while the drummer redoubled the pace of his drumming, and everybody danced a little faster. The clarinet joined in when the dance was fairly

going, and that was the signal for everybody to pick out
his particular group of friends, break the circle, make tight
little hugging groups with them, which went off dancing
on their own. When the whole pattern of the dance had
been lost, and groups of shouting or wailing friends, men
with men and women with women, were prancing from
end to end of the compound and falling over one another in
confusion, the dance came to an end. Everybody was ex-
traordinarily happy,and shouted for another tune. Our servants ran about giving more bottles of drink to persons who
looked exhausted, and serving Catullus, Bay and myself
with brandy and soda. The drummer pretended that he
was tired, at which the large man, who had made himself
master of ceremonies, seized him again and poured half of
another bottle down his throat, the drink running out of
his mouth, over his body and dripping from the drum that
hung by a cord from his neck. He spluttered, and struck
up a new rhythm. This suggested a new sport, and the
master of ceremonies came to me and said that if I would
lend him some properties, they would do a play.

They went into the house and came out with one of
my curtains. A man put his hand into the ashes of the fire
and blacked his face. He put on a torn shirt, and the curtain
was bundled up inside it to give him a wobbling paunch.
Another man kneeled down, and the actor, who was now
representing an official of the administration, lowered himself with dignity on to the man's back, until he sat as if
on a seat, though the seat was the kneeling man and
remained so throughout the drama. The man with the
paunch nodded for proceedings to begin, and Bay and I
shouted with laughter because it was so exactly the slow
"Now-I-think-we-can-declare-the-bazaar-open" nod that
Catullus used at official ceremonies. The drummer played
a bar or two, and some other actors shouted extempore
lines. They were asking the official for some favor (we
could not gather what) and he was refusing. They insulted
him, and at each particularly choice hit the drummers rolled

out an appreciative stave or two on their instruments, and the audience laughed.

The official now made a particularly silly excuse, and the other actors set upon him and beat him. The drums thundered, and the dialogue began again. Once again the official made a lame excuse, and once again was beaten. Then, winking broadly to show that at last he was a perfect echo of Catullus making a speech, he said, "How can you dare pester me in this manner. This is no time to ask for favors." "Why? Why? Why?" howled back the petitioners. "Because," he said in Catullus' most outraged and treble inflection, "I am about to go to the lavatory."

He walked off stage to show that that was the end of the play, and the audience almost stood up with laughing. Our servants sent round more drink, including brandy for us, and we all began to feel very happy indeed.

There was another dance of concentric circles, while Bay, Catullus and I talked enthusiastically of the spirit of a people that could perform such an excellent satire in the very presence of a high official. We noted how very expressive the acting was, shouting our remarks at one another over the noise of the band. Then Bay got up and said, "*Now*, I think," and went into the house. A few moments later he came out with one of my bedspreads draped round his shoulders in the manner of a cloak. A great cry of delight went up from all the small boys when they saw him, and the dance was immediately stopped. The master of ceremonies hustled all the adults back to their squatting places, and left the ground clear around the fire for some twenty boys that I noticed all came from my school.

Bay signalled to the orchestra, who played a few introductory bars; he then strode out into the open space, swinging his cloak, and turned to face me. The master of ceremonies dived at the seat that Bay had been sitting on, picked up Bay's hat, and gave it to him, ducking out of the way like a property man before the curtain goes up.

Bay accepted the hat and put it on his head. He turned to Catullus and myself and said:

"Your Honors," and bowed.

The clarinet started a rather sad tune, and, remarkably, the player contrived to keep the sound of the instrument soft and sweet-toned. The fire flamed up for a moment, making Bay's figure in his swinging cloak satisfactorily dramatic.

"*Beyond the isle of Prester John and his lordship of the wilderness that goes right East men shall not find but hills, great rocks, and other dark lands,*" said Bay.

"It's a play about heaven," Catullus whispered. "Limbo heaven."

The clarinet played quietly and sadly, and Bay, in a very fine and rich voice, went on.

"*This wilderness and dark land, where no man may see day or night, lasts to the land of Paradise Terrestre.*"

"How beautiful," I said. "Is it a translation of a Limbo poem?"

Bay had broken his recitation to move slowly round the fire, while the drummers beat in rhythm to his steps. Following came a train of small boys, each of them imitating Bay's mighty walk.

"No, not exactly a translation," said Catullus to me. "Primitive poetry is rather limited, I find. I did once take a lot of trouble to get an exact translation of one of the Limbo songs."

Bay was the far side of the fire now, admiringly watched by everybody in his audience. The music rose in volume and had touches of grandeur.

"I'd like to hear it," I said. "How did it go?"

"Well, it was rather obscure. It went:

> '*I and my grandmother flew away like a kite,*
> *Flew away so high, changing our color white.*
> *What did papa do to mama,*
> *Under the brinjal tree?*
> *Got the gun and shot the bastard,*
> *Under the coconut tree.*'

The change of vegetation is difficult to follow, but is probably significant. All primitive poetry is like that, don't you find?" said Catullus despairingly. "Anyway, Bay thought something rather better was called for in this play about heaven."

Bay had made a full circle, leaving the boys in set positions behind him as he did so. He now came forward again and faced us.

"*Of Paradise Terrestre I cannot speak properly for I have not been there, but that which I have heard I shall tell you.*" He took off his hat and bowed deeply. "To be accurate, what we are about to show you is not Paradise Terrestre but Paradise Celeste. However, I did not like to tamper with old Sir John Mandeville's admirable prose, from which, as you no doubt already know, I have been quoting."

He paused, and a servant ran out and gave him some brandy, which he tossed back in a worthy imitation of the drummer.

"The boy in the middle," he announced simply, "is the Creator." I noticed a boy standing on a chair and wrapped in two of my bath towels.

"That is, the Limbodian Creator, and being this, he is attended by two parties of demons: a Left Wing, and a Right Wing."

Two groups of boys stood round the boy on the chair, gazing at him in awe.

"The Creator is bored," Bay announced, and the music made loud yawning sounds, while the boy slowly and wearily stretched himself.

"He asks, 'What are they doing down there in the world?'"

The clarinet made a loud and pompous noise, and the boy opened and closed his mouth. Then the whole band broke into a slow dance measure, and for the first time the big drum that needed two men to beat it was brought into use. It gave a very solemn and heavy tread to the music.

The boys began to dance, very well, very gracefully, the story of how God inquired after what was doing in the world he had made, and how the demons told him that there was a certain good man down below. The demons ran to and fro in front of the heavenly throne, bowing and bending their knee, courtiers in a palace as rigid in its etiquette as that which surrounded Louis XIV. The Creator received the intelligence of there being a good man with no great display of enthusiasm. A singer, in the shadows, took over from Bay as story-teller, and we could follow the meaning of the dance clearly from his words. In neat, formal gestures, the boys told how the Creator turned to the left-hand party and asked, "Is this really a good man?"; and they said that he was not. Then he turned to the right-hand party and they said that yes, he *was* a good man. Then the Creator sent out two devils, one to plunge the man into mischief, and the other to save him miraculously from the result of his folly. The demons ran about, came and went, and with short, stamping steps made their way to the foot of the throne again. The man, they said, had refused to listen to the bad devils, and had listened only to the good. The clarinet yawned prodigiously again, and the Creator stretched his tiny arms and opened his mouth in the extremity of boredom. Then he ordered that witches be sent to torment the man and so work up some amusement for him. Witches fled swiftly from the Presence and set about their business. This time the man, who was invisible to us, but very clearly seen in the eyes of the watching boys, who reported progress as they leaned over the ramparts of heaven, had no chance, succumbed, and committed a series of evils on which the singer dwelt lovingly, and not a little obscenely.

The news of the triumph of the witches was reported to the boy Creator, who, at a cue from the drummer, leapt in gladness from his throne and, surrounded by twisting and writhing demons, did a dance of happiness and contentment which brought the performance to a close.

The whole thing had been beyond praise beautiful, and I was enthusiastic at this unknown talent among my boys. I said so to Bay, who did not seem to hear me, but said, "They're starting another dance. Let's join."

As Catullus, Bay and myself pranced round the fire I said to Bay, "Did the boys think of all that themselves?"

"Well," Bay gasped as he beat out the rhythm with his feet, "it was really *you* who started it, telling me to write that pamphlet about the Manichees."

"Bay! Did you *invent* all that?"

"Basically," he panted; "basically the story is most Limbodian. But this afternoon" (the music got very quick and we were prancing higher and higher) "this afternoon, I *did* do a little work on the scenario."

We went dancing till three in the morning, when there was no longer enough left of the tree to give a really cheerful light.

CHAPTER SEVEN

"DO sit down," Bay said to the Judge, and indicated a tombstone. He spread a handkerchief over the head of a recumbent figure of Siva in the act of destroying the Universe, and sat down himself. "We can discuss the question while we admire the view. But I do wish you had seen the entirely impromptu dance which the boys of the school gave last night, a spontaneous and very charming illustration of my argument that this unfortunate man in prison is in no sense a murderer."

' The Judge that Catullus had sent for sat down on the tombstone, as he was told. He had arrived at midday, and Catullus, Bay and myself had booked him immediately to join us in our evening walk. We had made our objective a spur of the hill on which Catullus' bungalow had been built. The spur struck deep into a wide valley, on the other side of which range after range of hills lolloped away into the distance covered in trees up to their necks. On the very end of the spur was a very old graveyard, left behind by some Hindu community that had long since been driven out by the bows and arrows of the Limbodians. It seemed that the Hindus could have stayed only a short while: the tombstones, though very old, covered no great space of time. Most of them, to judge from the style of the effigies, were carved by the same man. Each dead man had been provided by the sculptor with a horse to ride upon, a sword to wave in his hand, an oval face, a triangular nose, and two almond-shaped slits for eyes with which to look back upon the living. No sooner had Catullus seen the Judge than he had seized upon a resemblance which he said he could trace between the Judge's face and those upon the stones. The Judge, small, dapper and old, with the abrupt and unnatural

113

movements of a man who does not wish to show his age by being slow, vigorously agreed to a quick walk to the end of the spur to see whether in fact he did look the same as the dead men. Now Catullus was looking from stone face to living face again and again, satisfying himself. There was some resemblance, but the little man rarely kept his head still long enough for it to tell. But Bay was pleased, because he thought the solemn setting would help his plan. He intended, as the first step in his defense of the murderer on religious grounds, to appeal to the Brahmin's spiritual depths.

"The boys," Bay continued, "did a little play to show that the Creator was not necessarily a good god, but maybe wantonly destructive, particularly if the world and the flesh were so unfortunate as to bore him. *You*, of course, will appreciate the rightness of such a view."

Catullus, to help along Bay's general tone, looked up from one of the memorial stones and said, with a touch of mystery in his voice, "I wonder, Judge—I wonder if these people who came and went and left no trace in Limbo but these fallen stones, I wonder if they could have been distant ancestors of yours? Do you feel any answering voice within you as you look upon these hills and this group of lonely graves?"

Bay took up the thread. "You say, Catullus, that they left no trace: but is that true? How like the Brahmin's view of the Trinity as Creator, Destroyer and Preserver is the Limbodians' picture of God? May not *this* belief of theirs in a destroying God be something left behind by the Judge's ancestors? Siva, the Destroyer, at least, of all the trinity, remains. What do you think, Mr. Bose?"

"Oh yes," the Judge said in a bright voice; "Siva remains. You're sitting on him."

Bay looked at the stone god on which he was sitting and jumped up in consternation. "I do hope you will forgive me, Judge. It was quite accidental. I trust you will not think that I intended any insult to your religious feelings.

Really, I do not know how I could have been so stupid."
He picked his handkerchief from off the statue's face and
began dusting down the torso.

The Judge got up himself. "I assure you, Mr. Leavis,
you need not worry. I am not an orthodox Brahmin. In
fact, I have given up Hinduism as an idle superstition. Oh
yes, I gave it up long ago, on the occasion of my first
visit to England." He looked round at us with bird-like
eyes. "I am a life-subscriber to the Rationalist Press
Association."

"Mr. Bose," said Bay, sitting heavily back upon his
statue, "do you mean to tell me you have abandoned the
metaphysical subtleties, the spiritual maturities, the scope,
depth and insight of the Brahmin faith for a subscription
to a crank society. What do you get in return for your
sacrifice?"

"I get their Quarterly post-free *and* the Annual. The
Annual comes once a year," the Judge added, to make himself clear. "Oh yes, I've given up all that Hindu nonsense
years ago. Really, you can't expect a contemporary man
like myself who's travelled and seen the world to believe
in humbug like gods with twelve arms and reincarnation."
He flung himself about vigorously to show that he was
contemporary with everybody, even a boy of twenty-one.

Bay put his hands over his ears.

"Do not say such things, I beg of you, Mr. Bose," he
said earnestly. "Have you ever thought of that dread
moment when, wafted to the abode of the immortals in
the Himalayan mountains, you are brought face to face
with your Maker? Have you imagined that awful question, echoing from ten thousand icy precipices, '*What,
Mr. Justice Bose, have you done for your God?*' And your
answer, 'I regularly subscribed to an irreligious book
society.' Again comes the mighty voice, '*And what else,
Mr. Justice Bose?*' And you say, 'Once I said reincarnation was humbug.' And then your Maker stretches out
one little finger of one hand of his twelve sky-embracing

arms and flicks you back to the land of the living again to
be reborn, Mr. Bose, reborn as a . . . as . . . a . . ."

"Printer's devil," said Catullus.

"Thank you, Catullus," Bay said; "yes, indeed, a
printer's devil." He shook his head in sorrow. "Have you
thought of that, Mr. Bose?"

The little Judge chuckled happily and said, "Well, it's
something to be able to say that an old man like me could
shock a lot of young men like you." He threw his arms
about to show that he was not, of course, at all old, but
really in the prime of life.

"We are not shocked, Mr. Bose," Catullus told him,
in a kindly voice, "but only very distressed."

"May I ask why?"

"But perhaps," said Bay, ignoring his question, "if you
do not believe in God, you at least believe in the Devil?"

"I do not believe in the Devil."

"Then you don't believe in witches?"

"I do not, Mr. Leavis, believe in witches." He looked
at Catullus in an amused fashion and said, "And tell me
sir, do *you*?"

"I believe," Catullus said in a depressed tone of voice,
"that there is a man whom you may hang for murder
before you leave Limbo, who, if you do hang him, will
have as much right to put you and me on a homicide charge
as I have to put him."

"Did he do it?" asked the Judge.

"If you mean did he hit somebody over the head with
a stone so that the man died, that's for you to say when
you hear the evidence; but I think I may say that he did.
But whether you think he is a murderer or not, to put it
shortly, depends on whether you, Mr. Bose, believe in the
Devil. And that of course depends on whether you believe
in God."

"Well, gentlemen," the little Judge said, kicking
vigorously at the ground, "I do not believe in God. In fact,
I must say that . . ." But Bay held up his hand for silence.

"Be careful what you say. Here comes a most worthy man of God, and you would not wish to offend his feelings."

Climbing up the hill came the missionary. He waved to us, and we answered him. He climbed the path and came up to us, standing for a moment on the very edge of the hill-top. He turned slowly, taking in the enormous panorama of untouched and uninhabited jungle. Then he said, "I hope I'm not intruding?"

"Not at all. Meet Mr. Justice Chandra Bose. Mr. Bose, the Reverend Small," said Bay.

We all sat down again, each on his own tombstone.

"The Judge was just telling us," said Catullus mischievously, "that he is a militant freethinker."

"Oh, come now!" the Judge said in embarrassment, "let's not talk about religion."

Mr. Small looked disheartened. "That's what everybody says," he remarked in a gloomy voice, "when they meet a missionary."

The Judge beamed at him. "But that's only because we don't want to offend you. We all know that you as a missionary are a good and sincere person who has devoted his life to a cause."

Mr. Small nodded. "Yes, I know. Madame Curie was a good and sincere person who devoted her life to the cause of research in inorganic chemistry. But I often wonder what she'd have felt like if everybody she met had said, 'Ah, Madame Curie, so pleased to meet you. Now let's *not* talk radium, *shall* we?' It seems to me if you don't talk to a man about his profession it means one of two things: that you're ashamed of it yourself, or you think that *he* is."

"Mr. Small," said Bay, "I quite agree, and we shall now discuss religion until darkness falls upon us, and devils come out of these ruined monuments to carry off the Judge for his blasphemies. Judge, you shall begin."

"Please believe me, Mr. Small," said the Judge, "when I say that I am not in the least a blasphemer. I merely say that a good deal of the religion one meets with in India, and in backward parts like this especially, is a lot of clap-trap for which I, as a travelled man who has kept in touch with progressive thought in England and America, can very well do without. I'm sure you'll agree with me." He leaned back with the air of a man who has extri-cated himself from a difficult position with the maximum of tact.

"Well, I don't rightly know that I can, Mr. Bose. You see, in the school where we were trained to be mission-aries, back in the States, we're taught that we're to tell people here that one religion is really as good as another, provided you serve God and your fellow-men."

"Really?" said the Judge, determined to keep the con-versation as pleasant as he could, "that is most interesting. Most progressive. Very broadminded."

"Exceedingly broadminded," agreed Catullus, "par-ticularly since, for a Muslim (to take just one of the creeds you missionaries will meet), serving God and his fellow-man involves, from time to time, slitting the throats of Christians like you and unbelievers like the Judge here, for the greater glory of Allah and the propagation of the faith. Mr. Small, when I turn over in my mind the peculiar-ities of religious beliefs at present held in the world and reflect on what practices you and your religious friends in America approve of, I wonder if you are fit to be admitted into polite society."

Mr. Small slapped a tombstone with the flat of his hand. "Exactly! I'm very glad you brought that up. It's just what I write to the folks back home. It's all very well to be broadminded over things you don't know anything about. I'm mighty broadminded about the theory of relativity. It doesn't matter to me whether Albert Einstein or Isaac Newton is right, so long as when I drop a rock it hits my toes instead of bouncing off my chin. But then they go and set me down in the middle of this jungle, where everybody believes in witches and the spirits of the

dead crowd around you so they don't give you elbow-room.
Just you take *that* side of Hinduism, if it is Hinduism, gentlemen. I reckon that what the folks back home don't know
about *that* would fill a couple of new Rig-Vedas. And yet
I'm supposed to say to my parishioners that it's all all
right in its way."

"What is your church, Mr. Small?" asked the Judge.

"The American Church of the Elected Children of God."

"Ah, then I take it that you, or rather they, are Calvinists. I have just finished reading a most interesting exposé
of Calvinism in the latest number of the Quarterly. I think
you should know——"

But Mr. Small interrupted him. "You say we're
Calvinists, Judge? Well, we are and we aren't, Mr. Bose.
You see, we're very independent-minded in the States."

"I'm glad to hear it," the Judge said. "Go on."

"Take John Wesley," the missionary continued. "As
you might know, John Wesley came over to the United
States after creating a considerable sensation in Europe.
He went down all right in England, but he wouldn't do for
us at all. No, sir. Some ancestors of mine got up a jury
and had him turned out for making himself an intolerable
nuisance."

"I didn't know that interesting fact before you told me,
Mr. Small, and with your permission I might work it up
into a little article of my own. But I heartily congratulate
your countrymen on their common sense. I wish that we
in India had the intelligence to make short shrift, in a
similar fashion, of every religious fanatic in our land, be
he who he may, brown, white or . . ." he stopped in embarrassment.

"Or translucent," said Catullus helpfully. "Trans-
lucency is a mark of the attainment of a high degree of
abstraction among Buddhists."

"I didn't know that either," the Judge said shortly.
"Anyhow, I wish we could clear out every bigot in the
country, in which category," said the Judge, making

amends for his previous slip, "I am sure that you know I
do not place Mr. Small."

The missionary poked at the ground with his foot.
"Oh, I don't know," he said. "I dare say I'll get turned
out sooner or later. We have been turned out of most
places we've been in. But when I do go, I hope I have the
Christian calm of John Wesley. Do you know, the day
before he had to sail, he didn't go around wringing his
hands or getting up a petition, or giving his parishioners
a piece of his mind. No, he just went to the market-place
and tacked a notice on the notice-board. It said, 'Whereas
John Wesley designs shortly to set out for England, this
is to desire those that have borrowed any books of him
to return them as soon as they conveniently can.' Maybe
my ancestors lost a good Christian when they threw him
out. They say a good Christian should heap coals of fire
on his enemies' heads. Believe me, what that man Wesley
didn't know about heaping, wasn't worthy knowing. But
you were talking about something when I came up the hill.
Don't let my ramblings interrupt you."

"The more I listen to you, Mr. Small," the Judge said,
"the more I realize you are a man of independent ·mind
and the power to think for yourself. A man after my
own heart, though we may be on different sides of the
fence. But in one thing, Mr. Small, I think I can claim that
you will be on *my* side. These gentlemen here were not so
much discussing anything as playing on what they took to
be my religious beliefs. Their object, I perceive, is that I
should acquit some alleged bloodthirsty homicide in whom,
for reasons best known to themselves, they have taken an
interest."

Mr. Small turned to Catullus. "Is that the unfortunate
man, sir, who says a witch made him kill his wife's . . .
er . . . paramour?"

The Judge answered the question. "It is, Mr. Small.
And they were trying to convince me that it was the proper
thing for me to do to believe in this witchery and flap-

doodle. But they forget that I am a Judge, used to patiently delving for the truth. I am not accustomed to being asked to believe in fictions."

"On the contrary," said Catullus, a trifle sharply, since the Judge had taken a high tone, "every time you sit on the Bench you willingly acquiesce in the fiction that the King-Emperor can do no wrong, although you must know from your history books that the Kings of England have rarely done anything else."

Mr. Small appeared to be about to speak, changed his mind, and then changed it back again. With a firmness new to him, he said, "If it comes to that, look at our Justices of the Supreme Court. Their job is to find out what the Constitution means. Personally, I take it that the Constitution means just what the men who wrote it meant when they put the thing together. Now the Fathers of the American Constitution were very re-markable men. I'm a good American, mark you, and I wouldn't have you think otherwise. But remarkable as they were, you can't ask me to believe that they had in mind a hydro-electric scheme in the Tennessee Valley when they were drawing up its clauses. No, sir, but does that stop the Judges? Not a bit of it. They search and search the Constitution until they find out whether Thomas Jefferson and George Washington and Alex-ander Hamilton had or had not any settled prejudices about electric turbines."

"You are wrong, Mr. Small," said the Judge, "and I may say that I am at last, in this extraordinary discussion, on my own ground. They do not look to see if it is in the Constitution. They are merely applying the general principles of the document to a special case. It is not a business of depending on the literal words."

"Well, Judge," the missionary said, "I'd like to see a Justice of the Supreme Court who would begin a judg-ment, 'Let's put aside the actual words of the Constitu-tion on this point. What it really means to say, in my

opinion, is this.' Mark you, I don't say that that's not
what they do in fact. But they don't say they do. They say
they're getting at what was in the minds of George Washington and Co., when one of those gentlemen said, 'And
now let's cover the question of power-dams.' No, Mr.
Bose, I respect the law, but I guess you'd be pretty safe
in holding that Judges are no more above believing a
convenient lie than the rest of us. That's why, when these
gentlemen ask you to believe in witchcraft and what you
call (and I don't say you're right and don't say you're
wrong) fiddlesticks . . .''

"Flapdoodle," corrected the Judge. "Fiddlesticks is old-
fashioned slang."

"Then, Judge, I'm sorry but I'm not on your side of
the fence. I'm on the side of these gentlemen and I think
you ought to believe it, at any rate for the trial. When I
came up here I thought I heard you discussing the poor
fellow, and I said to myself, 'Cuff Small, this is no place
for a simple missionary. Let the eminent Judge and the
distinguished Officer of the Crown and the clever gentlemen from Oxford and Cambridge argue it out between
themselves.' But then I said, 'No, Cuff Small, maybe
you can help.' So I stayed. Maybe I should explain
where I'd been before I got here. I'd been for a walk.
I wanted to get a few things sorted out in my mind. I'd
just been visiting that man in his cell."

Small paused for a moment and Catullus asked, "How
was he?"

"Low, very low at first. He couldn't make out why he
was shut up."

Catullus got to his feet with a nervous jerk and walked
away for a few paces. Then he stood with his back to
us, looking at the hills.

"He said," Small went on, "that it's the witches who
ought to be shut up, not him. He says he didn't do anything. At least, he didn't mean to. He was badgered
into it. Pushed and shoved and elbowed into it, and he's

no more to blame than a man that's standing on the edge
of a swimming pool and gets pushed over the edge by a
crowd is to blame for falling in the water. So he couldn't
understand why he's shut up. At least, he couldn't the
first time I paid him a visit. But the next day when I
went to see him he said that he understood. He had thought
about it in the night."

The Judge nodded his head quickly in approval. "I see
that you had put the case fairly before him in words he
could understand, Mr. Small," he said, "as becomes a
man of your cloth."

"No, sir," said Small quietly. "No, sir. I can't claim
to have done that. I can't claim to have explained why a
man is locked away in a room from the sight of the sky.
I can't claim to have explained why a man must have a
rope put around his throat and have his life choked out of
him by another man who does it for a day's pay. No, sir,"
said Small, and his voice was so quiet that we could barely
hear it in the silence of the evening, "*I* am only a missionary, It will need all *your* fine brains to do that, Judge,
and I was never any good with my head. That's why they
called me Cuff, on account of the way my school-teacher
used to box my ears."

The Judge fidgeted for a moment and then sat quite
still, looking at Small, as though waiting for him to go on
talking. But it seemed that Cuff had nothing more to say.

The five of us sat silent for a while.

Then we heard Catullus' voice, high-pitched and
strained. "But you said that the man understood why he
was in jail. 'Understood' was your word. *What* did he
understand?" He did not turn round to say this, but went
on looking at the hills.

The missionary looked at Catullus' back. "He understood that he is dead already," he said.

Catullus turned and faced Small, but did not move back
towards us. "Dead?"

"Yes," said Small, and his voice became cheerful again.

"He has worked it out. You see, it was this way. The first few days in the cell he spent in telling himself stories. He's reckoned a good story-teller in his village, so he kind of rehearsed his repertory. It kept him happy for a while. He told himself open-air stories about men who walked through the jungle, or gazed at the sky or swam in rivers. He always sees his stories in his mind's eye as he tells them, and for the first few days it went very well. He could imagine the jungle, and the sky, and the river. Then all of a sudden, he couldn't. He couldn't imagine the trees; they went all straight and smooth like iron bars. He couldn't recall the sky properly; it seemed to be made of cracked plaster, like a ceiling, and spiders crawled all over it. He couldn't imagine the river. It had grown hard and dusty like his cell floor. Then he knew that he had been taken away from the world, maybe while he was sleeping, and he was dead."

"Is he of sound mind?" the Judge asked.

"Oh yes," Small answered him. "He did something very rational. I'm sure you'll approve of it, Judge. He put his theory to the test."

"Interesting," the Judge said, and nodded rapidly. "Go on, Mr. Small."

"He asked one of his warders," said Small, "in a calm easy way, to let him run down to the local village and have a brief chat with a friend of his. He said that he had remembered something that would be very useful for the man to know. That was his test. You see, the headman argued it this way. If he were dead the jailer would be a demon and wouldn't let him do it, because it would be against the rules. The dead must not be kind to the living. They can only do them mischief. On the other hand, if he was alive, then the jailer was a man, and no living person could be so cruel as to prevent a man taking a walk down the road to do a friend a good turn. So he asked the jailer, just as he had planned. The jailer laughed at him, then swore at him, and went away, slamming the cell door behind him. That's when the headman knew that he was dead."

Catullus walked towards us and joined our circle again. "Did that make him easier in his mind, Mr. Small?" he asked.

Cuff looked down at the ground. "He sat in the corner of his cell and wept," he said. "He wept for several hours, so the jailer told me. I saw him towards the end of his weeping. He didn't sob or cry aloud. He made no sound at all. He just let the tears stream from his eyes, over his cheeks and on to the floor of his cell. It seemed," said Small, raising his voice very slightly, "not that he was sorrowing, but that he was weeping out all memories of being alive, so that the inside of him should dry and be truly dead."

It had grown quite dark, and the sky beyond the hills was the color of sheet metal where it caught the last rays of the sun that had set some time ago.

The Judge got up. He said nothing to Small. But he turned to Bay and Catullus and said in an impatient way, "Can't you get me something, somebody, some authority about this man and his witches that I can accept as *evidence*? Evidence according to the law. There must be somebody who knows about these things—an expert, an acknowledged expert."

He looked down at his feet for a moment, then said, "Anyway, my business is not to manufacture evidence, but to sift it. It is getting late and very soon we shall be caught by the darkness. Mr. Small, if you're going my way I'd be glad if you'd accompany me. These gentlemen go that way down the hill. We go this."

The Reverend Small rose and looked hesitantly round our circle. "It's very kind of you, Judge——" he began, and the Judge interrupted.

"Not at all, Mr. Small. Maybe you would care to dine with me?"

Cuff Small grew more embarrassed. "That's even

kinder of you," he said. "But the fact is I promised to go back to the headman and——"

The Judge interrupted again. "Of course, Mr. Small, I won't interfere with your work of mercy."

"I hope it's that," said the missionary. "Oh yes, I do hope it will be that. The fact is," he went on, stumbling over his words with nervousness, "I'd rather promised myself I'd take one of you gentlemen back with me. I hoped, if you saw him and talked to him . . ." He could not finish his sentence, but Catullus did so for him.

"We'd let him out, Mr. Small?"

"It's not for me to suggest that to you, sir."

"Nor can I go, Mr. Small. It's against the rules," said Catullus, but he sounded uncertain.

"Definitely against them," the Judge said crisply.

Bay said, "Let me go," but Catullus shook his head. "You're my guest," he explained. Catullus looked at me. His face lit up. "*You* go. There can be nothing wrong in that."

The Judge opened his mouth to say something, but Catullus put on his most official voice. "There can be *nothing* wrong in that," he said.

We went our various ways down the hill, I walking beside Cuff Small. The gravestones rose higher and higher above us, showing as fingers of shadow against the night sky.

CHAPTER EIGHT

"**S**IR," said the prisoner to the missionary, "please help me to be really wicked." Before Cuff Small and I could recover from our surprise at the headman's greeting there was a loud clatter at the cell door. The two jailers were trying to maneuver two of the office chairs through the narrow door. One chair had a cushion tied by tapes to its seat. The other had not. This was to distinguish between the missionary, who was not in the official hierarchy, and myself, who was. With one voice Small and I told the jailers to take the chairs and themselves out of the cell. They did so, upsetting the hurricane lamp in their hurry, so that it rolled on the floor. It rolled to where the headman squatted in his corner, and the light, striking up against the sharp bones of his face, made his expression as diabolical as his words.

I picked up the lamp and hung it on a nail in the wall. The headman became a pleasant, obliging but very worried Limbodian once more.

"I sit here," he complained, "and sit and sit, trying to think wicked things as I should, seeing that I am dead. But I still think kind things about people," he said, as though he were shamefacedly announcing his failure in an examination that obvious fools had passed.

"How do you know that *we* are not dead, as well as you?" I asked him.

He looked at Cuff Small.

"You cannot be dead because your eyes are too kind."

"What about me?" I asked, perhaps too much in the tone of humoring him.

He was instantly suave.

"You," he said with a respectful inclination of his head, "are an Official. To you everything is possible."

It was a Limbodian phrase that one commonly heard when one was trying to refuse a request on the grounds that it was not practical, and he had twisted it neatly to his purpose. This, I took it, was to exclude me from the conversation, and I therefore fell silent.

"Headman," Cuff Small said, "I can see your difficulty. But I don't think you ought to ask a missionary to help you to be wicked."

"Why not?" the head asked.

"It isn't my job to make people wicked," said Small.

"What is your job?"

"To make people good."

"Do you think you yourself are good?" asked the headman, with nothing but innocent curiosity in his voice.

Cuff Small blushed. "I try to be," he said.

! The headman nodded. "You do very well. We all say so. You are a good man."

Cuff Small blushed more deeply and searched for something to say to turn the conversation. But the headman did not want it turned. He held up a finger to mark his point.

"Since you are a good man you must think some very wicked thoughts," he said.

Small rounded his eyes and stared at his accuser.

"That's quite right," he said at last. "But how did you know."

"It is simple. When I was alive, sometimes I was a good man, sometimes I was a bad man. When I went to stay in the house of my father-in-law-that-was-to-be, so that he could see if I would be a good husband for his daughter, I was a very good young man. I said 'You are quite right' when he swore at me when he was drunk, and I said 'Your wife has great strength' when she threw the grinding-stone at my head. But all the time I thought wicked things about them, like an old witch with the belly-ache. Now you," he said to Small, "always go around as though you wanted every man to think you good enough to marry his daughter. So I know you have some excellent wicked thoughts about people in your head. Tell me some."

The missionary deftly avoided his request, by saying, "In the land where I come from we do not believe that the dead become wicked demons, as you do here. We believe that when a good man dies he is more good than ever before, and when a bad man dies he is . . ." and Cuff Small paused for an instant, "he is sorry," he concluded.

It was the first time I had heard Small preaching in Limbodian and I showed by my expression that I admired him. He seemed pleased that he had an appreciative audience. He had certainly impressed the headman, who now sat frowning at the ground, as he went over this new idea in his mind. Small, encouraged, no doubt, by my approval, went over his neat description of the Christian idea of heaven and hell once more, using the same words. The headman followed him carefully. When Cuff said 'good man' the prisoner picked up a small stone and set it upright on the earth floor of his cell in front of him. When Small said 'bad man' he took another stone and did the same thing with it. Then he scrutinized both stones in silence. We did not interrupt him. The night was hot and the cell was small for three people. Cuff dabbed the sweat from his forehead in what, in another man, would have seemed a rather self-satisfied manner.

The headman, at last, drew a deep breath and expelled it slowly.

"In your country," he said to Small, in the manner of one announcing the solution to a difficult problem of mathematics, "in your country the women and children weep a great deal."

"Goodness gracious," said Cuff in English, "why?" He repeated his question in Limbodian.

"Why?" echoed the headman. "But it is very simple. You say you believe that when the good die they are more good and when the bad die they are sorry?"

We both nodded.

"Then," continued the headman, pointing his argument by holding up the stones one by one, "all the good men kill themselves in order to make themselves even more good, and their wives and children weep because they are dead. And all the bad people go on living because they do not want to be made sorry, and their wives and children go on weeping because they are alive."

We both had nothing to say. The headman felt from our silence that maybe we had not quite understood his reasoning. "It is quite simple," he began again, picking up the stones again to illustrate his points. But Cuff interrupted him.

"Thank you, headman, but I think we follow you."

The headman smiled.

"Good," he said. "It seems to me with all the good men killing themselves and all the wicked being left, your country must be very wicked. Am I right?"

"Well, yes," Cuff admitted. "Yes."

"*Very* good," the headman said, with the look of a scientist who finds a new but predicted planet just where he said it would be found.

"My country is certainly a wicked country," said Small, obviously rallying his wits, "but not for the reason which you give. The good men do not all kill themselves."

"No?"

"No. It is," said Small in a desperate rush, "considered a wicked thing for a good man to kill himself."

The headman raised his eyebrows almost to the edge of his red turban.

"It is considered wicked for a good man to want to be more good?"

"Yes, if you put it that way, yes," said Small. "At least, I suppose so. I don't know. It seems to be nonsense, doesn't it?" he asked the headman, almost appealingly.

"No," the headman said judicially. "It is not nonsense. I have often thought so myself. It is not really wise of a good man to want to be a *very* good man. It might annoy the demons. That is what you think in your country?"

"By this time I don't know what they think in my country," said Small in a hopeless voice. "Do you mind giving me those stones of yours? I'd just like to work it out for myself once again." Then, as the prisoner smilingly passed him the stones, Cuff said to him in English, "I never was any good with my head."

"Perhaps," the headman remarked conversationally, as he watched Small place the stones carefully in front of him, "perhaps in your country they believe in witches as well."

Small threw down the stone that was in his hands.

"No, no, no!" he almost wailed. "Not *witches!*"

I felt it was time that I intervened.

"The truth is," I said, "that people in his country don't really believe that when a good man dies he goes to a place where he is a better man."

"So you have been telling me a story," the headman said pleasantly to the missionary.

"In a way."

"Thank you," the headman said. "I am very fond of stories. One day I shall tell you the story of the crocodile that drank too much strong liquor. It is a very good story, though a little too long to tell you now."

"I didn't mean that sort of story," Cuff explained.

"There are many sorts of stories," the headman agreed, and added boyishly. "I like all of them."

"The story I came here to tell you," Cuff said, "was about . . ." He broke off and obviously struggled with his Limbodian vocabulary. "God," he said at last, using the English word.

The headman rolled the unfamiliar word round his mouth.

"Gawd?" he queried.

"Gawd," Small agreed politely.

"Is it the Gawd you speak about over there?" The headman pointed in the direction of Small's church.

"Yes."

"The big demon that you sing to?"

"He is a good demon," said Small, relieved to be once more on his own professional ground.

"A *good* demon." The frown came back on the head-man's face as he thought about the new idea. "That is very strange. A good demon is very strange. You have met this Gawd?"

"No," said Small.

"But you must have met him," the headman said. "You say 'a good demon' and your face does not show that you think that strange. People go out into the forest and come back and say, 'I have been out into the forest and I have talked to a demon ten feet high with eyes that grew on long stalks.' Now that is strange, but when they say it their faces do not look as though it were strange, because they have seen it, and talked to it. So you must have seen this Gawd. He is not strange to you."

Cuff looked silently at the headman for so long that I thought I would again have to say something. But he spoke before I did.

"You are a remarkable man," he said to the prisoner, and stopped, silent again. "Yes," he said at length, "I *have* seen him."

The headman beamed. "Tell me," he asked.

Cuff nodded absently.

"It is a long story," he said, "and you must take some more stones and put them in front of you to mark the people that I shall tell you about."

Obediently the headman gathered some small stones around his feet, and Cuff Small began.

ii

"When I was a boy," he said, "I had to sing in the stand-up-and-sit-down dance which we used to do at big festivals."

After a moment or two I saw that Cuff was fitting Limbodian words round the idea that he once was a choirboy.

"But I could not sing a note. I had no ear for music."

"Then why did you sing?" asked the headman.

"That was because of the quarrel between Mum and the daughter of my maternal grandfather. The daughter of my maternal grandfather's name was Martha. Please put down two stones so that it will be easy to remember: one for Mum, a big one because she was my mother, and one for Martha, but a smaller one."

As the headman placed the stones, I remembered that the words 'aunt' and 'sister' are hardly decent in Limbodian manners. Martha, then, was Mum's sister.

"When they were girls," Cuff Small went on, "Mum and Martha had no rings to wear on their big toes. None whatever."

The headman shook his head sadly, while I delighted in the circumlocution that Cuff had used to say that his mother had been born in a poor family.

Silently translating, I found that Cuff was telling the story of his boyhood in a small American town. Mum and Martha had been poor, but Martha had never noticed it. Mum, I gathered, had thought of very little else. It may have been something to do with their looks, because Cuff described Martha in terms that could have meant that she was plain. But when he picked up the stone that represented Mum he spoke of her fine eyes and long hair and her lips, which remained young a long time after the rest of her face had grown old. Mum had a chance to make a good marriage; Martha would be lucky if she married at all.

But they both married and the headman selected two more stones for the new characters. Martha had married a man who was kind and poor, and a drunkard. Mum had married a student who was going to be a doctor. He never became a doctor because marriage (and the headman heartily agreed) costs money, and he never had money enough to take his degree. But Mum now looked upon herself as belonging to a much better class than Martha, so when Cuff was born he was not allowed to play with Martha's son Mickey.

As the boys grew up two things became clear. Martha's husband drank all the money he earned, and Mickey was much cleverer than Cuff. Mum thought that it was quite right that Martha's husband should drink and make the family poor, because Martha had never tried to better herself. Mum had always tried to better herself and everybody thought very highly of her for doing so. But it galled her to think that Mickey was so clever while Cuff was a fool. She loved Cuff, but she hated his school nickname, that he had got (as he had told us) because his master so often boxed his ears. The name made her angry. She thought of it especially as Cuff was doing his homework. She would try to help him, but he would be stupid and dull. So, in her exasperation, she would box his ears on her own account, thus making his name even more appropriate. Cuff did not mind. He knew he was stupid and he was sorry for it. He knew his mother was respected for always trying to better herself and he was proud of her. But he was no good at using his head.

Then, when the two boys were about thirteen years old, Mickey developed a beautiful boy's voice. He sang everywhere, particularly in church. Cuff heard him sing, and although he knew that Mickey was poor and his father drank and he was not the right sort of boy to play with, Cuff could not help feeling happy that Mickey was so successful. He knew he was successful from the way people spoke of Mickey. As for himself, he had no ear for music at all.

Nevertheless, he had to sing in the church choir; not Mickey's church, but the better-class one to which Mum went. Mum insisted.

Cuff explained to the choirmaster that he could not

sing, but the man said that he ought to try for his mother's sake, because she was such a good mother and did so much for the church. Cuff did try in his own way. He stood in his place in the choir, opening and shutting his mouth in tune with the other singers, but being careful not to utter a sound. The choirmaster found him out and was very cross with him. He told Cuff that if Cuff's Mum wanted him to sing, the least he could do was to try, instead of opening and shutting his mouth like a fish. So Cuff tried to sing, but then the other people in the choir made him go back to opening and shutting his mouth.

Whenever he heard music and people singing after that, he felt that he was being mean to his mother because he had no ear for music.

The choir, once it had got Cuff's position straight, turned out to be very good. It even won prizes. Cuff opened and shut his mouth assiduously and handed round glasses of water in the intervals.

Then, one day, when Cuff was about fourteen, the choir was singing at a festival competition. They had done well, and they were trying hard to win the final round. The words of the song were religious and Cuff concentrated on them hard so that he could make the right movements with his mouth.

All of a sudden, in the middle of the singing, he saw God. God was in the middle of the big chandelier that lit up the hall. Cuff had sat in church every Sunday and heard all about God, so that when he met Him personally, as he was doing now, he knew Him quite well. But never before had he known that God knew him, Cuff Small. Now he was sure of it: God knew all about Cuff's worry about hurting his mother and his having to make out that he could sing although he could not follow the music. God did not take it nearly as seriously as Cuff took it, but just laughed and said it would be all right.

Cuff understood all this just when the choir was getting into the last stanza, and he felt happier than he had ever been in his life. So he sang right at the top of his voice; he sang the words that he had learned, and he sang them right out loud. The fact that he was crying didn't seem to Cuff to make his voice shake a bit.

The next thing he remembered was that they were all in the changing-room at the back of the hall and Cuff knew they had lost the prize. His mother took him by the arm and said they must hurry home. When they got into a dark street she looked at him in the way she looked when she was going to box his ears. But he told her about seeing God. She said nothing at all. She did not box his ears.

iii

Cuff Small leaned forward and turned up the wick of the hurricane lamp, which had burned so low that the cell was almost in darkness. When it was bright again he said to the headman:

"So that is how I saw God."

"It is just as I thought," said the headman. "You saw this good demon. He is very strange; he looks like three hundred hurricane lamps hanging from the ceiling, which I cannot imagine. But since you have seen him it is not strange to you and you talk about him calmly. But why did you come here? Why did you not stay in your own land? You will never see three hundred lamps hanging together in Limbo."

Cuff Small did not answer. The headman screwed up his eyes and looked at Cuff closely. Then he picked up one of the stones in front of him and held it in his hand.

"Mum?" he asked.

Cuff smiled slowly and nodded his head.

"She told everybody about my seeing God," he said. "Everybody was very interested."

The headman nodded.

"Just as when one of our boys is picked to be a witch-doctor," he said. "Everybody gives him sweet things to eat. Go on."

Mum had made Cuff go to church three times in the week and twice on Sundays. What with this, and the story that he had seen God, people began to say that Cuff was well on the way to being a saint. Mum was very proud, and this made Cuff happy. But he was very bored in church.

One day a dark man with a beard, calling himself the Swami-something, came and talked to members of the church about India. Afterwards they had a meeting and decided that they would have a mission station in some place that the Swami had particularly mentioned. They set about raising money, and Cuff, who discovered in it something that a young and growing saint could do with propriety besides going to church, raised more money than anybody.

Mum was happy and Cuff was happy and then Mickey got a job.

"Mickey," said the headman carefully, and picked out a stone from the group on the floor.

"Yes," said the missionary, "Martha's son. He got a job, and a very good job. But as for me, I could not get a job at all."

Martha had not let the opportunity for triumph slip past her. She had come to Mum's house and she had talked a great deal about Mickey's new job. Then she had asked when Cuff was going to earn his living. Mum said, "My Cuff is the stuff that saints are made of." She always said that when Cuff's name was mentioned. Usually people lowered their eyes respectfully when they heard her say it and agreed with her warmly, especially church people. But this time Martha, inflated with her triumph, did not lower her eyes. She looked at Mum and said, "Oh yes, and how are you going to make *that* pay?" Mum had been wonderful in the way she had taken the insult. She stood still for a moment, very upright, and then she said, very quietly, "My son is going to be a missionary."

Cuff had been so pleased at the way Mum had handled the situation that he had overlooked the fact that he did not in the least want to be a missionary. But once Mum had told Martha, he could not very well let her down. He went through his training in an agony of boredom. For some time the hope that perhaps he would see God again kept up his spirits. But he never did see God, not even on the day when he was made a minister and given Limbo as his cure of souls.

"That was twenty years ago," said Cuff Small, "and I've been a missionary ever since. I've decided to give it up twenty times in these twenty years, but I've never done so. I've gone to bed sick with loneliness and determined to pack up and go the very next morning. But when the morning comes I always stay. I dream of Mum in the night, and how sorry she'd be if I let her down. She died ten years ago, but it's still the same. I'm still lonely, I still dream, and I still stay." His voice failed him for a moment, but he quickly recovered. He got to his feet laughing, and said, "But I always am tempted to let people down. This evening, for an instance, I came here to help you," he said to the headman, "and instead I spend the time talking about myself."

The headman rose with Cuff.

"Help me?" he asked.

"Yes. But I've failed." He picked up the lamp and it shone on his face. He looked more weary and alone than I had ever seen him. "But failing's nothing new to me," he said.

"You say you have not helped me," said the headman quietly. "Perhaps I can help you."

We both stood and waited for him to continue.

He held up one of the stones that he had used to mark the characters of Cuff's story.

"Mum," he said. "Mum was a *witch*."

iv

I walked back with Cuff Small to his bungalow. He was quite silent, except for one occasion when he repeated the headman's last words. He said them, not in the prisoner's warning tone, but as if they were a sort of revelation.

For myself, I was busy with a brilliant new theory in sociology which had occurred to me and I was grateful for his silence. As soon as we had said good-night I almost ran up the hill to Catullus' house.

I found Catullus and Bay sitting in long cane-chairs placed in the clearing in front of the house. They were sitting in the dark, and for once they seemed to have no conversation.

A servant placed a chair for me; as soon as I had got back my breath I told them what had happened in the cell. I gave most of Cuff Small's story, much as he had told it. Bay interrupted me once to ask me to repeat the part in which a dark man had come lecturing to Cuff Small's town. I went on to tell them of my brilliant theory. The headman, I explained, was perfectly satisfied with being a Limbodian. He could explain everything in Limbodian terms. He had no use for any other. His society was closed, whole and eminently satisfactory. I enlarged upon my theme. I drew comparisons, I pointed warnings to more civilized people. I grew oratorical. I paused for breath.

"Yes, yes, of course," said Bay mildly, and said nothing more. It is the sort of remark that people always do make when they hear my theories. I am quite used to it.

Then Catullus spoke out of the darkness.

"What we need to convince the Judge is not an expert, it's a miracle," he said.

I had quite forgotten the Judge. I had forgotten that the man was to hang. I sank in my chair and was glad of the darkness.

Then Bay said suddenly, "Catullus! You're right! A miracle. It's the only thing a pig-headed lawyer could ever be got to believe. We have got to convince him that what the Limbodians believe is a real religion, a religion in the eyes of law."

Bay swept on in his enthusiasm.

"We can't dress the witches in copes and mitres. We haven't time to write them a holy book. But we can make them work a miracle. Like Lourdes, for instance. Healing the sick. The Judge may not believe in it, but with his reputation for scoffing at holy things in a country like India he dare not say so. He'd be accused of allowing his private beliefs to distort his judgment. He'd be forced to retire. Yes, that's *just* what we want—a miracle." He fell silent for a while. Then he said, "Of course, it will have to be faked." He was again silent for a full minute. Suddenly he threw his heels in the air. "Catullus!" he shouted. "How far is the nearest telegraph?"

"Fifty miles," said Catullus. "The telegraph is a wonderful invention, but perhaps the Judge has seen one and would scarcely rank it as miraculous enough."

"Can we send a runner to the telegraph-post with a message?" asked Bay.

"Certainly. Why?"

"The Swami-something of poor Cuff Small. I've suddenly remembered who he is. Wire to him to come immediately—all expenses paid."

CHAPTER NINE

"WHAT do you make of this?" asked Catullus. It was some three days after we had met the Judge, and a runner had arrived just before dinner with an answer to the telegram to the Swami.

Catullus passed the paper, remarkably dry, across to me. The office of origin was Bombay and the message ran:

THE BLESSINGS OF THE INELUCTABLE BE UPON
THEE SHALL ARRIVE TUESDAY TERMS AND CON-
DITIONS STATED YOUR TELEGRAM 8TH INST VIZ
ALL EXPENSES PAID MAY GOD PROSPER OUR WORK
OH MY EXCLAMATION MARK

SWAMI ANANDA

"It seems the message is for you, Bay," I said and gave it to him. He read it carefully, polished his glasses and read it again. Then he shook silently for a while and we gathered that he was laughing.

At length he took off his glasses again, wiped his eyes and said, "The Swami never fails me. What is today?"

"Tuesday," said Catullus. "No, Wednesday. No, we had mutton today. It must be Tuesday." There was always a controversy over the day of the week in Limbo. What with the papers coming late and letters taking anything from a day to a fortnight to arrive there was no method of keeping check. It is difficult to explain to anybody who has not lived in Limbo why nobody kept a calendar, but perhaps it will be sufficient to say that if one did one would forget to tear off the sheets. There was a calendar in the Administration's office, but that added to the confusion rather than straightened it out, since it was altered daily by an orderly who could not read. But there were two effective checks, and we got by

141

with those. The first was that the mission bell, which struck the time hourly, rang sixteen instead of eight on Sunday mornings to show that there was a service The other was that on Tuesdays and Fridays a goat was killed for the very few officials who ate meat. This goat was called mutton. Tuesdays and Fridays were mutton days, the rest were chicken days. This was Tuesday.

"Then the Swami is late," said Bay. "I think you'll like him."

"Yes," said Catullus, "I have never met a man who says 'Oh my' so habitually that he puts it in telegrams. He probably also say 'Pshaw.' "

"I think you owe that to your telegraph clerk, who probably not only says 'Pshaw' but also, when he is surprised, says 'Golly!' and when somebody pinches him says 'Ouch!' because he has clearly been reading English schoolboy fiction. What the Swami said was 'May God prosper our work. Om!' Om is a sacred syllable which has various meanings, of which the most poetic is 'Hail, Jewel of the Lotus!' In Tibet it is said that adepts, by saying 'Om' with sufficient emphasis, can make their souls fly out of the tops of their heads. Your telegraph clerk did his best with it."

"I shall speak certain syllables with sufficient emphasis to make his heart sink to his boots if he mutilates any more of our telegrams. I should like to have preserved a telegram ending in 'Om,' " said Catullus. "Your Swami sounds the least bit bogus."

"He is the most delightful charlatan I have ever met," agreed Bay. "I doubt whether he is sufficiently adept at saying mystic formulae to make his soul fly out of his head, but he has certainly said them, and in the most sophisticated capitals in the world, in such a manner as to make a considerable amount of money fly into his pocket. He is," Bay said with enthusiasm, "in my opinion, the biggest quack since Cagliostro."

"What is his line?" asked Catullus.

"Mysticism: blue light beating around the initiate's head: visions and angels. He does it all very well."

"I am delighted. I hope he isn't one of these silent sages who write on slates."

"He wasn't the last time I met him. Not by a very long way. In any case, even if he had taken a vow of silence, he would not write on a slate. He has always moved in the most expensive society. He would be much more likely to refuse to conduct a conversation except through the medium of the radio-telegraph."

"I'm so glad," said Catullus. "I shall be able to hold long conversations with him. I have always wanted to hear a sage answer Charles Lamb's question 'Whether the higher order of seraphim ever *sneer.*' But tell me, Bay, why did you ask him?"

Bay rose from his chair and said:

" '*It's mystic fudge,*
Wherein we'll catch the conscience of the Judge.'

Come, let us go in to dinner. Tuesday mutton is on the table."

"It's all very exciting," said Catullus, and, waving his glass, led us into the dining-room singing in his high voice, to a lugubrious tune:

" '*Fierce anthropophagi,*
Spectra, Diaboli,
What scared St. Anthony
Shapes undefined:
Hobgoblin, Lemures,
Dreams of antipodes,
Night-riding incubi,
Troubling the fantasy,
All dim illusions,
Causing confusions,
Figments heretical,
Scruples fantastical,

Doubts diabolical,
Abbadon vexeth me,
Mahu perlexeth me,
Lucifer teareth me,
Jesu Mariae, libera nos ab
His tentalionibus orat, implorat,
R. Burton Peccator.'

"It's a little thing," he said, recovering his breath, "that Charles Lamb wrote for poor Robert Burton after reading the *Anatomy of Melancholy*," and with that he butterflyed off on a topic that lasted through dinner and I heard no more about the Swami until next morning, when a servant brought a note from Catullus which said, "The Om man is here. He's brought his own telephone box. C."

He must have sent a note at the same time to Bay, because I met Bay running up the hill. When we got to the top of the hill we saw that a truck was standing outside Catullus' bungalow. Helped by one or two servants, a man was unloading a very large packing-case. He was white-haired, with a large white beard that covered most of his face. He was dressed in a white blouse that seemed many sizes too big for him, and had wide flowing sleeves. This, at his waist, was tucked into a pair of khaki shorts. Beneath that he was bare legged and wore sandals. He thus gave the appearance of a Boy Scout carrying a stained-glass window adorned with a picture of an Old Testament prophet, in such a manner that the Scout was visible only from the waist downwards.

"Is that the telephone box?" asked Bay as he ran up, pointing to the package being unloaded.

"Why, it's Bay," shouted the old man, and then, "Yes, it's the box."

"What a charming compliment! The best I've ever been paid," said Bay and flung his arms wide. The old man ran forward to meet him, and they embraced. Bay kissed him on both cheeks, or rather, what would have been his cheeks had they not been inches deep in beard.

When Bay was disentangled, the Swami said, "Yes, I brought the telephone box along for more or less sentimental reasons."

"How very kind of you." said Bay.

"Not at all. I thought you'd like to see what I've done with it. Of course the whole thing's on a much smaller scale than it was in the good old days. But I've retained the essential idea, I think you'll find. Come and see."

"Immediately," Bay said, "but first I would like to introduce you to the Education Officer."

The Swami saw me for the first time, and gave a little jump of surprise. "Oh! just a moment, please. I must tidy myself up." He turned shyly aside and fumbled with the belt which held up his shorts. When he had loosened it, he began to haul out yard upon yard of white material similar, and in fact part of, that which made up his blouse. Then he shook it all loose and it fell to his feet, making a wide, loose gown that fell round him in becoming lines. He then combed his beard with his fingers, and with a little cough of satisfaction, turned to face me. He was now all Old Testament prophet and was not a little impressive.

"This is a very great pleasure, sir," he said in a soft voice.

"Swami Ananda, my very old and very dear friend," said Bay introducing him. The Swami folded his hands in the Indian manner of greeting, then, seeing that I had put out my own hand, dexterously changed to the Western mode and gave my hand a hearty grasp. He then gazed at me in silence for a while, his eyes glowing. They were very young and dancing eyes, which led one to investigate his smooth brown face, or as much of it as the beard showed; one saw that his face, too, was young. It seemed possible that he had bleached his beard.

"Let me look at your face," he said. "Ah yes, it is written plainly for anyone who has eyes to read the story that a face has to tell. Love of the innocent and weak, devotion——"

"Whoa! Swami," said Bay, "he's not a school-teacher. I'm sorry, I should have explained that he's a member of the Indian Civil Service."

"Service," the Swami went on without the slightest change of tone; "the stern touch around the lips which comes to the man of firm but kindly will, the leader, nay, the father of a simple people."

"After one hundred miles in a Chevrolet truck on roads built by those simple people, you are doing very well, Swami. But you really needn't bother, because I've already explained to him that you are entirely bogus. I didn't want you wasting your talents on officials. You have serious work to do."

"But, Bay, why don't you let the young man have his fun? Everybody likes having his face read," said the Swami, with the faintest trace of petulance. "I find that it goes much better than palmistry, and besides it doesn't tickle. Now tell me honestly," he said to me, "didn't you like being told you have firm lines round your mouth. Because, apart from the bogusness that Bay talks about, you have, you know. It doesn't need a Swami to see that. Any fool can."

I began to see why Bay liked him so much. "I was delighted, Swami, and Bay is being very rude."

"There," said the Swami, still holding on to my hand.

Catullus put his head out of a door.

"Swami, where do you want me to put the telephone box?"

"In my bedroom," the Swami said briskly, and began to draw me towards the house. "Now tell me all about yourself," he said to me.

I was just in my second sentence when Catullus appeared again. "What about the connections, Swami?" he said. "How do I fix the wiring?"

"It just plugs in to the electric light. It has a universal fitting, and you'll find it quite easy."

"But we haven't got electric light."

"Oh dear," said the Swami, quite dismayed. "I hadn't thought of that. But never mind, an oil lamp will do just as well. Perhaps I had better come in and help you." He disappeared after Catullus.

Bay and I were served with a drink, and in five minutes Catullus and the Swami were back.

"I think I've fixed it," said Catullus.

"You've done wonderfully well," agreed the Swami. "Now let us all go in and have a look at it."

It was a real telephone box. It had three glass sides and a small roof with slits to let in the air. The actual telephone was rather better than the usual model. It was white and had a pattern of intertwined roses and lotus buds painted on it. In the place of the usual framed instructions for operating the dial was a highly colored painting of Buddha, seated, and with his eyes closed in contemplation. The inside of the box, where it was not glass, was covered in a quilt of red silk, while in the place where one usually stands to telephone was a high seat, very comfortably upholstered. A small glove at the top was obviously intended to act as a light, though it was not on at the moment. An attachment in front of this, resembling those used on spot-lights, permitted the user of the box to make the light red or blue by merely pushing round a circle of colored transparencies. Outside was the customary hook for the telephone directory, on which the Swami now hung a bundle of leaflets, the first of which, in distinguished lettering, was headed:

SORRY YOU'VE BEEN TROUBLED
By Swami Ananda.

"Now," the Swami said, "I'm sure you're dying to know what it's all meant for. Shall I tell them, Bay, or will you?"

Bay, who was sitting on the guest bed, leaned back on the pillow and put his feet up.

"No, Swami, *you* tell them. It seems to have changed so much. And in any case you describe it very well."

"This," said the Swami, turning to Catullus and me and indicating the booth, "is a modern meditation box."

"How very sensible," Catullus cried, "and what a charming idea!" He bounced forward, opened the door of the box and sat down on the chair. "Is this how you use it?"

"Shut the door," the Swami said.

Catullus shut it. Then the Swami said, "Oh, but it's no use, we haven't got the light yet."

Catullus looked inquiringly through the glass and made gestures as if to say "What do I do now?"

"It's no use," the Swami shouted—"*No use*. We haven't got any *sunrise*."

Catullus opened the door and said, "What was that?"

"We haven't got any sunrise because we haven't got the lamp fixed. You begin in the glow of sunrise, and then as your spirit calms down you move the little thing over your head and you get moonlight. With moonlight comes peace. But we haven't got it working yet, so you won't be able to try it. I think perhaps I'd just better explain it in words."

Catullus came out of the box. "I'm sorry I can't try it. Nevertheless I must congratulate you, Swami, on a very brilliant idea."

"Oh really," said the Swami deprecatingly, "I owe it all to Mr. Aldous Huxley. You remember," the Swami said when we had settled ourselves in chairs, "just before the war, Mr. Huxley was publishing some books that dealt with the mystical side of things. Now, I am no judge of literature, but I understand from people who are that those books and others by the same author are so well done that of all the things written in our time they have the greatest chance of surviving. Well, when an author as great as that starts talking about something, the whole world listens to him: and some part of the world will want to follow him, too.

"I often wonder if great authors know what they're starting when they write a book. For instance, this business of mysticism. Mr. Huxley laid great stress, you may remember, on contemplation, and pointed out how if there was one thing that got in the way of the con-templator more than any other thing it was what he called *distractions*.

"Now, usually when I get to this point I talk about the Cloud of Unknowing, but since Bay has very kindly given you details of my biography, perhaps I may take that part of my explanation for granted." He smiled at us with the greatest good humor, and went on. "Now, distractions are almost anything that comes into your mind when you set out to do some contemplation. Mr. Huxley in one of his books gives quite an interesting list of the things which personally distract him. The list includes the French name for henbane and a scheme for catching incendiary bombs in mid-air. Now, that brings out my point very well. Take the ordinary man or woman. When he or she sits down to contemplate the infinite do you think that they are worried by the French name for henbane? Do they seriously consider methods of catching bombs? Gentlemen, believe me as a man who has worked among the common mystics, they do nothing of the sort. Now, with Mr. Huxley it is different. I quite believe him when he says that such thoughts come to dis-turb his equanimity, because he has a powerful brain, a world-exceptional brain. Now, for a man like him, it is comparatively easy to get rid of distractions and he recom-mends a few methods. But they are suitable only for men of extraordinary will-power and mental attainments, not for the ordinary plain seeker after infinite Beatitude."

"I like that phrase," said Bay from the bed; "it appeals to the man in the back row."

"I try to move with the times," said the Swami, and resumed. "During the period when everybody was reading these books, I, myself, was beginning to win, in a small way, some reputation for knowledge of the occult. People came to me with their troubles. They wanted to find one peace; they wanted to be contemplatives; they agreed with the eminent author that it was very necessary that they should no longer neglect the deeper things of life. But what about those distractions? Could I recommend any easier method of attaining bliss than that which they found in the books I have already alluded to? Now, I am not a deeply read man. My life has been spent on a plane in which books seem, as the preacher says, indeed vanities of vanities. But I knew of one or two methods which the great mystics of the past had used. What were they?"

"St. Simeon Stylites sat on top of a pillar," I said. I knew he had not meant the question to be answered, but I was carried away by his beautiful voice.

"St. Anthony buried himself in a tomb for twenty years," Catullus added.

"Since interruptions seem permitted," said Bay, "the case of Alfred Lord Tennyson may not be out of place. A gentleman with the improbable name of Mr. B. P. Blood wrote to Lord Tennyson and asked him, since it was common knowledge that the poet had mystical experiences, how he induced them. The poet replied courteously to the letter, and said that he found the best method was to repeat his own name slowly, and several times, to himself. Thus," Bay richened his voice, " 'Tennyson, Tennyson, Alfred Lord *Tennyson*.' In his own words, his individuality then seemed to dissolve away into boundless being, death seemed to be an almost laughable impossibility, and he became absorbed in the only true life. When the famous and sceptical Professor

Tyndall was one day so rash as to suggest that there might be some delusion in the matter, Lord Tennyson thundered in reply, 'By God Almighty, there is no delusion in the matter at all!' ''

The Swami raised a graceful hand. "Exactly. Lord Tennyson had, I have no doubt, a superior mind. What suited him would not suit everybody. It is much the same with tombs. Twenty years in a tomb would not suit everybody."

"It suited St. Anthony," said Catullus. "When the anxious populace broke down the walls and dug him out, he stepped through the breach and, clearing the dust from his throat with a cup of water, went straight on to preach what I must say has always struck me as a rather ordinary sermon."

"And as for pillars——" I said, taking up my turn.

"Most people have a bad head for heights," the Swami interrupted crisply, "so that settled that. No, if I was to be of any use to these poor seekers after the truth I must think of something neat, compact and unobtrusive. One day, turning over this problem in my mind, I had occasion to make a telephone call. I was in a noisy hotel lounge and I made my way through the throng to a telephone booth. I went in, shut the door, and remarked thankfully on the peace that descended upon me. At that moment the idea was born. It was, if you like, a coincidence that I should have to telephone just when I was turning over my problem."

"Nonsense. It's Newton and the apple all over again. A million apples dropping in front of a million men but only one Newton to deduce a theory from it," said Bay.

"Thank you. As a matter of history, the actual notion of the box did not come to me all of a piece. It rather hung about in the back of my mind. The actual moment when I saw it plain and whole I remember very well. I was delivering a public lecture. My subject was the relationship of the disciple to the *guru* or teacher in the attainment of mystical knowledge, and I had taken for my theme the position of Yajnavalkya in the Brihadaranyaka Upanishad."

"Good Lord," I said, "did you get many of the public to come?"

"Oh yes," he said mildly; "I called my lecture *Dial o if you cannot get your Connection*. And while I was elaborating my simile, I *saw* it. A neat, comfortable telephone box, where the average man could close the door and be shut off from the world, and which would form an inconspicuous and even tasteful article of furniture in the contemporary home. They went very well. The original design did not include a telephone. That only came in with Bay's scheme." The Swami looked at Bay mischievously and added, "But that I shall leave to him to describe."

Bay shook his head. "No, Swami, you are too modest. My contribution was not more than a tiny flourish in the corner of your grand design."

Catullus said, "What was the flourish, Bay?"

The Swami sat down and spread his robe tastefully round him. "Really, Bay," he said, in his silkiest voice, "since you have given our friends your version of my biography before I arrived, you cannot very well refuse to give a little of your own."

Bay laughed but said nothing.

"How did your part begin?" asked Catullus. "With the publication of a poem by T. S. Eliot?"

"Well, no, I wouldn't say that," Bay answered. "I suppose, if anything, it began with the passing of Part One of the Married Women and Tortfeasors Act in 1935." He turned round and punched up the cushion to make himself comfortable.

"What is a tortfeasor?" I asked him.

Catullus said, "I am not sure, but I imagine one feases a tort very much as one flushes a bird? Am I right, Bay?"

"I am afraid I cannot be sure of the legal details. The man to tell you about those would be Jasper Hadow. He knew all about the Act, because it provided him with his bread and butter. He really was called Jasper; it was on his birth certificate. I rather think it twisted his life, because Jasper was at heart a kindly and even sentimental man. It was the expression of deep human pity on his face that first attracted my attention. I was having a rather early drink in a bar in Piccadilly, and I remember that an edition of the evening papers had just come on the streets. A man came in and handed one to Jasper, who was sitting in the middle of a small circle of well-dressed and clean-looking young men. Jasper took it, and reading a headline shook his head in sorrow, and his face took on the look that I have mentioned. I glanced over the shoulder of a man at the bar to see what it was that could have caused his sadness, and discovered that it was the report of the sentencing of a notorious share-pusher for a stiff term of penal servitude."

"They came down on them very heavily," said the Swami regretfully.

"That was what the circle of young men were saying. One of them ordered a round of drinks. When they were served, Jasper took his and raising the glass said, 'Well, here's to poor old So-and-so,' mentioning the name of the man in the newspaper, and all present gloomily drank the toast. Well, naturally I was interested in a man who could feel so deeply for a share-pusher, and I was wondering how I could make his acquaintance when I noticed that one of the young men was a person who had been pointed out to me as a notorious confidence trickster. I need not say that of all the people in the world to strike up an acquaintance with, a confidence trickster is the easiest. I let him swindle me for a guinea on the spot: there's a word they use for it . . ."

"He 'conned' you," the Swami said. "Would it have been Teddy by any chance? Teddy *Rust*, I think his name was."

"No. I can't quite remember his name, but I'm sure it wasn't Teddy."

"Pity," said the Swami, stroking his head. "I always

wondered what became of Teddy. Nice boy. Very nice boy."

"Yes, indeed. Well, from the 'con'-man I was passed on to Jasper Hadow, and Jasper was quite ready to explain his sorrow over the share-pusher. It appeared that the share-pusher had been a client of his (Jasper was a lawyer) and he was regretting that such a criminal should ever have had the impertinence to come to him, a respectable solicitor. That was his first explanation, and obviously a lie. About three hours later, when I was beginning to wonder if I had the money to pay for yet another round, he could restrain himself no longer. I had a kind face, he thought, so he told me the truth. He was the solicitor for a whole firm of share-pushers. But business was not what it had been. There was a drive on, and one by one the big guns were going to jail. The news this evening had been an almost crushing blow. They would have to close the office now, and then where would everybody be? I had no idea that a share-pusher had an office and I was eager to see it. That, with a little sign-ing of bills at the bar for another round or two, was arranged.

"It was the most extraordinary office I have ever been inside. It was done up in that style of leather and satin-wood luxury that is favored by the most wealthy combines. There was a whole corridor of executive's offices with dis-creet nameplates on the doors. Most of them were empty. This side of the thing was done for the benefit of any client who happened to call in while on a visit to London. Most of their clients lived very far away from London, as those that ran the swindle took good care to see. But the offices were just in case the organization broke down."

"They wouldn't have been that place in the Strand?" asked the Swami.

"They were near the Strand, but not in it," Bay answered.

"Oh. They did things well at that place in the Strand.

They looked after their staff too. Gave you a handsome bonus when they went into voluntary liquidation. Not many of them used to think of that."

"The staff of this office," Bay went on, "worked in a single room at the back. It was furnished with two long desks on which stood two rows of telephones. When business had been good, Jasper told me, I would have found a young man at every one of those telephones, working six hours a day. Now there were only two. Both were talking into the instruments, in a soft, persuasive manner, making a noise rather like the cooing of pigeons. That was where the Married Women's Property Act came in. The law had recently provided that the property of a married woman was exclusively her own. With the aid of a telephone directory and other sources of information peculiarly their own, these young men would find the telephone number and a a little of the personal history of suitable women. Such was the greed of these women that it was perfectly possible for a young man with the right kind of voice to contact them by telephone, and in the course of two or three rather long conversations, get them to buy, with their brand new property, the particular bogus shares that were being pushed at the moment. It was not entirely women that they telephoned: clergymen were a good second string. But women made the business go.

"Well, now, with the police drive on and succeeding, they were in a poor way. The two young men, when they had finished their duty at the telephone, both begged me to do something for them. Very soon it was inevitable that they would be out of work. It was a poor prospect for them. They had, they said, specialized. Their whole assets were in their voices, and they were going to be as hard put to it to find a job as a lion-tamer without any lions. They were desperate; and in addition they were, as the Swami quite rightly says, nice young men. I felt very sorry for them.

"Then I met the Swami. He was doing well as an occult consultant—I think that was what you called yourself, wasn't it, Swami?"

The Swami nodded.

"But he was doing, if anything, too well. He simply did not have the time to interview all the customers that wanted to talk to him and benefit by his contact with the world beyond the veil."

"It wasn't that I minded work," said the Swami. "I may say that nobody has ever accused me of that. It was the hours that were the difficulty. It did not look good to make appointments right through the day. One had to put aside certain hours for retreat and contemplation. And it was the way those women talked! They were shameless about taking up a busy man's time. And when they'd done, one had to do a fair measure of talking oneself."

"The result was," said Bay, "that the Swami had to put his fees higher and higher, to make a bare living out of it."

"I didn't want to do it. It meant that I cut out a lot of people who were badly in need of help. It used to make me feel very bad to have to turn them away. And there was no free clinic to which I could give them a letter of introduction. So you can imagine how relieved I felt when Bay here put up his brilliant idea."

"Shortly, that idea was that the Swami should open a more popular business at lower prices. After all, what his clients wanted was a soothing and strengthening chat. I saw no reason why we should not call in the aid of modern inventions: and one very good reason why we should. It gave my two poor young men a job. We installed two telephones in the Swami's consulting chambers, and set the young men to work."

"They needed training, of course," the Swami said, "but they were good boys. It took a little time for them to get familiar with the spiritual difficulties of all my clients, but I must say they learned the patter very quickly. Of course I insisted on my clients occasionally having personal contact with me, but we could run for weeks on the telephone alone. Sometimes clients got awkward to handle; that is, for a novice. It usually happened when they got it into their silly heads that they had had a Revelation of Glory in the night. But the whole beauty of the telephone consultation was that my young men had time, when anything like that occurred, to press a bell and bring me in. Then just a note or two on a scribbling-pad, and while they were talking I could lend them the whole benefit of my experience. The cost was low, and the charge was likewise. Bay's idea was a public benefaction."

"The Swami had already hit upon his telephone box idea, which fitted in neatly."

"It did indeed. Most of my clients already had modern meditation boxes. All that was needed was to wire them up with the Government telephone system."

"And that, you see, is how the telephone got into the telephone box," said Bay.

"So you see," said Bay to the Swami that evening, "what we want is a fake miracle. And from what we've heard this morning," he went on, speaking to Catullus, "I think you'll agree we've got one of the best possible men to do the job."

"Two," said Catullus.

CHAPTER TEN

"THE trouble with the Swami," Catullus said with irritation some two days afterwards, "is that he can't *concentrate.*

"He's enjoying himself," Bay said. "He likes the Limbodians. He keeps on calling them 'Nature's gentlemen.' From the way he says it I think he thinks he invented the phrase himself."

"Unfortunately the Swami is not one of Nature's Messiahs, and unless he studies his part your excellent plan for a miracle will prove a failure. I do believe he hasn't an idea in his head about *what* miracle he is going to fake."

"Well, I asked him again this morning. He seemed to take it seriously enough."

"What did he suggest?"

"Of course he's only just limbering up, you know," said Bay apologetically. "He got as far as suggesting that he knew how to do Sawing a Woman in Half. But I think we want something more canonical."

Catullus looked worried. "Don't raise the dead," he said. "I don't know the legal position."

"If only he'd rehearse a little, I think we could manage to drive out devils very nicely."

"By the way," said Catullus, "where is he *now*? I've got an appointment with the best witch-doctor in Limbo at twelve. I can't keep him waiting."

"I don't know," said Bay. "He went off in the direction of the village."

Catullus called a servant and asked him if he knew where the Swami was.

"Yes, sir; he's in the village."

"What's he doing?"

"Sir, he is giving away turbans."

"Turbans?"

"Yes, sir."

"Good God," said Catullus. "I bet they're red ones. He's making everybody in Limbo a headman. Bay, do you know anything about his political antecedents?"

"I didn't know he had any," said Bay, but rather anxiously. "He hadn't in England."

"What newspaper did he read?"

"It didn't matter. He only used to read one paragraph."

"What was that?"

"The one giving the time of high tide at London Bridge. He used to take the figures and then look up the corresponding page number in his edition of the *Bhagavad Gita*. That gave him his Text for the Day. He had great faith in his system."

"We'd better go and see what he's doing. Come on!"

As soon as we came in sight of the village we could see that something novel was happening. It was market day, and the local vendors had as usual spread out their goods on the ground near the village well. They made a sort of street, setting up small awnings on bamboo sticks on either side, and usually there was a trickle of villagers passing up and down the full length of the market. Now, everybody was gathered in a packed circle around one particular stall. When we got closer we could see that their attention was fixed on somebody hidden from us, and in the middle of the group. When we got right up to them, we found that it was the Swami. We came up on the side to which he had, just then, turned his back and he did not see us. Spread around his feet was the entire stock of one of the men who peddled lengths of cloths for turbans. Catullus noticed with relief that they were not red.

The Swami had one particularly attractive piece of cloth in his hand, and he was talking rapidly and persuasively to the people around him.

"Now, who's next, who'll have a try, who'll chance his luck?" he was asking them. "On my right is a satisfied customer, and on my left another lucky man. It costs you nothing to enter, and you may win this fine handsome turban that would grace the brows of a Prince. On the other hand you may not, but if you're unlucky there's nothing to pay. Never in the history of Limbo has such a generous, such a magnanimous, such an open-handed offer been made. You may say I'm crazy. All right, I'm crazy. But who'll have a try? You, sir? Thank you, sir! Here's a man who knows a good thing when he sees one."

A giggling youth with a great bunch of uncombed black hair stepped forward, and the Swami gave him the turban length.

"Put it on, boy, put it on and see if it suits you."

The boy wound it carelessly round his head, and then, giggling helplessly, stood still for the Swami's inspection.

"Is that how you like to wear your turban?"

The boy nodded, and the cloth nearly fell off.

"Are you quite sure? If you are going to a wedding, is that how you would put on your turban?"

The boy nodded again.

"Then you can have it," said the Swami, "free of all charge, and may you be lucky with the ladies." With a final string of giggles the boy disappeared in the crowd.

"Is it a swindle?" whispered Catullus.

"I don't *think* so," said Bay. "He's not dishonest, except about God and the soul and blue lights beating round people's heads. Moreover, look, he's paying for it."

The Swami had hitched up his robe on one side and was feeling in the pocket of his shorts. He took out some coins and threw them to a man who was squatting by the pile of undistributed turbans. The man took it and seemed very pleased.

"And now, who's next?" asked the Swami. A handsome young man stepped forward, throwing back his long coiled hair as he did so. He was well-built, and around his narrow waist he had twisted, instead of the usual loincloth, a piece of flowered print. The Swami looked at him admiringly, and saying to himself, "Now let me see, green, yes, green. Ah, I think this one will blend very well," he picked out a pale primrose length of cloth and handed it to the young man.

"Put it on," said the Swami.

The young man shook out the cloth and began bunching it in long folds. When it hung to his satisfaction, he flung it in the air once or twice to see that the folds stayed put. Then, with a delicate movement of his wrist, he twisted it once round his head. He patted this circle into place, and then, with quick movement, wound another circle on top of it. This he repeated two or three times, patting the circles each time until they fell exactly into the place on his head which he desired. When all the cloth had been made into a turban, he threw up his chin and said to the Swami, "Well?"

The Swami studied the turban for a moment and then said, "Amazing. Quite amazing." The young man did not understand him, and put up his hands to alter the shape of the folds.

"No, no, no, don't touch it, don't you *dare* touch it!" said the Swami in great excitement. "Just stand still, stand quite still like a good boy." The Swami pulled up the other side of his gown, and felt in the other pocket of his shorts. He produced a paper of pins, from which he took several and put them in his mouth. Then, going up to the young man, he began inserting the pins with great care into the turban, walking round the wearer as he did so, and muttering "Amazing" through his mouthful of pins.

When he had made the complete circle, he carefully lifted the turban off the young man's head. As he did so, a fold came loose. "Dear, oh *dear*," he said, and then to the young man, indistinctly because of the pins, "Put id ba'." He repeated this urgently once or twice, and the young man at last understood. With the Swami holding the rest of the turban together, the young man patted the loose fold back into its proper position. "Goo'," said the

Swami, and took the turban off in one piece. Carrying it with the care a boy might use in handling a bird's nest he had taken complete from a tree, he brought the turban over to where a basket lay upon the ground. Several other turbans, all of them held together with pins, were already in the basket, and the Swami carefully laid the new one beside it. Then he straightened his back and rubbed his hands in a satisfied manner. He noticed us.

"Oh, hullo!" he said. "Isn't it a beauty? Worth twenty guineas, I should say, and that's putting it low."

"What on earth are you doing, Swami?" Bay asked.

"They're for Max."

"Max?"

"Yes, you remember Max. That nice young man who keeps the hat shop. The hat shop all done out in black-and-white on the corner of the Ritz-Carlton. Surely you remember Max?"

"Why, yes, yes, I do. But why this?"

"But, Bay, just look at them. Look at the line, the *chic*, the dash in these turbans. Max is a genius at making hats, but I've seen him spend all day winding a piece of cloth on on and off, on and off his head in front of a mirror, and he's never got anywhere near these. Moreover, the poor boy's had so many business worries he's going stale. He's even fallen to doing things like all the other hat-designers do. You know, seeing a crabshell and saying, 'Ah, I see Lady So-and-so in that hat, all it needs is a twist of chiffon.' Well, Max has always been kind to me. He always put in a good word for me, and I always put in a good word for him. 'It doesn't suit your aura,' he would say when a woman came in and wanted to buy a cheap hat. That led round to me. 'Go and buy yourself a new hat, my dear young lady,' I would say when I thought a client couldn't really afford my fees, 'it will do you more good than I can.' So when I saw these absolute geniuses at hat-designing, I thought I would do Max a good turn. I shall pack them in cotton wool and ship them to Max, and Max can copy them. I dare say he'll give me a commission."

Catullus fought to control what might have been laughter or might have been the beginning of hysteria.

"But, Swami," he said, "I could have got you dozens of turbans. I could have sent a policeman round to take off every tenth man's turban in Limbo. You needn't have come to market to get them!"

"That is very kind of you," said the Swami, "but you could not have done what I wanted. To tell you the truth, I very nearly failed myself. You see, I asked these people to tie a turban, just bluntly like that, and they got embarrassed, like all true artists, and produced the most monstrous three-and-eleven-three shopgirls' bonnets you have ever seen. This method is much better. You see, they don't know what I'm after. I just get them to put on a turban, and if I don't like the result I give them the cloth free. If I *do* get what I want, well . . ." and he pointed with pride to the basket. "Every one different, and absolutely exclusive, as dear Max would say."

"Swami," said Bay in a firm but friendly voice, "you must remember that twenty-four hours from now you will be performing feats by virtue of your spiritual exaltation that will beggar the imagination."

The Swami looked down at his feet guiltily. "Oh yes, I forgot."

"In the Middle Ages," Bay went on, "this is the time that you would have undergone the trial of temptation by the Devil. He would have appeared to you in the alluring guise of women, in the horrifying incarnation of a man with the head of a wolf, as seductive music, as scented zephyrs, as a melodious voice whispering the attractions of evil. To you, Swami, he appears in the guise of a hat."

"That's right," said the Swami. "We must move with the times."

"We must move with the times. Hats, Swami, are Distractions."

"That's right," said the Swami.

"And now come home or I shall lock you up in your own telephone box and not give you any lunch."

"No more today, boys," said the Swami to the crowd. "I shall be seeing you tomorrow . . ." and then, catching Bay's eye, he added "with a new and sensational line of merchandise." Then, confidentially to Bay, "That fixes it."

We moved away. Catullus hung back a little and then said, "Bay, let him keep the hats."

Bay nodded.

"Thank you very much," said the Swami gratefully, and Catullus signed to a small boy to carry the basket behind us as we climbed the hill.

ii

"Bay is considering the Laws of Nature," said Catullus, driving his car cautiously over a bad piece of road, "to see which one it would be best to suspend. So he couldn't come with us."

We were going to see the leading wizard in Limbo. He lived on the extreme edge of the country, and we had several hours' drive ahead of us.

"I think we can safely leave it to him to choose. We were up at Oxford together." Catullus steered cautiously past spears of broken bamboo that jutted out from the surrounding forest and threatened to impale us.

"All we want *you* to do," he said to the Swami, who was sitting beside him, "is to talk shop to the witch-doctor that you're going to meet, and get the patter correct. It's most important from the Judge's point of view that the whole thing is done according to local custom and belief."

For the next two or three hours Catullus gave the Swami a résumé of the Limbo religion. By the time we had arrived at the place where the wizard lived it was already evening. The boundary of Limbo is marked by a great wall of hills. The witch-doctor had retired to the highest of these, and lived there with a few disciples. The hill he had chosen ended in three distant peaks, and between them, like a nest high up on a tree, was a shallow depression, some half a mile square, covered in soft green grass with two or three springs of fresh water that ran all the year round. He had built for himself and his pupils a neat cluster of huts, and from one of these he emerged to greet us.

He was not immensely old, as I had somehow expected that he would be. His hair, which was barbered trimly, was iron gray, and his face had more wrinkles than was usual with Limbodians. In fact, his whole face was more finely cut than any I had seen among the people in Limbo, and he appeared to be taller. He was plainly, almost austerely dressed, his only ornament being a chain of human little-finger bones around his neck. He saluted us with dignity, and chatted for a while with Catullus as one official to another. When he was introduced to me and he was told I was the new Education Officer, he said that he was a bit of a schoolmaster himself, and pointed to four little boys who were in the group of retainers that stood behind him. He was teaching them magic, he explained, all of the white magic and a little of the black. But frankly he thought that two at least of the boys would never do any good at the course. For his part, he always said that a witch-doctor was born, and not made. But it was traditional that the leading wizard took on pupils and he himself was a conservative in such matters. But he thought that if I were to look into the matter, as I no doubt would when I got well into my duties, I would think that it was rather an old-fashioned system to load an important functionary like himself with pedagogical duties, however desirable it had been in times past. Perhaps it would be possible to set up a separate school, under my control. But in any case, I must come to the annual ceremony, after the rains, when all the novices showed what they could do.

Then he was introduced to the Swami, and he took him by the arms in a most friendly fashion, saying, "There can be no formalities between *us*," and led him to a rise in the ground that had been covered with bamboo matting. He invited us to sit down, and offered us some of the local liquor in brass cups. He was altogether a most courteous host.

"Well," he said, shortly afterwards, "you didn't come here to listen to an old man's prattle. You want to see some magic. I understood from the runner you sent," he said to Catullus, "that what you want is the gist of the thing. Of course, I am not allowed to give you the details, but I have arranged a program which will give you a general idea." He hesitated, and then leaned over and spoke in Catullus' ear. Catullus nodded, and the witch-doctor smiled and waved his hand. Instantly someone lit up a bonfire which blazed as though it was saturated in oil, drums started thundering from positions which I took to be on the three peaks of the hill, a man flung himself in dizzy circles round the fire, rattling on a small hand-drum as he did so, and all the retainers began a wailing chant. Under cover of the noise I asked Catullus, in English, what the witch-doctor had whispered to him.

"He said that he hoped it was understood that, from the point of view of the law, all this was strictly off the record. I assured him that it was," said Catullus.

Now a group of retainers came up close behind us, sat down and began playing musical instruments. Most of the instruments were long tubes across which wires had been strung lengthwise: two gourds, one at each end, prolonged the note which the instrument gave out, so that every touch upon it made a long whine. One or two of the men were shaking sistrums, while another, with his fingers, stroked a brass rod held against a metal tray. This made the sound of a cloud of insects flying through still night air. More drummers gathered round the fire, and the noise became very great.

The Swami was sitting on the far side of the bamboo mat, with myself between him and the witch-doctor. The

Swami leaned across me and said something to the wizard, but could not make himself heard.

The witch-doctor put his hand to his ear, and leaned nearer to the Swami.

"What did you say?" he shouted above the noise.

"I said, I see you use music," the Swami shouted back. The witch-doctor nodded.

"Do you find it *helps*?" the Swami asked at the top of his voice.

"People like it," yelled the witch-doctor.

The Swami nodded in complete understanding. They both watched the performance for a while and then the witch-doctor leaned across me and said, "I don't use it when I'm by myself."

"No," bawled the Swami, "neither do I. As a matter of fact, I don't use it at all. But it's an idea."

The witch-doctor nodded in his turn. "Not too much of it, though. Makes it too much of an entertainment."

The Swami shouted "Quite. They'll be expecting dancing girls next."

The witch-doctor laughed heartily.

They both returned to watching the performance with expertly critical expressions.

A man ran out from a group towards us and sat down a few feet away, facing our hillock. He took off his turban, and the drummers struck up a new and insistently regular beat. He began to jerk his head from side to side with great violence, as though at each beat he had been hit.

"What's this?" the Swami asked the witch-doctor. And then, as the witch-doctor was about to speak, "No, don't tell me. Let me guess." He screwed up his eyes and studied the rocking man for a moment. "I know. Trance."

"That's right," said the witch-doctor.

"It looks painful. Do *you* have to do this?"

"Yes."

The Swami watched the man for a minute or two longer in silence. The man's head was jerking now so hard that one could feel a sympathetic pain travel down one's neck and spine.

"Have you ever tried a crystal ball?" the Swami asked, leaning across me.

"No," the witch-doctor said with interest. "How does it work?"

"You just look at it. It gets you in a trance in no time. Only you mustn't use it if you're tired. You'll just fall asleep. And if there's anybody else watching when you wake up you feel rather silly."

"I must try it," the witch-doctor said.

Some of the members of the orchestra now began an undulating melancholy chant, which they seemed to be addressing to the man who was still tossing his head about.

"They are asking if the spirits of the dead are willing to come into this man's body," the witch-doctor explained.

"One-knock-for-yes-two-knocks-for-no," the Swami added professionally.

"Not quite. You'll see how we know."

The man on the ground stopped shaking his head. He held it upright for a few moments, and then it lolled over on to his shoulder. His limbs began to stiffen, his legs reaching out slowly in front of him. He began to breathe very heavily, and the firelight showed that his pupils had rolled back under his eyelids, leaving only the whites of his eyes. Sitting in a rigid attitude that could only be held by a trained gymnast, he began to whimper.

"The spirits are ready," said the witch-doctor. "A woman is now in possession of him."

A boy from the watching group got up and went to the man in the trance. He had in his hands earrings and bangles, which he put on the man.

"When it is a woman, we put woman's jewelery on him."

Then one of the drummers stood up and went over to

the possessed man. He sat down in front of him, placed two hands on his shoulders, and began to murmur in his ear. The man whined, and said a few indistinct words. The drummer began to weep, and kissed the medium on both cheeks. The music started with a shiver of the sistrums and a twanging chord on the guitars. The drums from the hills rolled more loudly than they had done before. The hand-drummers beat furiously on their instruments and the whole assembly broke into a rhythmic shout. Throwing down his sistrum, a musician leaped out towards the fire, seized a burning piece of wood and, to a stamping dance, began to chew flaming splinters from off the end of it, spitting them out when he had held them in his mouth for a considerable time.

"He too has become possessed. It is the first time that he has done so, and he is giving us proof that the possession is genuine."

The fire-eater had now taken another and more flaming piece of wood from the fire. He waved it in the air as he danced, and came close to us, passing the brand in front of our faces so that we could test the heat. He made a few more steps of his dance, and then slowly passed the blazing stick up and down his bare arms and legs. He shuddered as he did so, and bit his lips. He prodded the thick part of his thigh with the tip of the stick several times, next applying it to his bare belly. He came near to us once again and we could see that there were no marks on his flesh. He danced a little more and suddenly began to stagger. His legs sagged and he almost fell. The drums beat faster, and he managed to right himself and dance with nearly the same vigor as he had shown before. Once again he prodded his thigh with the burning stick. He stood quite still for a moment, then prodded low down in his belly. He gave a violent shudder, and fell prone on the ground. A boy ran forward and threw water over him. He rolled over on his back, shook the water from off his head, slowly got to his feet, and walked back to his place in the orchestra, picking up his sistrum on the way. There was a long silence. It was broken by the voice of the Swami.

"*I* can eat glass," he said.

"Glass?" the witch-doctor said incredulously.

"If it's thin enough. I learned it when I joined a magician's act once. Of course, it's just a trick."

"But a very good trick, *if* it can be done," the witch-doctor said.

"Have you got a glass?"

"I've got one. It was given to me as a present. But I should be very glad if you would eat it."

"Bring it," said the Swami, and "and a glass of water."

The witch-doctor gave orders that this should be done, and that the music should begin again. The man who was possessed by the spirit of a woman began mumbling in a high-pitched voice, and the musicians struck up once more on their stringed instruments.

The glass and water in a brass cup were brought. I got up and allowed the witch-doctor to sit next to the Swami. The witch-doctor handed the glass to the Swami, who broke it with the heel of his shoe. He took a draught of water, and then a mouthful which he used as a rinse. Then to the amazement of the witch-doctor, and not a little to our own, he put some pieces of the tumbler in his mouth, and crunched them, his vast beard wagging in what appeared to be enjoyment.

The musicians faltered, watching this demonstration, but at a sharp word from their leader went on, if somewhat inaccurately. The witch-doctor, with little exclamations of surprise, alternately handed the Swami a piece of glass and the cup of water. Once or twice the Swami smacked his lips, and remarked in a stagey voice, "Good glass!"

A man from the group around the fire approached the hillock on which we were sitting and said something to the witch-doctor, who did not hear him. The man coughed nervously and then said, in a louder voice, "Sir, the man is still possessed of the spirit of the woman, and she asks if you will say the words that will release her."

"Oh don't *bother* me," said the witch-doctor; and selecting a particularly choice piece of glass he went on feeding the Swami, his face glowing with admiration.

iii

"Sir! Sir! Come quickly, come quickly!"

I had got up very late the next day because we had not arrived back from our visit to the witch-doctor until three in the morning. I was awakened by the urgent voice of a servant, Catullus' servant. I tried to find out what had happened but the man was incoherent, and all that I could gather was that Catullus wanted me to go to his bungalow as quickly as I could.

I called for my own servant, but there was no answer. I looked in the servants' quarters but they were quite empty, a plate of half-eaten food in the middle of the floor. I bathed and dressed as quickly as I could and, almost running, went up the hill. All round Catullus' bungalow was a crowd of Limbodians, trying to peer inside. In the front rank stood all my own servants. As I drew near, Catullus came out and held up his hand.

"He is resting," he said very solemnly. "He is very tired. He asks that you go away." Nobody moved.

Then Catullus saw me and shouted. "Thank the Lord you've arrived. Bay's just come, so I don't have to tell the whole story twice."

"What story?" I asked, running up to the veranda. "Has anything happened?"

"The miracle's happened," said Catullus in his highest treble, "and the Swami—the *Swami!* I can't tell you how good he was. Come in, come in, come in and hear all about it."

The Swami was sitting, utterly relaxed, in an easy-chair,

being vigorously fanned by Bay. As soon as he saw me he waved and said, "Well, how do you think it went?"

"I don't know anything about it," I said.

"Neither do I," said Bay, a remark which the Swami and Catullus greeted with delighted laughter.

"It was brilliantly organized, Bay," said Catullus, "and it was a pity that you couldn't be there to savor your own immense success. But I quite see that you couldn't. It might have spoiled everything to have too many of us around. As it was, the whole unnatural thing happened as naturally as possible."

"Besides, if you had been there, Bay," said the Swami, "it would have put me off. But, the way it turned out, I didn't miss a trick, did I, Catullus?"

"You were so good I nearly clapped."

"Considering I went on at a moment's notice," said the Swami.

"With no breakfast," added Catullus.

"I wonder I didn't burst into tears," said the Swami.

"That is exactly what I shall do if somebody doesn't tell me soon what happened. Sit *down*, Catullus, and begin," I said.

"They brought him along just as I was starting breakfast," said Catullus.

"Who?"

"The boy."

"Poor little chap. But what an actor!" said the Swami.

"There were about twenty people with him, mostly Limbodians, but some who came from just outside. In the middle of them was the boy on a sort of rough hammock, moaning and writhing and throwing himself about in what was the exact imitation of an epileptic fit. Well, that gave me the clue. You were very quiet about it all, Bay, but you let one thing slip. You remember you said you'd prefer it to be casting out devils?"

"So I did," said Bay. "So I did."

"I went outside and asked them why they had come.

'There is a holy man with a white beard staying with you. We hear that he is so holy that he can cure the sick,' one of the men said."

"I know where they got *that* from," the Swami said, looking archly at Bay.

"I said," Catullus went on, "that such a person was here but that he was resting. He had spent the night in vigil on a mountain-top with their own great witch-doctor. I did not mention that you had also been eating glass."

"We are *now*," said the Swami, combing his beard with a theatrical gesture, "in legitimate drama. Our music-hall days are a dim and amusing memory."

"But they begged me to bring out the holy man. They showed me the boy, who started groaning dead on his cue, and there was even a weeping mother. How you got them all together I don't know, Bay!"

"All stars; and in the same cast," said the Swami.

"Well, I said that I would see if the great man was awake. Then I ducked into the Swami's bedroom and ripped the bedclothes off him. 'You're on,' I remember saying, 'get up! You're on.' Then I started to get his clothes together."

"And me without a clean robe," said the Swami. "I could have screamed."

"I got him dressed, or nearly dressed, and I sat him down for a few moments to relax and get himself in the mood. Then we couldn't find his shoes."

"Talk about distractions," said the Swami, full of self-pity.

"Then I said, 'Never mind, bare feet will fit the part just as well.' "

"But I think a good costume is *so* important, it *gives* you something. We must get it right next time," the Swami impressed on Bay.

"Yes, we must," said Bay. And then to Catullus, "Go on."

"Well, I didn't want to keep that poor lad acting far

too long. I guessed that a good many of the crowd were perfectly genuine. Of course I knew you'd bribed the boy. But I also knew you'd arrange that some quite innocent villagers would be there to see what happened and spread the news. So that the Judge would hear of it. I liked your subtlety in not having him present. I liked that very much."

Bay, who was listening intently, nodded.

"So," went on Catullus, "I hurried him out of his bedroom to this room here. Just as he passed that window, the crowd caught sight of him, and a mighty, awed cry of 'Oh!' went up. To judge from the tone of it some people had fallen down on their knees at the mere sight of his beard flashing past the window. I don't know because I didn't look. I hadn't got the time. I was telling the Swami here that he'd have to do some witch-divining by throwing rice in a winnowing fan, the way that the witch-doctor had shown us just before we left last night. So I said to the Swami, 'Where is your winnowing fan?' and the Swami had a temperament. 'You don't expect me to find my own props, do you,' he screamed at me."

"I did *not* scream," said the Swami.

"You screamed," said Catullus.

"It was just nerves, nerves," the Swami apologized and sank wearily in his chair.

"I ran into the kitchen for a winnowing fan, but I couldn't see one, and I couldn't remember the Limbodian for it to ask the servant. I made up my mind we should have to do without it, and ran back to this room, and there was the Swami sitting on the floor *there*," said Catullus pointing to a corner, "sitting on the floor and swearing at me."

"Really, Catullus, I don't know how you can tell Bay such things. I was not swearing at all, Bay. I was saying 'Om! Shanti! Om! Shanti! Om! Shanti!' which means Hail Peace, Hail Peace. I was practicing Detachment. It was very soothing."

"Not for me," said Catullus. "I got him to his feet and

I told him there was no winnowing fan, so he would have to mutter spells instead. Then he said, 'How shall I make my entrance? I know, I shall go out to them and say quite simply, "Which of you is in pain and suffering?" ' 'There's Bay's boy out there bellowing like a bull,' I told him, 'they'll think you're deaf or something. No. Be practical. Act like a doctor. Don't overdo the spook stuff. What does a doctor say when he comes into a house of sickness?' I asked him, just to be helpful, and the Swami says, 'Sorry, I'm late. I had a confinement.' "

"But they *do* say that, Catullus. At least they always do to me," said the Swami, grinning in his beard.

"Anyway," went on Catullus, "I knew by that that the Swami was his old self again, so I wished him good luck and pushed him through the door. Nothing I shall say now can do justice to his performance from then on. It was beyond praise and almost beyond description. He walked out on to that veranda, stood there a moment as though he had just awakened up from sleep-walking . . ."

"Meditation," corrected the Swami.

". . . and then suddenly saw the crowd. His expression was like that of Rip Van Winkle waking up, if Rip Van Winkle had been Florence Nightingale."

"I was concentrating on the Florence Nightingale side," said the Swami, a little hurt.

"Never mind; whatever you looked like the crowd thought it was terrific. They bowed and saluted you and one or two actually knelt down. Then the Swami made his way down the steps, straight to the boy.'

"Straight?" the Swami cried. "It just shows you what art can do. Let me tell you that what I was thinking at that moment was that if somebody didn't step aside pretty soon and let me see just where that boy was, I should have to stop and ask my way. Still," he said airily, "if it didn't *show* . . ."

"Nothing showed except a very saintly figure moving towards an errand of mercy. The crowd did fall back, and there was the boy. He grew quiet, and then lay absolutely still. He nearly stole the scene, Swami."

"I'm not a selfish player," the Swami answered. "I helped him along with a few whispered words."

"Then the Swami put his hand out for silence. Nobody was making any noise, but I can only say you hadn't *noticed* the silence till the Swami put his hand out. He bent over the boy and began saying incantations. He didn't scamp them. He gave a good two minutes to incantations, but he could have taken five: he had the audience in the hollow of his hand, even those who knew it was a fake. Then he laid his hand on the boy's brow. I wish you could both have seen that gesture. It was something like this," and Catullus waved his hand downwards.

"No, *no*," said the Swami; "go *out* with your *wrist* first towards the object you want to touch. Then, when your wrist is almost there, bring round your hand so," and he waved a languid hand at the end of his wrist. "It's Gerald du Maurier's advice. I got it from an old actor who was in vaudeville with me."

"That boy," said Catullus, "lay quite still for a while. Then he opened his eyes and tried to rise. The Swami put his arm behind him, and tenderly helped him to sit up. Then, with an intense light in his eyes . . ."

"I was *living* that part, you know," the Swami said.

". . . he took the boy's feet and placed them on the ground. The boy hesitated, looked at the Swami, smiled, and stood up. He tottered for a moment, and leaving the Swami's protecting hold, walked over to a woman who was kneeling in tears some distance away, and bent down and kissed her. Then he stood up straight. When the crowd saw he was well again, they went mad with joy. Bay, I take off my hat to you!"

"Oh, Bay!" I said, "I wish you'd told me. I would so like to have been there to see it."

"So would I," said Bay. "Yes, indeed. But you see, I didn't know about it."

"You mean you didn't know when they were going to do it? Hadn't you arranged it?"

"I hadn't even decided what miracle would be best, much less the time it should be worked. And as for the boy—well, I wonder who the lucky little chap is?"

We none of us said anything for a moment. Then the Swami raised himself slowly from the chair and said:

"Bay . . . you don't mean . . ."

"Yes," said Bay, "the credit is entirely yours. I didn't fake that miracle, Swami. It was real."

CHAPTER ELEVEN

"I'M AFRAID you can't see the Swami, Mr. Small. He locked himself in his room just after it happened this morning. And he's been there ever since. Unless, of course," said Catullus, "he's travelling abroad on the astral plane."

The missionary said he was sorry. He wanted to pay him his respects.

"You can try. You can hammer on his bedroom door if you like, but he's not seeing anybody."

"Oh yes," said Cuff Small, "I quite understand. I suppose he's in retreat."

"Full retreat," said Bay; "he's packing his bags."

"Surely he's not taking his wonderful gift of healing away from Limbo? We need it so much. Surely, Mr. Leavis, you're an old friend of his, surely you can persuade him to stay. Tell him of all the terrible sickness that these poor people suffer."

"I've tried that," Bay answered. "I spent most of the afternoon arguing with him through the door. I told him about enough medical cases to stock a hospital."

"What did he say?"

"He said he'd send us some penicillin as soon as he reached a good chemist's shop. He said he'd heard it was very good."

"Well, naturally, he'd make light of what he's done. I've never met him, I'm sorry to say, but I can guess he's a modest man. It's a trait of the saintly character. They realize their power comes from Outside themselves."

"So does the Swami," said Bay, "and he says Outside's played a damn dirty trick on an old man who never did anybody any harm. He says, with all the people in the world who've made their lives miserable being holy, why pick on *him* to work a miracle? He says it's his beard, that's what it is: he says it's just typecasting, like they do in pictures."

"Well," said the missionary, "I suppose he must deliver his Message to us in modern terms; we can't really expect him to talk the language of the Bible."

"My dear Mr. Small," said Catullus, "if some of the Old Testament prophets had had the Swami's flow of language when they were warning Israel we should have had no Jewish problem."

"Surely he's not blaspheming?"

"When I last heard him he was working his way up through the Cherubim and Seraphim. It may have mounted to blasphemy by now."

"But perhaps it is our fault and we do not understand him," Cuff said. "I've always thought that the people who worked miracles called for a certain amount of quick-wittedness from the onlookers; and when everybody didn't immediately grasp the theological implications, the saints were very liable to get cross and sarcastic. They strike me as being somewhat *hasty* men."

"This one's too hasty by half," admitted Catullus. "He'll be gone before the Judge has a chance of meeting him."

"Or any of us," said Cuff.

"Particularly the Judge," Catullus corrected him.

Cuff Small blushed. "Oh yes, of course. Particularly the Judge. I didn't mean to push myself forward. It's really very rude of me to come running up to your bungalow, sir, like this. I should have waited till I was asked. There must be so many important people waiting to see the Swami. . . ." The missionary became inarticulate with his embarrassment.

Bay intervened kindly.

"No, no, Mr. Small. Catullus did not mean that at all. It is just that we had a plan to help that poor man in jail. The plan has gone well. I might almost say surprisingly well. But it is essential for its full success that the Judge should meet the Swami. It does not look as though he will."

Small got to his feet.

"Of course I don't understand fully about your plan, but I'm sure it's brilliant, and if it's anything to do with the man in prison, I'd like to help. Can I run down the hill and find the Judge?"

"That is kind of you," said Catullus, "but the whole police force of Limbo is running up and down every hill within five square miles of this house trying to find the Judge. He went out riding this morning and I'm having the roads searched by every constable in the place."

"All six of them," said Bay admiringly.

"There are only three roads, so that makes two to a road," added Catullus.

"Most efficient," said Small. "Is there any news?"

"They're to run up a flag over the police-station if he's found. I have a man posted on a tree outside with binoculars, watching."

Years of experience in Limbo darkened the missionary's eyes.

"Is the man in the tree a reliable man?" he asked.

"I gave him a personal interest in his job," said Catullus. "The police-station has no flag so I made him give them his shirt. He is now anxiously watching to see that they hoist it carefully."

"That is really far-sighted of you," said Small with grave approval. Bay looked at his watch.

"We can give the Judge fifteen minutes at the most. The Swami's all but finished his packing, and farewells, I feel, will not be protracted."

The missionary sat down on the edge of his chair and screwed up his forehead. After a few moments he said, "Couldn't we have some sort of ceremony when he leaves?"

"He's in no mood for it," said Catullus.

"Oh, I don't mean anything elaborate. But perhaps you

could make a speech. A longish speech, as Political Agent.
It might give the Judge time to arrive. You made a very
good speech at the Durbar."

Catullus began to shake his head, but Bay slapped the
table with his open hand. "Speeches!" he almost shouted.
"Mr. Small, hitherto, in common with the Judge, I have
respected you as a man of intelligence. Now I must pay
homage to you as a genius. *Speeches!*" he repeated with
deep admiration in his voice. "The very thing." Cuff Small
beamed happily. Bay lowered his voice. "They're the one
thing the Swami can never resist. Oratory is a sort of
hobby with him. It has its practical uses for a man in his
profession, of course, but the Swami has a love of long
speeches that is pure beyond the thought of personal gain.
He used to sit for hours in the Distinguished Strangers'
Gallery of the House of Commons, just drinking it all in."

" 'Distinguished,' " Cuff Small remarked. "So he is
already a famous man?"

"Not quite. He used to present himself at the public
entrance to the House, dressed in his white robes and
twirling a prayer wheel. The Swami says that the Sergeant-
at-Arms used to take him for the Tashi Lama. At any rate
he was always shown straight into the best seat over the
clock. He bore himself very well. He used to bless the
policeman as he left. But he left only after many hours.
The more pompous the speeches the better he liked them.
He simply revelled in the flow of words. From time to time
he would say in a deep voice, 'Yoi!' He maintained it was
the Tibetan equivalent for 'Hear, hear.' Anybody else
would have been thrown out, but not the Swami. The
House got used to him. Young members making their
maiden speech would wait anxiously for that deep 'Yoi'
coming from the bearded figure way up in the gallery.
When it came they felt that they were doing well. Catullus,
you shall be the first speaker, Small, the second, and I shall
wind up."

"Oh dear," said Small in dismay, "and a moment ago I was so happy. I do see it's a good idea, but what on earth shall I speak about?"

"Anything. In political oratory—and that's the sort the Swami likes—it doesn't matter what you say: it's the way you pause before you say it."

"Quite right," said Catullus. "I always imagine I am dictating to a particularly stupid stenographer."

"But you've had so much practice, sir," said Cuff. "I must have some sort of theme. Something like a text, perhaps. Did the Swami send us any sort of Message?"

"Yes," said Catullus.

"What was it?" asked the missionary in an awed voice.

"He asked if I would lend him a packet of razor blades."

"Oh dear," said the missionary, "what could he have meant by that?"

"I meant that I wanted to save my face," said an exasperated voice behind us. "Can't a man have a sane request taken in a sane manner in this place?" It was the Swami, dressed in a bush-shirt and trousers, and without his beard. He looked a man who was just in the prime of life and not finding it much to his taste.

"Catullus," he said, putting down the grip he was carrying, "if I were in a civilized place instead of this little bit of heaven I would now shake you by the hand and go outside and whistle myself a cab. As it is, I have to ask you to extend your hospitality so far as to send your servant for one of the Administration's trucks to convey me and my luggage out of Limbo. By that," he said in an awful voice, turning to the missionary, "I do not mean that I wish to be carried off in a chariot of fire or pulled through the air by strings of doves. I mean that I want a truck, preferably motivated by an internal combustion engine. I am sorry if I disappoint you."

Bay said, "Let me introduce you to the Reverend Cuff Small."

"At any other time, Mr. Small, I should be willing to

show you the respect due to your cloth. But just now you must pardon me if I look upon you with the same suspicion as a dog looks at a small boy swinging a tin can on the end of a bit of string. *What* are you up to *now*, sir?" he said, pushing his face close to that of Mr. Small.

Mr. Small stepped back a pace. "Oh, nothing at all, sir, I just came on behalf of the Mission to pay my respects."

"Mr. Small," said the Swami, and his eyes were terrible, "I may, through no fault of my own, be gone to glory, but I assure I am not yet dead. So there is no use," he went on more calmly, "in coming for my relics. In any case, I am bequeathing my body to the Royal College of Surgeons, where I can rest assured it will be in reverent hands."

"Why, of course you're not dead," said the missionary cheerfully.

"Thank you. Thank you, Mr. Small. They are the first words of human kindliness I have heard today."

"I just came to inquire about your future plans."

"You should know better than I, Mr. Small. What plans can I make? It is merely a question of waiting for my gridiron or my posse of lions. That, I believe, was the future which lay before my predecessors."

"But, sir, this is the twentieth century . . ." said the missionary.

"Oho no," the Swami replied with a ghastly smile, "you can't fool *me*, Mr. Small."

"Of course, you have proved to all of us that the Age of Miracles is not dead," said the missionary.

"You must make a wonderful preacher, Mr. Small."

Catullus sent a servant for the truck.

"But what are you going to do now that this marvelous thing has happened?"

The Swami watched a servant carrying out a basket. "I am going back to London," he said, "and if I don't find Max leaning on a gate and watching Henry V ride out on his way to France I shall buy a partnership in his hat business and lead a quiet, retired life working in his shop, where the only miracles that happen are that silly old women do actually pay his prices—and they happen a satisfactory number of times each day. I shall, in my more inspired moments, design hats of my own, and if one of them happens to glow with an unearthly light as a customer tries it on I shall merely describe it as an exclusive model and double the price on the spot."

"I wonder," said Small, "how I would have felt if it had happened to me. After twenty years as a missionary," he added wistfully.

Catullus said, "Look, the lorry will be a little time in coming, so let's all sit down a while."

ii

"If it had happened to you, Mr. Small," said Catullus, "you would have felt the virtuous pride of a man who, after years of honest labor in the cause of his fellow-men, opens his newspaper to find his name in the Honors List. The Swami here doesn't feel like that."

"I can't," said the Swami, but he spoke more kindlily than before. "I see your point, Reverend, and it makes my tantrums look pretty cheap, I grant you that. But I *am* cheap, Mr. Small, I *am* what Bay called me. I'm a charlatan. You're not. Loving your fellow-men comes easy to you. But don't deceive yourself that it comes easy to everybody else, or even that it ought to. Loving your fellow-men and wanting to do them good is a trick, like . . . like eating glass. It means you can swallow a lot that other people can't."

"Yes, it is a trick. In fact people pay to watch me do it every Sunday," said the missionary. "But you're not being asked to preach loving-kindness from a pulpit: you're being asked to use your power to heal the sick. You're like a very wonderful doctor. Doctors don't throw away their gifts."

"Very wonderful doctors," said Bay, "have to be bribed by very wonderful fees before you can even get them to promise that they'll try to see if their gifts will work. And the better doctors they are the higher the bribe they demand, until the very best of all can only be persuaded to work for people who can spend enough money in curing a cold in their silly heads to endow a bed in a hospital for twenty years."

"What he's trying to say," said the Swami bluntly, "is that there's no money in being a saint."

"That's what they told my mother," Cuff answered "when I was such a good boy they thought I might be one. So to prove them wrong she put me in the Church. Well, it didn't come to anything because I wasn't a saint, but *you* might rise to be an Archbishop."

"Name me one Archbishop who could work miracles."

"Thomas à Becket," said Bay.

"Not until he was dead," the Swami said. As he spoke a servant came up behind him. The servant looked dishevelled and hot. In his hands he held a pair of binoculars. Catullus caught his eye and silently asked him if there were any news. Equally silently, the servant indicated there was not. Catullus, with a gesture of his head, sent him back to his look-out post in the tree.

Bay coughed meaningly. Catullus got to his feet, hooked one thumb into the pocket of his bush-shirt, extended his other hand in an arresting gesture, and said:

"Exactly. It's a fundamental principle of society that you cannot have exceptional men at the top. I am a Civil Servant, and I run society and I know. We talk about the Greeks as being the most civilized people in all history but we forget that they impeached, ruined and exiled almost every man of genius who dared to show his hand in Athens. We don't do that nowadays, not because we are more tolerant of men of great gifts, but because we have learned a better way of dealing with them. We give them toys to play with: we set them to writing novels for women to read in the afternoon, or plays for people to go to after dinner to escape the deadly boredom of their own conversation. We give scientists vast playgrounds in the shape of laboratories, and ask them to solve questions that will take up their lifetime, paying them salaries that would not cover the annual breakages account for the apparatus, so that they can never cut more than grotesque and impoverished figures of fun in a society that glitters with the brilliance it has filched from them. And if by sheer force of his genius one man does thrust himself into temporary prominence by inventing a panacea for sickness or a mathematical formula that lays bare the secrets of the Universe, we tell him that it is becoming for a man of his high-mindedness to publish his secrets freely and openly for the good of the human race: by which we mean that he should give it to business men to sell and grow rich and become peers of the realm, to manufacturers to twist it to make a fortune out of a new kind of bomb. There is not one man in England who cannot name twenty of England's poets and authors and painters: he would be hard put to it to name ten Prime Ministers. Yet the Prime Minister is the greatest power of his time: he can send a million people to their death through an error of judgment and be held to no more severe account than the loss of his constituency at the next election. The poet, the painter, the scientist, the geniuses who are molding their own and future ages, are considered well rewarded if they and their wives and families do not starve in the streets. This is a pity, and we know it, but we know that it is necessary. Although we are bitterly aware that the man we place at the head of the State is no more than a fool chosen by a party to stop two clever men fighting for office, we unite in praising his wisdom, his grasp, his shrewdness and his balance of judgment, when his wisdom is the platitudes of street-corner orators, his grasp of affairs no stronger than his grip on the Depart-

mental notes with which Civil Servants like myself supply
him, his shrewdness the cunning of a stupid man hiding his
foolishness, and his balance of judgment the inability of a
man who cannot make up his mind which of two opponents
is right, because he is too stupid to know what either of
them is talking about. We paid court to Kings until the
Kings of Europe got so dangerously ignorant that they
could not impose even on their own flunkeys. We do it now
to politicians although for half a century we have been reeling from one catastrophe to another, following their guidance. Now that we tire of politicians, we shall do it for
another century to charlatans who will forsake the maneu-
vers of the party committee for posturing before cameras
and employing the technique of actresses before the micro-
phone. We know them all: Kings, Presidents, Prime
Ministers and Leaders, to be outstanding only in cunning,
and otherwise fools who began their careers through their
inability to make an honest living; but we shall go on
doing it. We must; we know what we are. We know that
after six thousand years of being given good advice we
are naturally capable only of following bad. Our grandfathers used to deceive themselves that those six thousand
years had been spent in building the City of God: now we
know that we have only been extending its sewage system.
Our grandfathers spoke of progress: now we know that
the only progress we have made is in our vices. We have
men today who in an instant have caused more slaughter
than Genghis Khan could in a year. We have perfect devices
for the torture of individuals which surpass the rack and
the strappado as much as they in their turn surpass the
schoolmaster's cane; we fill our magazines and newspapers
with advertisements so fraudulent and lying that the tricks
of the old alchemists seem like the subterfuges of children:
we have debased our arts so that we spend enough money
to buy a gallery of masterpieces in making one film of a
story written by a literate maidservant for the delectation
of other maidservants. We have produced the biggest wars,

the worst famines, that history has ever seen, and we have
rewarded the victims of our cruelty by providing them with
prisons of unparalleled size. We no more want the interference of men of intelligence and virtue in our de-
baucheries than a brothel-keeper wants a resident chaplain.
We know ourselves, and we know our men of genius have
no particular love for us. We know that a Dante, inventing Hell line by line and peopling each successive circle
with the persons he did not like, would not shrink from
putting real persons in a real hell if he were given the
opportunity, and would think he had rendered his God and
his conscience a service by doing so. We turn the pages of
Leonardo da Vinci and hold up our hands in horror that
so great a man could invent a submarine and a machine
for slicing off the legs of soldiers; we hurry over the
monstrous caricatures of men and women that he has
drawn on the back of the sheet, but we know that these are
as true as his drawings of dissected bodies, and more cruel
than any of his toys for soldiers; we know that a man who
saw his fellows as such vice-sodden hags and monsters
would not mind very much chopping off some of their legs.
We read the philosopher who spent a lifetime denying
that we possessed reason, and, knowing it to be true,
wonder why he took so much trouble to prove it. We
read him, and determine that it would not be safe to make
philosophers kings. We read the lives of saints and marvel
not how such men and women could rise to such wisdom,
but how men and women could show such a derisive contempt for the things that the rest of us hold so dear. We
laugh and clap at the poets and playwrights who display
such a deep knowledge of our nastiness, but we would
prosecute them in a cout of law if by chance we could
recognize ourselves in one of their characters. We dis-
trust our geniuses, and with reason, because we know that
they must hate us. It is not that we do not want to hear the
truth: that would not be so serious a failing; but we are so
sunk in lies that we regard the truth as an entertainment, a

titillation to our appetite for further and more monstrous falsehoods. We are like the debauchee who will sometimes tell his friends that his mistress is a bitch, raising himself up above the mire in which he wallows to make his next plunge all the deeper. No, Swami, you are right, there is no future in being inspired, there is no room for saints until they are dead and can be lied about, there is no room for a genius except he be a pander or a clown. You had best stick to being a charlatan, for that way there will be fame and money and honor for you. And who knows? One day, maybe, we shall reward you with the highest honor in our power and let some actor make a film about you, proving that, although you did see God once, it was quite all right because it was only because you were so upset at the frustration of your passion for a chorus-girl."

"Yoi!" said the Swami in deeply satisfied manner. "Yoi! Yoi! Yoi!"

He relaxed in his chair like a man basking in the first warm sunshine of the year.

"And now," he said easily, "after all that, will somebody please tell me if Catullus was meaning to be rude to me or to be nice?"

"Well," the missionary said, "he put you in some pretty distinguished company: Kings, Presidents, Prime Ministers and the like."

"Not to mention chorus-girls," said the Swami, feeling his newly smooth chin.

"As you say," Mr. Small agreed, "and as for the Kings and Presidents, why, I can't argue with you, Catullus, because you should know, Government being your profession. But when you come to wallowing in vice, that's *my* profession."

"Mr. Small," said the Swami, "you disillusion me."

"Why do you think that the priest has held his place in society even when his Churches have collapsed about his ears? Why do you think that my folks write to me every month to tell me about some new evidence of what they call the revival of religion?" asked the missionary. "I'll tell you. The priest is always fascinating to an adulterous generation because they think he knows more ways of committing adultery than anybody else. It's logical. He deals in sin as much as a dustman deals in garbage. If there weren't any garbage for the dustman to carry away he'd be out of work. And it's the same with the priest. I agree with Catullus about our sins, but who's to carry them away if it's not the priest? Who else would soil his hands? And if Catullus really means what he says, then he should put his trust in religion and do his best to make you, Swami, use the power that has been given you in religion's cause."

"Now don't you go twisting Catullus' words, Mr. Small," said the Swami, "and let me tell you that when you begin talking about religion, that's *my* profession too, and I don't agree with you. People aren't turning to religion to get rid of their sins; they don't go to the priests to save their souls, they go to save their reason. Has it ever struck you that a very strange thing has happened in our lifetime? A lot of very clever men spend their young lives in lunatic asylums and come out with degrees as psycho-analysts. Then they write books about all the loonies they've known and the rude things they do and dream about. So far so good. But what happens then? Young ladies and young gentlemen, and a good few old ones too, get the books from the Public Library and read them from cover to cover. Why? Because they want to become psycho-analysts? Because they want to find out why Aunt Matilda always leaves her knitting in the w.c.? Don't you believe it. They read the book because plain, honest-to-God naughty books aren't allowed by law. And the first thing they turn to is the bit on their own special fancy. Just you take one of those books off the shelves of a Public Library. Choose one of them where all the vices are laid out neatly, one chapter one vice, like the Seven Deadly Sins of the Catholic Church. Then just you look at the thumb-marks. I hope you gentlemen don't think I'm being indelicate, but a man in my profession has to get a good working knowledge of human nature and he can't wait until he's an old man. That's how I got a lot of mine and it's stood me in good stead. Now, I don't say that all those people do anything about it: I don't mean they put down the book and start sending orchids to the milkman's cart-horse. But I do say it's a sobering thought that hundreds of thousands of people find books about the doings of lunatics nice, homey reading for a wet Sunday afternoon. Now suppose that a woman of forty, married to a stockbroker and the mother of three strapping lads, finds herself winking at soldiers in the Park? That's not really the right example, but I modify it out of respect to the reverend gentleman on my right."

"But I know exactly what you mean," said Mr. Small brightly.

The Swami raised his eyebrows, but went on. "Now suppose she gets worried and goes along to a psychoanalyst. 'Ach yes,' he says to her," the Swami mimicked, assuming an accent. " 'there vos a gase like yours in the Wiener Schnitzel Sanatorium in 1926. There is nothing to vorry. You will be all right if you gome to me three times a week for two years. The other woman, she had to be put in a strait-jacket, but there is nothing to vorry.' That is not what she wants to hear: she hasn't the money to go to him three times a week; besides, it would leave her no time for walking in the Park. So she leaves the psychoanalyst and goes to the parish priest. She can't tell him exactly what the trouble is because she doesn't know if she can trust him, so she says that she hasn't been to church since she was married and now she feels the urge for spiritual comfort. So what does the priest do?"

"Knocks her down for a fifty-dollar subscription to the fund for repairing the church roof," said the Reverend Small promptly.

"I shall leave out the technical details," said the Swami.

"He tells her we all stand in need of spiritual comfort, which she takes to mean that the clergyman winks at nursemaids in the Park as well (which he probably does), and so she goes to church. It's cheaper than the psychoanalyst and more convenient, being only once a week. In church she hears stories of sinners who've done everything from A to Z in the index of the looney books, but it does not sound so exciting, because instead of being called Miss Z. and Mr. A. they are called impossible names like Rehboam and Jerboam. Most of them come to a bad end. Then there is Hell. She can never quite get that clear. Hell seems to be a custom on the point of dying out yet not quite dead, like standing up and offering a lady a seat in the bus. So she goes to the priest and says, 'What about Hell, Reverend, do I stand in danger of Hell?' And he leans back in his chair and smiles and says, 'My dear Mrs. Brown, we *all* of us stand in danger of Hell of one sort or another,' and then . . .'"

"He knocks her down for a *hundred*-dollar subscription," said Cuff Small.

"Mr. Small," the Swami said to him patiently, "if you feel that you must keep a cash account as my story proceeds, please keep it mentally, and when I have finished you can let us know the total in round figures. To resume, Mrs. Brown is now in a fine predicament. She has the alternative of ending up in a strait-jacket or on the end of a toasting-fork. She tries to pull herself together. She tells herself that winking at soldiers is a sin. She stops going to the Park, and annoys her family by switching off the radio every time a band plays military marches. For weeks she goes around with a spiritual expression on her face. When she plays bridge and the other women gossip about a neighbor she doesn't join in but says 'Poor soul' and 'We must be kind' till all her women friends think she knows something really spicy and is meanly holding out on them. She is just beginning to wonder if saints are canonized during their lifetime, when she goes to church and hears the clergyman preach about the woman of the town whom Jesus forgave because she loved so much. She goes home, kicks the cat, stamps on her hat, and books herself a seat for every performance of the Aldershot Tattoo."

"But why?" asked Catullus; "surely she should have been pleased that her sins would be forgiven her."

"That's just the point," said the Swami; "if the clergyman had followed up his first good impression and told her, 'Yes, Mrs. Brown, we shall be glad to have you in our congregation; we're all such a jolly lot of sinners I'm sure you'll fit in. We meet every Thursday afternoon in the vestry to compare notes,' why, that would have been fine and she need not have troubled about being a good woman. But as it is she doesn't know where she stands. It she goes on winking at soldiers she might burn to all eternity, but if she stops she might find some painted and peroxided Moll Flanders stepping on her toes and being preferred in heaven before her. Believe me, Reverend, if you gentlemen want to make sure that the Return to the Church is lasting, just get up and preach the New Testament, plain and simple without any trimmings. Just say Christ died to save sinners once and for all, and add that when he was talking direct to God he did not say, 'On behalf of certain persons who have realized that their way of life is not what it might be and are genuinely sorry for it, I ask you to extend your Heavenly clemency.' Just point out that he remarked, with a common sense which makes every other statement in every other religion sound like a lawyer splitting hairs, 'Father, forgive them, for they know not what they do.' "

iii

Cuff Small opened his mouth to say something, then, catching Bay's eye, changed his mind and was silent.

"I didn't say it was theologically accurate," said the

Swami looking at him, "and for all I know St. Athanasius or St. Chrysostom may have spent their entire lives writing books to prove that it isn't. All I say is that that is what Mrs. Brown goes to church to hear and she doesn't hear it. And not only Mrs. Brown but a lot of other people like the man who pressed the bomb button that Catullus was so hard upon, and the man who earns his living writing advertisements for bogus patent medicines, and the man who keeps his wife and family writing salacious lines for a cinema company because he finds he's got a flair for making puns. All those people that Catullus flung rude names at, they want to hear that *they don't know what they're doing*. They don't want to confess their sins. Only the little sinner wants to do that, the man who's so unimportant nobody knows anything about his peccadilloes and nobody would care if they did. There are plenty of other people whose sins don't *need* confessing. They're written big across the face of the earth these days. Whole cities stand blackened and ruined to bear witness to them, crosses rise over mass-graves filled to the brim with evidence. Catullus is right when he says that now one little nobody can commit a more heinous sin in an afternoon than an old-time king could commit in twenty years. But he's wrong when he says they like it. They don't: but if they thought that by going to church on Sundays and not cheating the ticket-collector for the rest of the week, by reading the Bible and loving what they've left of their fellow-men after six years of trying to kill as many of them as they could in the shortest possible space of time, they could wash their conscience clean and hold up their heads, then they would be devils, not men. But they don't. Everywhere you go you see they don't. Everywhere you turn you see it in people's eyes: 'What have we done? Where are we going? Why can't we stop it?' They're like people bewitched. I don't know who the witches are. Maybe the wizard on the hill could get busy on an outsize winnowing fan with a shipload of grain and find them for us. But even

if we can't name them we know they're there, sticking pins
in our wax images, muttering spells. Then, before we
know what we're doing, we're garrotting men in the dark,
disembowelling little children as they sit at school learning their lessons, shooting down half-naked black men in
their own villages, or, worse even than that, spreading lies
that we know are lies to say that all this is very regrettable
but is the only thing a civilized man can do. You talk of a
return to religion, padre, and you may be right, and people
may be going back to the churches. But when you hear the
tramp of their feet on the stone floors of your cathedrals
you should tremble in your cassock. There's something
that Queen Elizabeth wrote to a bishop that I've always
remembered, maybe because I'm a man who's had many
rude things said to him in his time and I've become a
connoisseur. She wrote: *'Proud Prelate, You know what
you were before I made you what you are. Do what I ask
or I shall unfrock you, by God.'* They'll do that to you and
your brother priests if you don't give *them* what *they* ask.
There was a time not so long ago when you churches were
empty and you were wondering how long your jobs would
last. Now you find yourselves praised in books, in films,
and you get as good a price for writing in a daily newspaper as a man who can describe a boxing match blow by
blow. But take care: those who made you will destroy
you if you fail them. I know, because those that you disappoint come to me. I meet them in a white robe, blinking
my eyes as though I've just been a million miles away
talking to a Buddha the other side of the Dog-Star. Mrs.
Brown and all the rest come to me, and they know I'm
bogus. They tell me their troubles and the sins on their
consciences. I don't show them how to wash themselves
clean of sin; I don't tell them to pray for forgiveness; I
don't tell them that they're no better than lunatics at large,
because they know that already. I tell Mrs. Brown that
it doesn't matter a damn if she winks at soldiers provided
the soldiers wink back, and if they don't she'd better try

sailors or Chelsea Pensioners. I tell the man who has bad dreams of the men he's killed by pressing a trigger that that doesn't matter either and that he's got about as much real sin on his conscience as the sten gun that he used to do the killing. I tell them all it doesn't matter, because God doesn't give a rap. He's as sick of you as you are of yourself. He's tired of the whole thing, and he can't even remember whether it was the gigantosaurus or the mammal under its toe-nail that he killed off. Whichever it was, it was the wrong choice. As for sin, you can no more help that than the baboon can help having a red behind: neither is very pretty; but then, neither you nor the ape need crick your necks trying to look at it. Do as you like, only don't bother so. If you want to see it God's way you've got to be as bored with the whole thing as he is."

"You obtained this information from Buddha behind the Dog-Star?" asked Bay.

"Oh, I admit the charlatanry. I tell them that God is a cloud and he isn't a cloud, I tell them that God is a blue light, and I tell them to sit on their bare hams for two hours a day, being careful to put a layer of silk and a layer of cotton on the floor before they do so. I say that this is to keep in the psychic forces, but really it's to keep out the rheumatism, because I cannot afford to have my clients laid up in bed. But Catullus has justified me in that, even if he did it in a back-handed way. People won't listen to the truth unless it has all the appearance of a thumping lie. I explain that God really wants them to do nothing at all. I also add that, just to tease, God has made it impossible to know him through thinking, so they had best go home and sit and do nothing for a bit and wait for something to happen. Nothing happens, except that they have time and leisure to see that their husbands are not dashing young men of twenty but bald and prosy men of forty-five: or their wives are no longer capable of giving them unendurable pleasure infinitely prolonged as they thought they would when they were walking out together. Then they begin to get stiff in the joints and make up their minds that they have experienced the First Stage of Illumination and that will do for today. Actually I have given them a quiet half-hour to themselves, and if I do that by selling them fancy telephone boxes I'm not doing them any harm. It's cheaper than a hotel bedroom and, for obvious reasons, so free from any suspicion of immorality that not even the King's Proctor could find anything wrong in it. Then, of course, they realize that God no more cares about their sins than a professor of mathematics worries about who gave the cat her kittens. So they sin around a bit more, and feel rather proud of it. But that doesn't last long, because they've got the feeling that they're not really interesting anybody, God being, as I told them, bored. They come to me and say, 'You know, you're doing me a powerful lot of good, Swami. Tell me more about this Indian philosophy of yours.' I tell them to come back tomorrow and I will initiate them. Their cure is finished, and what I've got to do now is to get rid of them. I know they won't go on paying me the sort of fees I ask for a tutorial course in the Vedanta, which they can get out of a book. So when they arrive next day I burn a few incense sticks and read to them for one solid hour in Sanskrit, or what I hold to be Sanskrit and shall continue to hold until somebody knows enough of it to contradict me. They listen and listen, and what with my Sanskrit and the incense they develop a headache fit to split their craniums. They say, 'It sounds very beautiful, but what does it mean in English?' Then I read them for another whole hour an English translation done by one of those Europeans who come and live in ashrams. At the end of the hour they say, 'Thank you very much. I understood it so much better in Sanskrit. I am going abroad on business for a while, so maybe I should settle your account—I mean, could I . . . well, if you won't be offended, Swami, I'd like to make a little contribution . . .' And then, as the padre has re-marked at less suitable points in my narrative, I knock

them down for a hundred dollars. Catullus had the kindness to rank me among the charlatans and so did Bay, and
as for the padre, he seems to think he knows better what
I should do with what is left of my life than I do myself.
I've put *my* cards on the table, gentlemen. I've told you
the little part I play in helping to keep a distracted world
sane. I don't say my work is very noble, but I do say it's
practical. Have you anything better to offer?"

iv

The Swami looked to Bay for an answer.

Bay said "Yoi" in a rather dubious manner. He looked
behind the Swami's head and all of us save the Swami saw
that the man with the binoculars had come back. He had a
happy look on his face.

"Sir," he said.

We held our breath.

"Sir," he said again, "may I go and get a drink of
water?"

Catullus, with an effort at self-control, said that he
might, but he must go back to his post.

The Swami looked at his watch.

"Have we," said Catullus to him in a rather forced
voice, "anything better to offer? Well, for my part, I'd
shoot the Kings and the Presidents and the Prime Ministers
and pay the best artists in the world fabulous commissions
to depict them as they weltered in their gore. Just for a
start," he added.

"That's because you're a Civil Servant, and every bank
clerk and office boy thinks the world would be a better
place if he could shoot his boss," said the Swami. "What
about the padre?"

"Me?" said Cuff Small, blinking with dismay. "Oh,
please leave me out. I was so enjoying myself, just listening. And it's scarcely fair. It's not Sunday and a clergyman only makes speeches on a Sunday." Bay sadly shook

his head at him, but Cuff was too nervous even to be
abashed. The Swami saved us.

"Here am I," he said, "opening the secrets of my soul
and my art to the world and you talk of it as though I
were opening a new bridge. But never mind. Tell us in
a sentence."

"Oh!" said Small. "A sentence? Well, how about 'Love
your neighbor'?"

"Who were your neighbors in your home town?"

"Mr. and Mrs. Schultz and the Van Adamses. The
Schultzes had a Miss Carcopino staying with them as a
paying guest," the missionary said obediently.

"Then why didn't you stay at home and love *them*?"

"Well, I might have managed to love Miss Carcopino,
but she was very temperamental. I don't think Mr. and
Mrs. Schultz *wanted* to be loved, and if I'd loved the Van
Adamses they would have said I only did it for their money.
Altogether it would have been very difficult."

"Exactly," said the Swami, "you missionaries find it
difficult to love your neighbors at home, so you settle on
the somewhat eccentric belief that it will be easier to love
a bunch of semi-nude savages."

"Well, I admit it does seem odd, but when I said 'Love
your neighbor' I was only taking you at your word and
preaching the New Testament straight."

"Floored!" said Bay delightedly. "Swami, the missionary's put you out for a count of ten and you richly
deserve it. Never take on a clergyman about the Bible.
He's always in the pink of condition."

"Which brings me," said the Swami unperturbably,
"to you, Bay. What have you to offer to the solution of
our problem other than ring-side ejaculations?"

"I have listened to both of you," said Bay, "and I
agreed with both of you until each of you, separately, by
your own devious routes, reached a point at which you
began talking in the manner of one of the most silly women
that I have ever come across. She was much sillier than

your Mrs. Brown, Swami, but she was very like her in
that she asked questions in philosophy. You will remember
her, Swami. She comes in your favorite Brihad-Aranyaka
Upanishad, and, now I come to think of it, you are a
much better person than me to repeat the story."

"Possibly," said the Swami urbanely, "but you had the
courtesy not to interrupt me so why should I interrupt
you? Tell it," he said generously, "in your own way."

"Thank you," Bay said, and, sinking lower in his chair,
went on. "Her name was Gargi and she had attached herself to the sage Yajnavalkya, because she had heard that
he was conversant with all the secrets of heaven and earth.
Though, as is the habit of Indian sages, Yajnavalkya was
by no means a taciturn man, Gargi could not rest satisfied
with what he said freely from his wisdom, but must needs
pester him with questions. He had spoken of the weaving
of the worlds of the sun, warp and woof (two good words
for you, Swami, warp and woof) and she began to question
him. 'On what, Yajnavalkya,' she asked, 'are the worlds
of the sun woven, warp and woof?' 'On the worlds of the
moon, O Gargi,' said the sage. He called her O Gargi
because it was the polite thing to do in those days and a
little politeness helped him to keep his temper. He needed
all the help he could get, for the egregious Gargi went on.

"'On what then, pray, are the worlds of the moon
woven, warp and woof?'

"'On the worlds of the stars, O Gargi,' said the sage.

"'On what then, pray, are the worlds of the stars
woven, warp and woof?'

"'On the worlds of the Gods, O Gargi,' said the sage.

"Now Yajnavalkya felt that if this woman said 'warp
and woof' just once again he would forget who he was
and strike her. But she went on:

"'On what then, pray, are the worlds of the Gods
woven, warp and woof?'

"'On the worlds of Indra, O Gargi.'

" 'On what then, pray, are the worlds of Indra woven, warp and woof?'

" 'On the worlds of Brahma, O Gargi,' said Yajnavalkya, not really knowing or caring what he was saying.

" 'On what then, pray, are the worlds of Brahma woven, warp and woof?' asked Gargi, and the sage was terrible in his mildness.

" 'Woman,' he said, 'do not ask so many questions or your head will fall off.'

"Now whether the sage," said Bay, "knew the answer to her question or not I cannot tell you. But what he did know was that the woman was throwing words about for the pleasure of the sound of them and not because she wanted information. Just so, I think, did you and Catullus use the words sin and God, hell and salvation; not because you thought that they were important to make your meaning clear, but because they boom and thunder strikingly in the ears of your listeners. The Devil, said someone, has all the best tunes: he might have added that God invariably has the best prose styles. Even the Polynesian savage, thumping his hollow tree-trunk and praising his God, does so in poetry that sounds well despite a scientist's clumsy translation. The better the style, the more obscure the meaning, and so much of a vice did God-language become that the prophets of the Jews found the more deathlessly beautiful their denunciations became, the less and less could their listeners understand what they were driving at. It got so bad that Hosea, not himself a mean stylist, determined to put an end to it. He went to live with Gomer, daughter of Diblaim, and had three bastards by her in order to demonstrate unmistakably the meaning of his statement that the Jews had gone a-whoring after strange gods. The loveliness of religious prose, the purity of religious poetry, the artistry of parables and the drama of the legends of gods almost persuade one that human beings talk their best only when they have not the least notion of what they are talking about. Because neither Catallus nor you, Swami, *do* know what you meant. Catullus knew only when he spoke of things which, had he time, he could have proved from history. It is true that civilization has no need of genius and every child would know that in his schooldays if, instead of teaching him Virgil and Racine in order to inculcate the excellent lesson that literature is in a large part deadly dull as well as being unimportant, they had taught him the history of Byzantium. It is said that we teach history only when it concerns Kings and Generals and that this is harmful. But we do worse: we teach history only when it can be made into an entertaining anecdote, a procedure which is about as sound as leaving the teaching of sexual hygiene to a commercial traveller. If we taught dull history the world would know that for a thousand years the Empire at Constantinople was the center of all that was civilized: for a thousand years it lived a life of leisured splendor while the rest of Europe wallowed, hungry, in the blood-stained mire of its darkest ages. But Byzantium had no geniuses. It built cathedrals of surpassing beauty, but the man, if there was a man, who drew the plans was forgotten before the roof was on: they painted, not well but powerfully enough, but we do not remember the names of the painters: they wrote, voluminously, but if anybody but an antiquarian or a theologian read a line of it, the book will certainly be the vicious backbiting gossip of Procopius, who has survived because he has the merit of being worse than even his own bad times. It was not that they had no artists alone: they did without great men of any kind. Of their endless list of Emperors, their lives are all so petty and ignoble that the ennui of reading about them can only have been equalled by the tedium of living in their courts. Two we remember: Julian, who detested his people and their civilization so much that he was called the Apostate, and Irene, because our fathers considered it a pretty name for a girl; an odd choice, and one which makes my point, for the original

Irene blinded her own son to make certain of the throne. It has happened once, then, that we have done without genius, and lived comfortably enough: Catullus is right, it can happen again and indeed may already have happened for all that we can tell. But he is wrong when he hurls accusations of sin at people that he does not like. Strangely and not a little frighteningly wrong, because the word sin was much in the mouths of the people of Byzantium, and anathemas as common as votes of censure are among us. It seems to be true that when evil is so commonplace, and the dislike of it so weak that there is no zest left in its condemnation, that you must sauce your arguments with the sharpest words that you can draw from the vocabulary of your forefathers: you must describe things which no longer cause a man to lift an eyebrow in words which in past and better days would have frozen his soul with horror. It seems that this must be, but you should remember, Catullus, that to claim to know a man's sins is to claim to know what is virtuous: to be wise enough to tell a man what not to do, you should be wise enough to tell him what he should."

"I have my principles," said Catullus; "any man has. True, as a Civil Servant, I may not keep to them all the time."

"By all means doubt the honesty of other men's principles, Catullus, but surely it is foolish to live as though you doubt the honesty of your own? But I am forcing you to claim to be a sort of person that you are not, and do not want to be. Or rather, you are forcing yourself by using these words, sin and God and salvation and the like, as a lover might send his mistress a poem he had copied out of a book and find himself owning to a tumultuous and exhausting passion when he was only trying to save himself the trouble of thinking out another love letter. And you, Swami, who this morning was blessed by three gifts beyond the price of rubies, the gift of healing, the gift of being a successful trickster, and the best beard since Karl

Marx. You have thrown away the last and you intend to throw away the first. What are you doing with the gift that is left to you? You advise the missionary solemnly on the meaning of the New Testament, you erect a theology of your own on the foundation of Mrs. Brown's military predilections, you thunder warnings about the duties of the Church. You once told me that you knew the trick of sawing a woman in half. What would you say to the illusionist, Swami, who would not let his wife play the part of the woman on the grounds that he preferred her in one piece? They tell me that you can eat glass: what would you think of a man who asked, before he ate it, whether the tumbler was a Czechoslovakian manufacture, and if he was told that it was, took a pill or two after his performance because he found Bohemian glass deficient in vitamins? There is only one disgrace in being a charlatan and that is if you come to believe in your own tricks. You should take a lesson from the early Pope who wrote letters to all his earthly supporters announcing that the world would surely end at the turn of the century, when the year one thousand would arrive: and then bought up all the lands and estates that had been thrown on the market at dirt cheap rates, thus laying the foundation of the temporal wealth of all the Popes who came after him.

"When I met the Swami," Bay went on, turning to the rest of us, "I thought that he was the only man I had ever known who did not bother about right or wrong, sin or salvation, God or the Devil. He did not bother his *soul* about them, however much these words were on his lips. He seemed to me to be a man who, if he were not utterly devoid of all sense of decency, honesty, morality and feeling for his fellow-men, would have blown out his brains long before. But I see now that he was only a clergyman who had not had enough money to take his divinity degree and his charlatanry was nothing more than the dishonesty of a schoolboy cribbing the lesson he has not learned in time. I brought him here to give him the opportunity to do the biggest and most insolent fake of his career; he restored his sense of respectability by becoming a buyer for a hat shop. In spite of himself, a thing happened to him that shows that he is either a demon or a god. He answers that he is by taste and inclination a milliner."

Bay fell silent.

"I take it you are finished?" asked Catullus.

Bay mopped his forehead.

"Yes," he said.

"So are we," said Catullus sadly. "Here is the truck to drive the Swami away."

v

It drew up outside the bungalow and, before it had properly stopped, out of the driver's seat leapt Mr. Justice Bose.

"Quick, quick," he said in great excitement, "where's the Swami? He must come straight away. There are at least three hundred people waiting for him down by the big tree. It's the so-called miracle, of course. Mr. Leavis, you are quite right, quite right, these people's faith is a very real thing, a very real thing indeed, and if it isn't real in law, well then it ought to be. It's the most inter-esting example of mass hysteria and induced delusion I ever hope to witness. I'm making notes," he said, waving a jotting-pad. "I'm making notes, and I shall work the whole thing up into one of the most fascinating articles the Annual has ever had the good fortune to print. But where's the Swami?"

"Right in front of you, Mr. Bose," said Catullus and Bay simultaneously.

"Oh yes, indeed. Thank you for your message, Catullus. I jumped in the truck as it was passing in order to get up here all the quicker. Couldn't send a message, the mass hysteria is turning even the servants' heads. So you're the Swami, sir, congratulations, sir, congratulations," he said, seizing the Swami's hand and shaking it with the enthusiasm of a schoolboy greeting the captain of the First XI after he's made a century. "A most striking experiment in the artificial stimulation of religious mania. But they told me you had a beard."

"Well, you see . . ." said Catullus.

"But, my dear fellow, of *course* I see. Mass delusion, an ideal instance. Freud would describe it as the projection of the father-myth, I imagine, but what you've done today is going to make a difference to a lot of those theories, I'll be bound. We'll upset a few apple-carts when we publish this."

"Would you mind very much," said the Swami, "if I made my way to the truck?"

"Not at all, not at all; I'll come along with you."

"The Swami is leaving Limbo," Catullus explained.

"Leaving Limbo?" the Judge said, bewildered. Then, snapping his fingers, "But of course, of course, you're going down to the plains to bring up some psychiatrists. Most important, most desirable. We can check on the index of mental deficiency, and if my hypothesis is even half correct, we're going to find it pretty high."

The Swami had taken two steps towards the door leading to the veranda, but on hearing this he stopped. He turned slowly and faced us. With perfect courtesy but a voice of ice he said, "I regret that I did not catch your name?"

"Bose. Bose is the name. Chandra Bose J. Meaning Justice."

"Mr. Justice Bose," said the Swami, "in the course of this afternoon I have been insulted, successively, for being a charlatan and for not being a charlatan. I have been criticized for ignoring my responsibilities as a pillar of the Church and jeered at for my lack of knowledge of the Scriptures. I have been slanderously described as lacking every sense of decency and mocked at for having the mental outlook of a clergyman. I have been fleeringly

classed with Prime Ministers and dismissed with contempt
as a milliner. All this, Mr. Justice Bose, I have withstood
with fortitude, preserving the most admirable calm. But
of all the uncalled for and unprovoked attacks upon my
character, your suggestion that the purpose of my depar-
ture is to get the innocent and ingenuous inhabitants of
Limbo certified en masse as lunatics, I find the least possible
to bear."

"I beg your pardon if . . ." the Judge began in a bewildered voice, but the Swami held up his hand and
stopped him.

"Do not," he said gravely, "do not, I beg of you,
apologize, for you may start in the hardened hearts of
these gentlemen here such an agony of repentance that I
should weaken in my purpose. My mind is made up.
Bayard Leavis I have always known to be a bad influence
on me, but not until this afternoon, when he exposed his
wicked soul to the public gaze, did I see the depths to
which he was heading me. Mr. Justice Bose, I request
you to bear witness that I am henceforward determined to
strive might and main to make myself an honest man and
to put behind me for ever the evil communications that
have too long corrupted the good manners my mother
taught me. I am now going to the nearest town, and there
I shall buy a supply of epsom salts, jalap, potassium per-
manganate, aspirin, liniment and similar simple medical
aids. With these I shall return and take up the duties of a
male district nurse. And if any Limbodian or anyone else
should mention miracles or sin or any other theological
topic to me, I shall give him a double dose of castor oil."

He got into the truck and the engine started. As the
truck moved off he leaned out, and with a broad and
friendly grin, waved us goodbye.

CHAPTER TWELVE

THE next day Limbo seemed very empty without the
Swami. There was nothing to do except wait for the
runner to bring the post. He came each day in the middle of
the morning, a bag slung over his shoulder. He was called
a runner but nobody had ever seen him run: he covered his
distance in a steady walk, bending his knees at every step
like a man tottering to a collapse. His peculiar gait served
him very well and he brought our few letters very
regularly. Whatever the state of the rivers, he was always
on time. He delivered his bag at Catullus' bungalow, and
we gathered there each morning to see what it would bring.

On the morning after the Swami had left us there was
only a postcard and a letter. Catullus read the postcard and
said, "I do wish people would write me letters. I don't
mean clever or friendly or gossipy letters, but just any sort:
an envelope enclosing the week's washing list would do.
It would help the Indian Post Office to take us all seriously.
They don't, you know. Just look at the postmark." He
showed it to us. It said, EXPERIMENTAL POST OFFICE,
PRIMPRI.

"Primpri's a village just outside Limbo," Catullus explained, "and that Post Office has been experimental for
fifty years. But still, it gives one a feeling of insecurity. I
always feel that one day the Postmaster-General will say,
'This joke has gone on long enough. That man Catullus
invented the whole thing. There is no Limbo. Close down
the Post Office at Primpri.' Bay, you're not listening."

"It's very hot today," sighed Bay. "But I am listening."
He fanned himself with the postcard that I had passed on
to him from Catullus.

"You can't be. You haven't said, 'I must now tell you

of the man who invented an entirely new Republic in
South America.' "

Bay took a long drink from the glass of lemon-juice
and water at his side. "No," he said, "but I can tell you
of Du Haillau. He was a French historian, and he found
himself writing about a certain early French King called
Pharamond. Du Haillau quickly made up his mind that
Pharamond never existed, but he did not like to say so.
The French were going through a very nationalist period
at that time, and Pharamond was a popular hero. For all
his popularity, the details about Pharamond were very
thin, and Du Haillau prided himself on writing the most
convincing histories. So (like the sensible man he was)
knowing, I presume, that history, like the drama, is re-
written every two generations and so need not be true,
Du Haillau invented two entirely fictional and entirely
new Members of King Pharamond's Council. He called
one Charamond, which was not very inventive, and the
other Quadrek, which was. Now *you* are not listening,"
said Bay to Catullus, who was reading the letter.

"Yes, I was," said Catullus absently, and still reading;
"you were talking of a man who invented quadratics.
Really, Bay, your range of useless information is quite
astonishing." But he still went on reading the letter with
a helpless look on his face.

"My dear Catullus," said Bay, "whatever is wrong?"

"Wrong? Oh, nothing, nothing at all." Then, folding
the letter with great precision, and putting it back into its
envelope:

"Winifred's flying out from England."

"Winifred?"

"My wife."

"Really? It must be five years since I met her. She dined
with me, I remember. Charming woman. It was in my
rooms at Oxford, and she found some books under the
table. I remember she told me I was an untidy bachelor and

I think I made a bad impression. But I explained that I'd left them there for Fenstone-Brown, the authority in the third passus of Piers Plowman. He always read his books under the table," he explained to me.

"Yes," I said, "Catullus told me. Why?"

"Privacy, largely. He preferred a table laid for breakfast, not formal dinners. Tablecloths were used for breakfast, whereas the modern fashion is to have the plain polished wood for dinner. The tablecloth cut him off more from the world, he used to say."

"What did my wife say?" Catullus asked him.

"Nothing, as I remember. But she was charming throughout dinner, and I think she accepted my explanation. But why is she coming out here in this heat?" asked Bay, fanning himself again. "This is surely no place for a holiday."

"That's what she thinks," said Catullus, putting the letter carefully in his pocket. "She wants to know why I am staying here so long. She knows I usually only come here for Durbar Day, and she is suspicious, I think."

"Good Lord," said Bay, "whom does she suspect? A woman?"

"No," said Catullus. "You."

Bay chuckled and finished his lime-juice with relish.

ii

Then we were all busy getting Catullus' bungalow ready to receive Winifred. We moved the furniture around in her bedroom, trying to give the room a feminine touch. We had our separate opinions about what that was. We spent a good deal of time closing the door, then opening it and standing on the threshold, trying to see what it was like 'coming in at the door.' When we had got her bedroom arranged to our satisfaction we turned to the rest of the house. It was very bare and gaunt: the furniture had been made from the local teak trees by carpenters whose previous experience had been limited to making bullock carts, and was undisguisably clumsy. Catullus asked us both to bring any light and gay furnishings that we had in our own bungalows and to let him use them during his wife's stay.

I brought a large earthenware pot with a design of tigers and antelopes, which I had found in the village. I thought it would look very well if we filled it with flowers. Bay brought a long carved staff. He said it should be leaned against the table. Winifred could use it to rattle about with underneath, to see that nobody was sitting there at meal-times.

In the middle of the bustle the Swami returned. He had been as good as his word. He had brought packing-cases of drugs and bandages and one or two books on Tropical Medicine. He commandeered an empty hut in the village and made it his headquarters. At first he used a large white flag with a red cross on it to indicate his business. For two days no Limbodian came anywhere near the place. Then one morning he found the hut hideous with the squawking of dozens of chickens, each lying on the floor with its legs tied together. After some tactful questioning he found out the reason for them. A red cross in Limbo means that the place is inhabited by a devil. It is usually found on trees and stones, done roughly with two strokes of red lead. The Limbodians had taken it as quite natural that a man of his powers should have inter-course with demons and, since he was clearly a kindly person, he had run up the flag to warn the inhabitants of what was going on inside, that they might keep out of danger. The chickens were the usual sacrifice, and were meant to keep the demons inside the hut. A few extra chickens had been added as a mark of appreciation of the Swami's courtesy in running up the red cross.

The Swami gave back the chickens and took down the flag. Bay suggested that instead of it he should nail a winnowing fan to a post, as a sign that he practiced in the

divination of witches. But the Swami would have none
of it. He said he would have no truck with that sort of
thing, and that he would rely on his hard work to advertise
his purpose. Good wine, he told Bay, needed no bush. Bay
had said, "I must now tell you the interesting story behind
that saying." But the Swami had refused to listen and had
stalked off to his hut to roll bandages. There was no doubt
that he was a changed man, and a very happy one, but his
past sometimes dogged him.

Among his first patients was a boy. At this time he
still had to go out into the village and capture people by
main force in order to treat them. This boy had, as usual,
fallen from a tree, but since his fall had been broken by a
thick clump of six-foot jungle grass, he had not been seriously hurt. There was, however, a cut in the top of his
head. The Swami saw him in the village street, and, seizing him by the arm, dragged him into the hut. He looked
up a first-aid book and found that a cut on the top of the
head called for quite a considerable bandage. Placing the
book open on the ground he went to work, winding the
bandage up and down and round as the book directed. He
felt that he had done a good job of work when it was
finished, and came to have his lunch with us in a very
satisfied mood. He was even more pleased when, return-
ing to his dispensary in the cool of the evening, he found a
crowd of what he took to be patients. Only when he had
examined at least a dozen and found nothing particularly
wrong with them did he discover why they had come. They
had seen the boy that he had treated in the morning, they
said, and they thought that he was giving away turbans
again. If so, could they each have one. More or less as a
penance for what he now considered the frivolities of his
past life, he gave them each a bandage, winding it around
their heads in various fashions. He consoled himself for
the loss of medical supplies that this entailed by imagining
that each of them had increasingly ghastly wounds, and he
gave himself some practice in bandaging. For a day or two

afterwards, any group of Limbodians walking down the road had the appearance of part of an army straggling home after a disastrous defeat.

For the first few days the Swami had a lot of trouble from witches. Not that the woman who was the local witch ever came near him; but, whenever he diagnosed a complaint, the sufferer's family went to the witch and threatened her. They said that the Swami, who was the greatest witch-doctor in Limbo, had said that So-and-so was bewitched, and although he had named no names, not yet being sufficiently paid for his services, they knew quite well who had done it. They demanded that the witch take off the spell or else they would see about it. They would then go home and wait for the patient to get better. They were very puzzled when the Swami insisted on going on with the treatment; they mostly concluded that witches were getting very malignant and using double and triple spells. This disturbed the Swami, because he did not want to do the witch harm; but he was prevented from explaining himself to the villagers by the awe which surrounded him wherever he went.

But soon the Swami began to notice that the people were treating him as one of themselves. He was delighted. He put it down to the fact that now he was actually using a pickaxe and spade, as well as mysterious things out of books. Indeed, and most admirably, he was. He was determined to drain away the pools of filthy water which lay round many of the huts and bred mosquitoes. To set an example, he dug ditches and runways himself. But it was not so much this that had changed the villagers' attitude towards him as something that the witch herself generously explained to him the first time she visited his hut.

She came after dark, leading a goat. The Swami welcomed her and brought her inside. She brought the goat with her and the animal immediately broke two large bottles that the Swami had stood upon the floor. He asked her to take the goat outside, but she shook her head.

She was a handsome woman with a determined but pleasant manner, as of one used to exercising authority. She said that the goat was a present to the Swami. He refused it, saying he would not deprive her of so valuable an animal, but she said, no, take it, she had plenty more. In fact, she had so many she did not quite know what to do with them all.

Then she explained. For years past, of course, she had caused all the sickness in the village. Occasionally people died, and often they did not. Naturally, like all witches, she had been threatened with beating unless she made people well again. She was a just but kind woman, she explained, and if she could possibly see any reason for letting people off, she made them well. When she could not, then she did not, and she relied on the respect the villagers had for her powers, dead or alive, to save her skin. Recently much fewer people had died, very many more got well. She was, as everyone knew, responsible for this. Perhaps she was getting rather soft-hearted, but there it was. The villagers were very grateful for her kindness and were continually giving her the most lavish presents. For one instance among many, the goat.

Being observant and clear-headed people, she went on, the villagers had noticed another thing. The Swami: he, it was plain, was the instrument of healing. He made the necessary passes and gave the prescribed herbs to dissolve the spell. This was a new thing in witchcraft, but no man would be such a fool as to claim he knew everything a witch could do. The villagers had decided that she, their own witch, had put a spell on the Swami and by its means had made him her assistant. They were sure of this when they found him digging ditches. It was obviously a punishment she had set him for some slackness over his duties.

Now, she would be frank with the Swami. Recently she had been overworking. She had had all-night conversations with talkative demons, and she was feeling the strain. Maybe in a tired moment her tongue had slipped and she had said something which had the effect of binding the Swami to her service. She didn't know. She was sorry if it was so, but if it was, well, there it was. She did not mean to offend the Swami, and she hoped the whole thing could be arranged in a way that was fitting to a man who was, say what anybody might, a person of considerable influence. So she did not suggest that he go on being her assistant. She offered him a partnership, with a half-share in the gifts. Please, now, would be accept the goat?

Wisely the Swami did accept the goat, and we all subsequently had mutton on a non-mutton day. From the night of the witch's visit onwards the Swami's work went smoothly and undisturbed, and would have continued so if it had not been for the arrival of Winifred.

iii

She was a short woman with a rather big head. There were no hard features on her face, and when she was young she might have been pretty; pretty, but definitely not beautiful. She was middle-aged now, but both her hair and her figure looked younger. Mostly, her appearance was unimportant: what one remembered of her was her voice. It was very low, so that when she said anything to you, either you did not hear what she said, or you leaned over towards her, strained your hearing, and cudgelled your wits to fill in the missing words: in short you gave her your undivided and intense attention; which was exactly what she wanted.

When you did manage to hear her voice you found it full of sympathy and kindliness, not of the motherly type, but of a less possessive sort. She spoke in the tones that might be used by a young girl with a fortune of a million pounds, perfect health and kind parents, talking of a successful love-affair, to a devoted girl friend over lawn tea on a sunny Sunday afternoon.

It was in this voice that, coming up the veranda steps

and greeting Catullus, she placidly said, "How nice to see you again, darling. I am a little late but I was delayed by a tiger."

The servants came forward with garlands of flowers and hung them round her neck, as it is the custom to do with all visiting wives of Officials. But wives (and it is a common complaint among travellers in India) are at a loss to know what to do with them. The garlands are too bulky to wear with grace, and yet it is impolite to take them off. The usual thing that is done is to wait until the donor is out of sight and then hurriedly to take the garland off and hang it in the most conspicuous place in the room. If the donor returns, one casts admiring glances at it every so often, as though one had taken it off only the better to see it. If the donor does not return, one puts it in the dustbin.

Winifred received her garlands with quiet little exclamations of thanks, looking kindly and long at each servant, giving the impression that she was memorizing the face of a man who had been so very kind to her as to give her flowers.

"Thank you. Thank you, indeed, And *you*, what beautiful jasmine! Thank you!" she said to them severally, and then with so little change of voice that they all but missed the order, "Bring me some tea made with *boiling* water and some *thin* toast and I shall have it on a tray on the veranda."

Then Catullus said, "This is the new Education Officer," and she shook hands with me, speaking as she did so. I was not yet used to her intimate way of speaking, and she may have been saying "Oh yes, and a fine scoundrel you've picked for the post, too," for all I could tell. Judging rapidly from her expression, I said, "Yes, indeed!" She told me afterwards that what she had said, by way of a joke, was, "So you have an Education Officer. Well, we all of us stand in need of a little educating," and that she had been disconcerted by my reply. She had rather wondered if her husband had picked up with yet another friend like Bay.

Catullus said next, "And I think you've met Mr. Leavis," and Bay shook hands with her.

"Oh yes, Mr. Leavis asked me to a most charming dinner-party. These are very different surroundings to find you in, Mr. Leavis. So bizarre compared with your rooms in Oxford; or are they? And now, P.A., tell me all about what you have been doing."

Since Catullus answered her, we concluded that she called her husband by the name he is known by in his Service. Being a political agent, his equals refer to him as P.A., just as they would call me, as the Education Officer, E.O. It made Catullus sound very august to hear his wife speak of him in that fashion, saying 'P.A.' as one said 'The Duke' when talking of the Duke of Wellington in his lifetime. That, as I understood when I got to know Winifred better, was exactly her design.

"Well, my dear," said Catullus, "we have done some most interesting research into the anthropology of the Limbodians."

"Have you, P.A. How nice! You do take so much trouble over them. Who is the new Assistant P.A.?"

"Tony West. You remember him."

"Yes, indeed, and I'm glad to hear that he's getting on. So many people said that he never would when he married that Penny girl, but I always said she was the type to pick things up quickly. I hope he's doing well."

"I think so," said Catullus. "But slow in answering letters." She laughed a light little laugh, full of genuine pleasure, as though Catullus had said something witty.

"It's so good to hear you talking just in the same old way," she said, and poured herself some tea.

To me, and I think to Bay as well, Catullus could not have spoken more out of his own character, at least as we knew it, had he been doing an impersonation. She still wore the garlands, and as she was pouring her tea she said to one of the servants, "Bring me a flower-bowl, not *too* full of water, and some scissors, not nail scissors with bent ends, but ordinary scissors with *straight* ends." These were quickly fetched, at which she took off the garlands, carefully unsnipped the fastenings, and began transferring the flowers one by one to the bowl. The servants watched in dumb amazement. It is possible, I suppose, to receive a Christmas card, open it, write across it, 'Thanks, see you in the New Year,' and send it back again. Winifred, from the servants' point of view, was doing no less.

"How did you manage to get a seat on the plane so quickly," Catullus asked her. "I hear they're still very hard to come by."

"George, that nice young man at the India Office, helped me. He could not have been more kind. He told me quite frankly at first that I would have to wait a week. So I told him he simply wasn't to worry and just went on chatting about old times. You remember what a harum-scarum lad he was when first he joined the Service out here? Well, that's all behind him, as I reminded him, now that he's got such a responsible and serious job at the India Office. There's one thing to be said for us all, I told him: your old friends from India don't *gossip* when you get back home. He quite agreed that it was a very big point in our favor. The dear lad must have moved heaven and earth to get me a seat, for I was off and out of the country within thirty-six hours."

"I'm sure I don't know that George was so very harum-scarum, my dear. All I know is that he's got a much better job than I have, and he was my junior."

"Yes, dear, he has," said Winifred, delicately adjusting the flowers in the bowl; "are you working hard?" and she threw a quick glance over the flowers at Bay.

"It's been dreadfully hot," said Catullus hurriedly, and then, "Tell us about the tiger."

iv

She had wanted to drive through Limbo during the night to save her from staying at the verminous hotel twenty miles beyond the border. Catullus had told her that this could be done, when they had been laying plans for a previous visit. But now the driver bluntly refused to do anything of the sort. A man-eating tiger had been on the road the night before, he told her, and had killed a woman. Nothing would make him drive along that road in anything but the broadest daylight, and if she made a fuss he would just run away and leave her where she was.

"I had to promise, P.A., that I would not report him to you and you must take no official notice of it. I gave him my word, and these people trust us. Besides, nobody can criticize anybody for being afraid. We're all of us cowards about something or other. I'm *terrified* of epidemics," she said, laughing at her own weakness. "I'm sure that in a lot of things he's a very brave man. He looked a brave man. The way he talked was very bold. Even if he was afraid of tigers, he wasn't afraid of poor me. Oh dear me, no! I was afraid of *him*, with the language he was using. Of course I understood, P.A., that you have to let these people have a lot of freedom, but there would be some people who would think you let them do absolutely as they please. I'm glad the Resident's wife has never been driven by him. If she comes anywhere near the place, P.A., be sure there's another driver on duty. But I must not prejudice you against him, P.A. We made a bargain and he stuck to his side of it. He did not run away, and sportingly started well before the sun was up."

They had driven for two hours and arrived at the village of Chickrar. There was a flaw in the radiator and they needed water. They saw nobody in the village street and nobody outside the huts. The driver had shouted for some-one to fetch them water but there was no reply. The sun was up and it was unusual for nobody to be about. The driver sounded the horn, but still nobody came. This was not only unusual but sinister. Motorcars are rare in Limbo, and at the sound of a horn all the small boys in the village invariably come scampering to look. The driver wanted to go on and leave the village behind them. He did not like the look of things. But Winifred leaned on the horn control, and after a minute or so, a man appeared. He ran as quickly as he could across the space between his hut and the car, looking nervously to left and right of him. When he got to the car he began making confused explanations. The driver sorted them out and told Winifred what had happened.

The man-eater had been there two nights ago and had attacked a boy. The boy had run into the jungle and climbed a tree. The tiger had prowled round the tree for a while and then gone away. The next night, the one that had just passed, nobody went out till the morning came. The first to do so was an old man. He owned a buffalo and he had awakened up to hear it stamping and bellowing. At first he had thought it was the tiger, and then, peering through the cranks in the roof of his hut, he had seen that it was daylight. Thinking it safe, he had gone outside to see what was troubling the buffalo. It was the tiger. The spoor marks, and blood on the ground, told the villagers all that they could not gather from the man's single shout of terror.

"I asked him what he was going to do about it," said Winifred, "and the stupid man said that the next night they would tie up a goat as a sacrifice and hope that the tiger would be pleased and take the goat and go away. Well, I told him pretty sharply that I could stand guarantee that the tiger would be pleased all right, and the superstitious fool said he hoped so, because the tiger was a powerful demon."

She cross-questioned him until she found out that there

was a Forest Ranger two miles up the road who had a rifle. She had driven to his bungalow and found him sick.

"I had never known such a maddening thing," she said. "The man was lying in bed looking perfectly healthy when we arrived, and had probably been too lazy to get up. As soon as he heard what we had come for, his face went green and he said he had a fever. As a matter of fact his brow was as cold as ice, but there was nothing that would make him get out of bed. I couldn't wait all day, so I borrowed the rifle and some ammunition and drove back to the village."

"But, my dear," said Catullus in alarm, "you didn't propose to shoot the tiger yourself."

"No, P.A., not then, but that was how it turned out. In any case, I've been on shoots with you, dear, and I haven't done so badly."

"But they were Princes' affairs with a hundred beaters and elephants, and in any case we weren't shooting at man-eaters."

"Well, I didn't mean to. When I got back to the village I called everybody together and told them to get up a hunting-party. Nobody would go. Poor children, I felt so sorry for them, they looked so scared. Then I spoke to one young man who was rather better looking and cleaner than the rest, one that I thought looked most likely to have the feelings of a gentleman—some of them have, when you get to know them. I said, 'Young man, I'm going after that tiger: are you coming with me?' That's all he needed, a blunt question, and the fine fellow said 'Yes.' Well, that got the rest in, and we made a party. The young man led the way because he was good at pugging."

'Pug' is the local name for an animal's spoor and this young man had quickly led them to the river bank.

"He was about four hundred yards in front when he threw up his hand. Then he leaped for his life at a tree and clung on to a branch. It was the man-eater all right," she said, "and a more disreputable-looking tiger I never did see."

"Man-eaters are usually old," said Catullus.

"Well, I had the gun and I raised it. 'Don't shoot,' shouted the man next to me and started jabbering something. Prayers, I shouldn't wonder, for the tiger to grow wings and flap peacefully away. I had no time for that sort of thing, so I fired. And," she said, giving the flowers a last touch, "I hit the tiger."

"Well *done*," said Catullus.

"I *think* it was his foreleg, but it may have been higher. I fired again, but I missed."

Catullus put his head in his hands. "A wounded man-eater," he said, "it's just hell in a striped skin, Winifred."

"Well, dear, if you think you could have killed it at that range, you should have shot it yourself."

"That is just what I shall have to do," said Catullus with no enthusiasm at all.

The tiger had given a roar of pain and leaped at the person whom he thought had hurt him, the young man clinging to the branch of the tree. The tiger jumped short and missed the man, except that he scraped him with the claws of one forepaw. He laid open the man's thigh from hip to knee.

Winifred had been very practical. As soon as they were sure the tiger had gone, she had roughly bandaged the young man, using the villagers' turbans to do so. She had put him in the car and brought him to our village. She had not troubled to come to Catullus' bungalow, but had gone straight to where the village headman had pointed.

"I thought it must be the dispensary," she said, "but I do not think it could have been. It was just a hut with at least a dozen goats tied up outside. Really, it was quite disgusting, P.A."

"Never mind," said Catullus, "I'll have the man sent out of Limbo to a hospital today."

"I wouldn't have taken him in at all if a man had not

come out, quite respectably dressed, and talking very good English. I thought he must be a doctor. As soon as he saw the man he pushed me aside and he and the driver got the man into the hut. Well, considering I'd taken all the trouble I had, I expected to be treated better than that, and I was most put out, I can tell you. But it's *never* right to lose one's temper. The next minute, there was the man asking me if *I* could tie a bandage. 'We can't do anything with him,' he said 'except chloroform him and I haven't got any.' The man was making an awful noise and wouldn't let them touch him. But as soon as I got to work, he stopped. By the time I'd finished bandaging him up he was actually giggling."

Winifred looked round at us with modest pride. But then, with changed expression, she turned to Catullus and said, "P.A., do you know what that man whom I supposed to be a doctor was doing? He was just kneeling over that poor young man and pretending to take an egg out of his ear and make it disappear. P.A.," she said in the severest voice she had yet used, "are you allowing an unqualified man to practice in Limbo?"

CHAPTER THIRTEEN

"QUALIFIED to take eggs out of his ears?" asked Bay, to create a diversion. Catullus looked at him gratefully. "Oh, but most highly qualified, I assure you," said Bay.

"Well, P.A.?" Winifred pressed Catullus and ignored Bay.

"Oh yes," said Catullus, showing a trace of spirit, "anything about eggs. Bay will explain."

"That would be kind of you, Mr. Leavis."

"Well," said Bay, "the Swami is a friend of mine."

"How nice for you, Mr. Leavis. *I* know a bishop. But we were not discussing our spiritual advisers, Mr. Leavis. We were talking about that man in the hut."

"He *is* the Swami," said Bay. "Or rather, was."

"Was?" asked Winifred. "Do I take it that he has been unfrocked?"

"I have never heard him call it a frock. He always called it a robe. Disrobed would be a better word."

"Let us by all means choose our words carefully, otherwise we might all grow a little confused," said Winifred. "Why was he disrobed?"

"He worked a miracle," said Catullus.

"You mean he faked a miracle," said Winifred intelligently.

"That's what he meant to do, but it didn't come off. It turned out to be a real miracle."

"So he was unfrocked?" said Winifred.

"He disrobed himself," corrected Bay.

Winifred considered this for a moment. "I've had a hard day," she said.

"My dear, of course *you* wouldn't understand," said Catullus.

"No, P.A., I'm much too stupid. Any other Civil Servant's wife would grasp the whole situation in a flash. Miracles are a commonplace in the modern Administrator's life, I'm sure, dear. I can't think why George at the India Office went to all that trouble to get me a seat on the plane. I wonder he didn't just send round a flying horse."

"I didn't mean it that way, Winifred. I meant that you couldn't be expected to understand it unless you had been here when it happened."

"P.A.," said Winifred, pouring herself a third cup of tea, "it is possible that, if I had been here, a vaudeville artist who had left Holy Orders under a cloud *might* be practicing conjuring tricks on aboriginals in a village dispensary. But I don't think so."

"No, Winifred," said Catullus.

"So you'll have that man turned out of Limbo immediately?"

"Well, I don't know. He's doing a lot of good."

"You cannot possibly give him your support. You're an official, P.A."

"I know. But the Administration has never troubled to set up a proper hospital."

"The Administration," said Winifred, "has never troubled to build a bridge across the river five miles down the road. But there is no reason for you to import a troupe of circus aerialists to teach the natives to cross the river by means of the flying trapeze. No, P.A., think of what the Resident will say. The man must go."

"But I can't just bundle him out on an externment order. He's Bay's guest."

Winifred looked kindlily at Bay. "I'm sure Mr. Leavis will understand. And he can explain it all to the Swami when they get back to Oxford. He can give one of his charming dinner-parties to *all* his interesting friends. And the catering will give him no trouble at all. The Swami can just produce eggs from his ear and pass them under the table to Mr. Leavis' other friends, who, I am sure, will prefer to eat them raw."

"I do understand," said Bay, "and I assure you, madam, it is not you who are old-fashioned, as you complained, but myself. You may say that I still live in the eighteenth century, when the Englishman cultivated eccentricity for eccentricity's sake, and became famous throughout Europe for doing so."

"And you *are* going back to Oxford, aren't you, Mr. Leavis?"

"I am."

"Then that's all right," said Winifred, "and it must be so interesting for you living in the past. They tell me, Mr. Leavis, that Oxford is the home of lost causes. But maybe they haven't looked for them properly. If they did I'm sure they'd find them all lying about in your rooms." She looked round her to find some topic, so that she could change the conversation.

"Such a pretty flower-bowl," she said, "where does it come from?"

"I got it in the village," I said.

"But how clever of you! Tell me all about the school." I told her.

"I think that's all very satisfactory. And it's very noble of you to work so hard for these poor unfortunate people."

I said something about being paid a salary to do it.

"Of course you're paid. I do think people talk a lot of nonsense about doing good works. Why should they say it's better if you do charitable work for nothing? It was all right for people like St. Francis of Assisi. The thing was just starting then, and it was only a sort of hobby, like motoring when I was a little girl. But nowadays it's different. When you pay people for doing silly things, like hitting a golf-ball and acting on the stage, why shouldn't you pay people for giving up their time to the world's unfortunates? I always say that if St. Francis were born today he'd be a permanent Civil Servant, like my husband. I think that the

way my husband ends his letters is very beautiful: 'I have
the honor to be, Sir, Your obedient servant.' It reminds
me of a monk standing with his hands in the sleeves of his
cassock and his cowl up. But there, you musn't make me
talk about my husband. Tell me about your school. Oh
yes, of course, you've told me. I think it's all very noble
and you're to be congratulated, P.A., on your vision in
taking these poor little mites away from slaving for their
parents in the fields. Their parents are such lazy people
and very bad farmers. I do hope you're teaching the children modern methods of agriculture?"

I said I hoped to.

"Do you get any vegetables these days, P.A.?" she
asked.

"Only on the truck once a week."

"There you are, you see," she said, "for years my husband has been trying to make these people start a vegetable
farm. But they're so lazy and insolent they just won't. They
say they can get all the vegetables they want by digging
around in the forest. But you can't expect Officials to live
on roots. We have told them again and again we will buy
all the vegetables they can grow for our own table, and
so we would. It would be much cheaper than getting them
in by truck. But they just prefer to sit idle and dig in the
forest like *boars*. I hope you're giving your boys a practical
education?"

I said I hoped I was.

"Well, why not start a vegetable farm and the boys
could run it all by themselves? We could buy the vegetables and they could make a little pocket money. Not too
much, of course. They're in school to learn, not earn. But
enough to buy sweets and things."

"I think it's a good scheme, Winifred," said Catullus,
then, catching my eye, he hurried on, "but we've got to
consider it from all points of view. I mean, wouldn't the
parents say we had taken them away from their fields to
make them work on our own?"

"But we're paying them."

"That makes it worse."

"Well, then, we won't pay them at all. We'll make it pure education."

"That's worse than ever."

"P.A., you're very difficult to please. The boys have got to grow something. What would you have them grow? Thistles?"

"No, dear, of course not."

"Then that's settled, isn't it?" she said, turning to me.

I said I supposed it was. Only it seemed to me, I said, that there was something wrong somewhere. Maybe, I thought, what was a sound argument outside Limbo wasn't so sound inside. I just thought that; I didn't know.

"Have you been out here long?" she asked me quietly. I began to wish that the woman would bawl and holler for just two minutes.

"No."

"Then I'll give you some advice. I give it to all young men who join the Service out here, and they always come back and thank me in the end. *Don't let the country get you down.* Just remember that, whatever these people may be, you're English. Now that's common sense, isn't it? Very well. Every morning when you get up just play a little game with yourself. Just say, this isn't Limbo, it's Hastings, or some place you're fond of in England. A nice, hot summer's day in Hastings. And what's right for Hastings is right for Limbo. Maybe you'll find these lazy Limbodians haven't got your bath water from the well or something really annoying like that. Don't just sit down and say you're a stranger in a strange land. Remember it's Hastings or Torquay or whatever you've chosen, and just think of all these people as *Trippers.* And for the rest of the day you won't give way a jot. None of us does, you know. We keep up appearances. You've got to, otherwise you'll go down and down. I do think people at home are so silly to laugh at that sensible man Stanley for what he said

when he found the missionary. 'Dr. Livingstone, I presume,' he said, and everybody thinks it no end of a joke.
But why? It's exactly what any of us in the Service would
have said. What do people expect the poor man to have
done? Crawl forward on his belly, knocking his forehead on
the ground?''

I said of course one could exaggerate the strangeness
of jungle life.

"Of course you can," said Winifred; "you must just
take it all in the day's work. Which reminds me, P.A.,
you must do something about these people's foolish superstition over tigers."

"It might be difficult," said Catullus.

"Not at all. You can start with the children. Tell them
that it's all nonsense about the tiger being a demon and
going away if you give him a goat. *You* can start the ball
rolling in the school," she said, coming back to me.

"I'll try. But I don't teach, you know."

"Get the masters to do it. Have them put it to the boys
in the form of a fairy-tale. Children love fairy-tales."

"But my masters are a dull lot. I don't think they could
tell a convincing fairy-tale."

"Well, then," she said, rising and shaking the snipped-
off stems of flowers from her lap, "get Mr. Leavis to do it
for you. *He* can." With that she turned and, saying that
she thought she'd lie down a little, she left us.

In the silence that followed, Catullus looked in an embarrassed way at Bay. Then he said, "I hope you'll go and
talk to the boys, you know. She'd appreciate it."

Bay thought for a moment and then said, "Of course."

ii

On our way down to the school that afternoon I
remembered that Bay had been there before. On that
occasion he had taught them the Dance of Good and Evil.
I thought of Winifred, and then impressed upon Bay

that, since he was with me, this would be a formal visit. He said he quite understood.

He found the boys drawing. I had not been there for some time (what with the excitement over the Swami and the general indolence of Limbo), and I had a guilty feeling that the unfortunate children might have been kept at drawing by their masters since Catullus had shown them how to do it, but gone away without giving them orders to stop. The floor was deep in sketches, and some of the boys were sitting on stools and working at easels that had been hastily made from pieces of the local timber.

The boys looked in very low spirits. I remembered giving orders that the boys were to have some clothes, not so much because I felt that they were unhappy in their jungle nakedness, but because I had promised that they should have free food and clothing. The headmaster was a solemn, slow-speaking man with a sense of the dignity of his calling, whose only drawback was that he considered himself immeasurably superior to jungle folk and had taken this post merely because jobs were scarce. Nevertheless, he was almost morbidly aware of his responsibilities as a servant of the Crown. He had walked many miles to a weekly bazaar in some distant village and bought up a bundle of ready-made clothing. This, it was only too clear, he had distributed to the boys. They now sat about sadly, fidgeting in cotton shirts and drill trousers, none of which fitted them. Indeed, their figures were so odd, with their long legs, sinewy from walking forest paths, narrow hips and protruding bellies, given them by their coarse food, that hardly any clothing ever invented in Europe would have fitted them, save perhaps a small toga.

As Bay and I entered the classroom, the boys stood up and said "Good night, sir" in English, a courtesy which I assumed the master to have taught them.

"We are honored by Your Honor's visit to the school," said the headmaster, who by this time had retrieved from his desk a small round black cap (denoting his social status in his own community outside Limbo) and put it on his head. "Thank you," said Bay. His eyes travelled critically over the boys.

"Tell me," he said to the master in a polite schoolmaster's voice, "do you have much trouble with drunkenness among the boys?"

I thought it my duty to rescue the master from his embarrassment. "Come now, Bay, you can do better than that. Just think back to the time when an important person visited your own school, and copy him."

"My headmaster," said Bay, "had the best cellar in the West Country. We always had trouble with drunkenness from the visitors, not the boys. Besides, every Limbodian drinks. It's a religious custom."

"There is no drinking in the school, Your Honor," said the headmaster with considerable dignity.

"I don't believe it."

"I assure Your Honor."

"Surely you don't lock the boys up at night? Well, what happens, then?"

The headmaster thought of this for a moment and then in his most official voice said, "Occasionally, in the course of taking my evening stroll, I pass a few of the boys lying drunk by the roadside, but there is *no* drinking *in* the school." He had the air of a man who has defended his accuracy against questions which, now all the facts were clear, might perhaps be considered rather too distrusting.

"I like 'I pass,' " said Bay; "I like that very much." He then went over to the boys and patted one or two of them uncertainly on the head. He smiled uncomfortably at some more, and then, reaching out his hand to pat another boy, found him approximately of his own height. He withdrew his hand quickly and instead took off his hat to him.

"You know," he complained, "I'm not really good at this sort of thing. I have no idea what to say to them."

"Well," I said, "you might give them permission to sit down."

"Good heavens, yes! I say, 'Sit down, boys, don't bother about all that fuss for me,' don't I?" He did, and the boys sat down. "It's all coming back to me. Now I turn to the headmaster and say, 'With your permission, sir, I'd like to declare the rest of today a half-holiday!' That's right, isn't it?"

"Quite right." So he said that as well.

The headmaster gave him a little bow and then announced the holiday to the boys.

"Now they raise three cheers," said Bay reminiscently.

But these boys did not. Maintaining a purposeful silence, they all stood up and stripped off their trousers. They then turned and helped one another in the more difficult task of getting out of their shirts. Not until they were clear of all clothing except the small modesty-bag which every Limbodian boy wears night and day, did their faces relax. Then with a universal grin and a shout they scampered from the classroom, jamming the door with a mass of naked deep-brown bodies and waving arms. In the middle of it was Bay, who, when he had recovered from his amusement at the boys undressing, had headed the rush for the door. When they were finally outside, an enormous clamor of voices began demanding a play, a game, a story, from Bay, while he was pushed and pulled in all directions at once. "Quiet! Quiet!" I heard him shouting, and then, when he had something like silence, "We can't have a play, it's much too hot. But I'll tell you a story."

The master, with tiny exclamations of dismay, was collecting the discarded shorts and shirts. I left him to it, and went outside. Bay had made the boys sit in a circle so that they were partly in the shade of the projecting eaves, partly in the shadow of a near-by tree. He himself, pulling up his trousers carefully to preserve the crease, and placing his black hat beside him, sat down on the ground in the middle of them. I thought for a moment how comically incongruous he looked, so elegantly dressed and so pale, in the middle of the circle of naked jungle children. But then

I saw by the faces of the boys, all intent upon him, that they saw nothing comic in him at all. He had been with them once before, and they had made up their minds, in agreement with his friends in Oxford, that he was a very likeable man.

He saw me and said, "Unfortunately I have forgotten what that silly woman wanted me to tell them."

"Something about tigers," I said, "with an uplifting and improving object."

"Ah yes," he said, "Tigers," and following with his eyes the master, who was crossing the compound, his arms full of the boys' clothes, "an uplift." He frowned at the tree for a moment, and then, when I had joined the circle, began.

iii

Once upon a time (said Bay) there was a discontented tiger. He was not only tired of living in the jungle— although he thought the jungle was indeed a very silly place, all trees, trees, trees; he was not only tired of having a striped coat—although he thought stripes were a silly design, just a lot of brown lines on a lot of yellow; he was deep-down-discontented with being a tiger.

He put his point of view to three other tigers.

"Don't you feel dissatisfied with just being a tiger?" he asked them.

One of them yawned so as to show off his magnificent teeth.

"Why should I be? Who has as lovely teeth as I have?" he said.

One of them pretended he saw something move in the grasses, and leaped thirty feet in one bound to find out what it was. "Dissatisfied?" he called back from among the grasses, "just find me an animal who can beat that leap."

But the last one was a thoughtful tiger and he put a paw on the discontented tiger's shoulder and said, "I know just how you feel!"

The discontented tiger was very grateful and said, "Do you really?"

The other tiger said, "Yes" in a sympathetic voice. "It's a sort of *empty* feeling, isn't it?"

"That's it. That's just it," said the discontented tiger. "Fancy you having it too."

The other tiger gave a shout of laughter (which sounded rather like laughing down a well) and slapped the discontented tiger on the back so hard that he fell over.

"It's nothing that a good hearty meal of buffalo won't cure," he said, and all the three tigers started laughing together.

The discontented tiger picked himself up, shook the dust from his coat, and said, "That's what I *mean*. Tigers have coarse minds," and he went off into the jungle with his head in the air.

But the pleasure of having been rude to the other tigers did not last for very long. He went on walking till he came to a road and then he sat down on his haunches to think things out. He curled his tail round so that the end of it lay comfortably across his front paws, and waited. Usually, curling his tail round his paws brought the most beautiful thoughts into his head, but not today. He unwound his tail and curled it the other way. But not even that did any good. He just sat there, feeling very low, and wishing that he itched behind the ears so that he could scratch himself with his hind leg. That usually passed five minutes or so quite pleasantly, but today he did not even itch.

He looked up and down the road to see if there was anything to take his mind off his troubles, but it was quite empty. A fly started buzzing round his head and he snapped at it. At the very first snap he caught it, so even that failed him as an amusement. Then he saw a dog. It was trotting down the road with the busy but worried expression which dogs always have when they're trotting by themselves, as though they are engaged on some urgent business which shows no prospect of being successful. When the dog was about level with him, the tiger said, "Well, hul*lo*!"

The dog leaped straight up in the air and fell down on his back.

"My!" said the tiger, "you did take a tumble. Won't you come up here and rest a bit till you get your breath back?" Seeing the dog hesitate, he added, "Please do. I must talk to someone soon or I shall burst into tears."

Now, the dog was a very ordinary dog, who had no ambition except to be left alone and allowed to go on quietly with his own affairs. He had found from experience that the best way to make sure of this was to agree with what everybody said to him, and never to get into arguments. Naturally, everybody liked him and thought him very intelligent, for a dog, and he was quite used to people telling him their troubles. He made it a principle never to say that things were not as bad as they seemed and never to say 'If I were You.' He was very popular with people in trouble. So the dog went and sat beside the tiger. He was rather nervous, of course, and he began the conversation in a somewhat confused manner.

"Well," he said, "you gave me a fright and no mistake. I thought you were a tiger."

"I am," said the tiger; "unfortunately."

"Ah," said the dog, nodding his head, "I understand," although he had no idea what the tiger was talking about.

"I wonder if you do," the tiger said, not wishing to be caught a second time that day.

"Oh yes," said the dog, "I understand. Not half I don't. It must be awful."

"*What* must be awful?" asked the tiger.

"What you said. Don't make me talk about it," and the dog shook his head again very sadly.

"But that's just what I want to do. I *want* to talk about it," said the tiger.

"That's right. Nothing like a good talk, I always say.

Two heads are better than one, if they're only sheep's heads."

"You're very confusing," said the tiger; "we're neither of us exactly sheep."

"You bet your life we're not," said the dog sagely.

"No," said the tiger; "you're a dog."

"Right," the dog agreed crisply.

"And I'm a tiger."

"Right again."

"As I remarked when we began this conversation," added the tiger, feeling they had not got very far. But all the same he felt better. "I'm so tired of being a tiger," he went on. "I don't suppose it's very exciting being a dog, is it?"

"It's terrible, just terrible," said the dog.

"Why?"

"No prospects. No variety. Nothing to it. What's it add up to, after all? Puppy. Dog. Dead dog—and there you are."

"I do feel we could do something better with our lives than just being a tiger and a dog. I mean, a dog and a tiger," he correct himself politely.

"You took the words right out of my mouth," said the dog.

"Now how would you suggest we go about it?" asked the tiger.

This had never happened to the dog before. People were usually so busy talking about themselves that they never stopped to inquire about his opinions. It worried him a good deal. He did not want to offend the tiger. He had heard that they were quick-tempered animals. Then he had an inspiration.

"We might walk on our hind legs," he said.

"Is that very inspiring?" said the tiger doubtfully.

The dog did not like the tone of the tiger's voice, so he just plunged on: "And use our front paws as hands."

"Oh yes, quite," said the tiger. He had no idea what

hands were, but he felt that the dog would think he was
not intellectual enough if he admitted it, and might stop
talking to him.

"Then we could live in houses," and the dog explained
what a house was. "We could wear clothes," and the dog
explained that too. He went on talking and talking, describing all that he knew about the village up the road and
the people in it, until the tiger thought he was the greatest
genius he had ever met.

"But all this is wonderful," said the tiger. "I don't
know how you can manage to think of such things. I'm so
very grateful to you."

"Don't mention it," said the dog, "anything to oblige."

"You don't know what you've done for me," said the
tiger, getting rather sentimental. "Before I met you I was
so depressed I could have lain down and died, I thought
that there was nothing beyond being a tiger. Nothing
higher and nobler. But now you've given me something to
live for. Do you think," he said anxiously, "that an ordinary
tiger like myself could ever hope—I mean, if he tried very
hard—to be a wonderful person like the ones you described
so very well?"

The dog looked at him critically. "I shouldn't wonder,"
he said.

"Oh, I'm so glad. I shall go away into the forest by
myself for a bit and practice. Hind legs, I think you said.
Yes, I can manage that, I'm sure. I've got very strong
hind legs," he said, thinking of his tiger muscles for the
first time with a certain amount of satisfaction. "Then
there's clothes," he said. "Clothes." Suddenly his spirits
went down again and he said, "Oh dear, oh dear, it's all
so difficult. I'll never be able to do it."

The dog felt a splash on the top of his head and he was
just about to say "Hullo, raining" as he always did whenever there was a shower. Then he looked up and saw that
big tears were running down the tiger's cheeks and dripping off the end of his whiskers. The dog felt really sorry

for the tiger, and for the first time in his life he broke
his rule.

"Oh, things aren't as bad as all that," he said. "Some
people manage it."

"Who?" said the tiger, sniffing.

"People," the dog replied, "in the forest. You'll meet
them one day maybe."

"Shall I?" said the tiger excitedly, wriggling his
whiskers to get rid of the tears. "How wonderful. But
I wouldn't like to meet them until I can do all the things
that they can do. Or at least some of them. I'd be so
ashamed to be an ordinary good-for-nothing tiger."

"That's the spirit," said the dog. "Never say die."

"I'll start practicing straight away."

"Easy does it," said the dog. "Well, I must be off.
It's been nice knowing you."

"It's been nice knowing *you*."

"Much obliged, I'm sure," said the dog, and he trotted
off down the road, worrying about his business, which
still did not look at all hopeful.

The tiger went back to the other three tigers and
poured out the whole story of how wonderful a tiger
could be if he only aspired to Higher Things and worked
hard to be like these people that the dog had told him
about, and who stood on their hind legs and lived in
houses and wore clothes. Of course they would have to
give up vulgarities like killing animals, because these
people were all Good and Kind and Loving and never
hurt anybody. The dog hadn't said that, but he knew it
must be so. It came to him as he was talking to his friends.
This time all the three tigers yawned, not because they
wanted to show off their teeth, but because they thought
he was talking the most appalling nonsense. But the tiger
was too full of his new ambition to notice, and went off
into the jungle to practice. He practiced twelve hours a
day. He stood on his hind legs until they ached, and he
tore down big leaves and put them all over himself and

tried to make them look like the things the dog had called clothes. He worked so hard that he almost forgot to eat. His coat grew shabbier and shabbier, his ribs began to show and his whiskers fell out. The other three tigers tried to argue with him, but he just stared over their heads and made silly answers. So they gave up arguing and took it in turns to watch him, not so that he would notice, but from the bushes. They were really quite good-intentioned tigers, and although they thought he talked a great deal of nonsense, they did not want him to come to any harm. They also left fresh-killed buffaloes in his path. As he was staggering along on his hind legs with his head in the air, he would trip over the dead buffaloes. Then he would say, "My, but I'm hungry," and one or other of the three tigers would watch to see that he got a good meal.

One day the discontented tiger (although he'd quite forgotten that he was ever discontented) was walking along in the forest, sometimes on his hind legs and sometimes on all fours, when he happened to glance between some bushes. Then he felt so weak with happiness he had to sit down: for there, in a clearing, standing on two legs, and wearing far more clothes than the tiger had ever imagined possible, was one of Them. The tiger blinked his eyes and dug his hind claw into his flank to see if he was dreaming; but he was wide awake, and it was true. He pulled himself together, bit off a big leaf and held it against his chest to look like clothes, and got ready for the moment he had been imagining for so long.

He got up on his hind legs, and was very proud to see that he could do it very easily. He tottered forward through the bushes and came out into the clearing.

"Well, hul*lo*," he said, but it wasn't very distinct, what with his excitement and the leaf in his mouth.

"There he is," said the man. "Look out!"

The tiger said the speech that he'd planned to say as he came forward. He had to drop the leaf to say it, but he thought the speech was worth it. "I've waited so long to see you," he said. "I've heard about how wonderful and kind and loving you are, and now at last . . ." But he could not finish the speech because at that point the man shot him dead.

"What an ugly beast it is," said the man as he lowered his gun.

iv

Bay finished. The boys looked at him with round sad eyes, and did not say a word.

"But," said Bay cheerfully, "one of the three tigers who were looking after the discontented tiger had seen the whole thing happen from some near-by bushes."

"Well!" said this tiger, "of all the conceited, rude, ill-mannered, snobbish animals I have ever seen, that thing on two legs standing over my poor well-meaning friend is quite the worst. Let me see," said the tiger, biting his whiskers, "just how far is he away? Ah-ah. Thirty feet, I should say. Yes, thirty feet," and out he sprang.

"Well, it was exactly thirty feet, and he knocked the man down and dragged him off into the jungle. And whatever happened to him there, he richly deserved it."

The headmaster, who had come back during the story, coughed quietly, and began ringing a little bell that swung from the veranda. In his arms he held the bundle of discarded trousers and shirts.

"Time to dress for tea, boys," he said, with an ingratiating smile to Bay and myself.

"SO you're off, Mr. Leavis," said Winifred.

Bay, who was watching his luggage being loaded into the back of the truck, nodded.

"I've told the Swami to be ready with his bags, and you'll be able to pick him up at the hut," she went on. "I quite liked him the last time I met him. He was so reasonable when I explained that a proper doctor will be coming and that perhaps it would be better if he went back to the stage."

"He might not have been so reasonable if you'd told him it would take a year to get the doctor's post sanctioned and then six months to find a doctor who'll take it," Catullus said. All morning he had been in an uneasy gloom, broken only by exaggerated politeness to Bay in passing him things at the breakfast table.

"No, P.A.," Winifred said, taking his arm, "if we advertised all the secrets of Administration, *nobody* would be reasonable. You should know that, of all people, P.A."

Bay superintended the stowage of the Swami's telephone box, and when it was placed to his satisfaction came back to us on the veranda, his black hat in his hand.

"Well, now," he said, "if I can only find the driver, who seems to have disappeared into the servants' quarters, I think I can start."

"Oh, do *hurry*, Mr. Leavis," Winifred said with an arch smile.

"That has less than your usual subtlety," Bay said to her. "You must be careful. Don't let the country get you down."

"Oh, I didn't mean it like that. It was just a little joke. You see, the police are after you, Mr. Leavis, all the six policemen in Limbo. At least they would be, only the poor dears are busy elsewhere this morning. But I wouldn't rely on them being busy this afternoon."

"Winifred," said Catullus, "what have you been up to? I do wish, you know, you would not play with the Administration of Limbo as though it were your own private doll's house. One day you will get people into trouble."

"I've *got* people into trouble," she said contentedly. "Mr. Leavis, for one, if he doesn't fly, fly, fly from the hounds of the law. I've had a chat with that clever man, Mr. Justice Bose."

A servant came in with a small hamper.

"Oh, thank you," she said, taking it. She gave it to Bay, "I've put a few little things to eat in it for you, in case you can get nothing on the way."

"That's very kind of you," said Bay.

"And there's a file hidden in a loaf of bread in case the worst should happen," she added in a whisper.

"My dear, what is the conspiracy?" asked Catullus.

"Not mine. It's Mr. Leavis' conspiracy. I explained it all to Mr. Bose. About arranging the miracle to impress him and all that. So eccentric and charming, I thought it. But Mr. Bose isn't an Englishman, of course, and anything but eighteenth century. He seemed quite annoyed. He talked about defeating the ends of justice. I can never understand lawyers. Can you, Mr. Leavis? As I tried to explain to him, you weren't defeating the ends of justice at all."

"That was generous of you."

"Yes. I told him you were defeating its beginnings. He wants to swear out a warrant or something, but he doesn't quite know his position with regard to my husband. Anyway, he wanted to swear all right, only he didn't like to do so in the presence of a lady."

"Of course you told him that Bay's plot didn't work?" Catullus said anxiously. "I mean, it was a real miracle."

"Oh yes," nodded Winifred. "But I don't think I really

impressed him. My faith had been shaken. You see, I had a talk with that witch-doctor with the nice manners. He's come down here for the eclipse of the moon tonight. Some devil-worship or other. But anyway, that's his business. What interested me was what he said when I told him how wonderful it was that the Swami had the gift of healing. He said, 'Yes. We did very well, didn't we? The boy was one of my students. I always thought he was stupid, but he showed great talents.' "

Bay put down the hamper and, pulling up his trousers to save the crease, sat on it. He put his hat on his head, then took it off again. He held it in his hands and looked at it as though it were a crown he was for ever renouncing. Then he said, "I see it all now."

"Then that makes two of us, Mr. Leavis," said Winifred sweetly.

"What about the man in jail?" asked Catullus.

"He'll probably get ten years, Mr. Bose thinks. Or be locked up as a lunatic. Mr. Bose seems to want to do a lot of locking up."

Catullus was staring at his wife in distress. He transferred his gaze to Bay. Bay looked up at him, and then quickly back at his hat. Catullus' eyes wandered to me. Then he jerked his head up and began to look like a Roman statue again.

"Go and find the driver, will you?" he said to me.

I went into the servants' quarters very willingly, because the farewell party on the veranda was growing very strained. The driver was not there, and I looked round the compound. No one was to be seen. I shouted his name several times, but there was no answer.

"It's all right, he's out front, shooting at a hedgehog with his bow and arrow," said a voice behind me. It was Catullus. "He'll be through soon. Don't worry about the driver. I only sent you here to have a private word with you. We've got to do something quickly."

"Yes, of course. About Bay. Is it serious?"

"No, not about Bay. I shall fix all that. I can't do anything about the Judge, because I mustn't interfere in the Judiciary, but the Police are under my control. I'll give them all a holiday starting at noon today."

"You have to give a reason."

"I'll find something. I'll say it's to celebrate the birthday of Sir Robert Peel."

"Fine. Then you mean, do something about the man in jail?"

"I've got that settled, too." He looked at me uncertainly, obviously not quite sure in his mind that he should tell me. The horn of the truck sounded to let us know that Bay was ready to go.

"The driver must have shot his hedgehog. Bay's going," said Catullus, with great rapidity. "Look. Go in the truck with him. Give any excuse so that Winifred won't be suspicious. Say you're looking for a site for a new school. Say anything, but tell Bay . . ." he paused, and the horn sounded again, "tell Bay I'm going to visit the man in jail and slip him the key to his cell. I hope he's got the sense to use it in the night."

"Catullus, that's wonderful. But what will Winifred say if she finds out?"

"That's just what Bay or you or somebody must do something about. *Get the woman away from here.*"

I was so surprised by his change of tone and the look of determination on his face that I could find nothing to say, just nodding my head. The horn clamored for us, and I took Catullus by the arm and led him back to the veranda to say goodbye to Bay.

ii

A few miles from the borders of Limbo we came to a valley that was still wet from a heavy shower of rain that had fallen the night before. The truck went very cautiously over the earth road, but soon sank into a mudpatch, axle-deep.

We got out and the driver tried to use the engine to pull the truck out of the bog, but he failed. Bay, the Swami, whom we had picked up as he stood forlornly outside his closed-up hut, and myself went into the jungle and gathered long poles of fallen bamboo. We brought them back to the road, trailing them behind us. We laid them around the wheels and behind the truck, until we had made a bamboo road some twenty feet long. It took us three hours to complete, and by the time the road was ready it was evening.

The truck moved a little when the driver put it in gear, breaking the bamboo poles and throwing off a dangerous shower of splinters. We watched for a while behind the shelter of a rock, but it was soon clear that the truck was not going to get out. The engine stalled, and the truck, bearing with all its weight on a single section of our road, broke through and was once more firmly in the mud.

We talked to the driver, who said that he would have to go back and get some bullocks from a small village which we had passed. He would be about two hours. We could wait where we were, or walk up the road to a village on the border where there was a small bungalow for the use of travellers. We had no torch, but the moon was up and we decided to walk.

Bay's black hat had fallen into the mud while we were building the road. He held it in his hand as he walked, waving it to make it dry. "Winifred mentioned David Livingstone this morning," said Bay, "and the most remarkable hat ever to come out of the tropics was that missionary's so-called consular cap. It had nothing to do with consuls, and, in design, nothing to do with anything but Livingstone's taste in head-gear. It had a peak, a sun-flap at the back, and was decorated with thick bands of gold braid. When Livingstone arrived in England after he had walked across Africa he was astonished at his fame. Everywhere he went people crowded to look at him. Very soon he professed to grow tired of the publicity and complained that he was never for a moment left alone. He might, perhaps, more easily have secured privacy, if, wherever he went, at dinner-parties, or driving in a car, or shopping in Regent Street, he had not insisted on wearing his extraordinary hat. An odd flaw in the character of a very remarkable man." There was a long silence.

"He's a fine man," said the Swami.

"Livingstone?"

"Who? Oh, the man you were talking about. No. I was thinking of Catullus."

"Then I agree with you."

"He's the only one of us who isn't bogus," said the Swami. "When he asks questions he wants to know. When we ask questions we want to talk. When he says he thinks he's wrong he wants to be put right: when we say it, we want to show how clever we are even about ourselves. He does good to poor people like that man in jail, not because they amuse him but just because they don't. He's got one thing that none of the rest of us has got, and that's pity."

"His wife is a clever woman," said Bay. "I wonder when she first discovered that Catullus had the makings of a saint."

"I wonder," said the Swami, "how long it took her to see that the saint should be a good Civil Servant."

"I don't like her, either," said Bay.

"I hope she never finds out about the key."

"She mustn't," said Bay. "She musn't. We must think of a very powerful exorcism."

We walked on for an hour, and we saw that the moon was turning red. The trees which grew on either side moved closer together, until one could see nothing between the trunks. The road went grey, as though buried under volcanic ash. Everywhere there were fire-flies, whole groups of them flashing in unison, each group with its own peculiar rhythm. Soon we heard drums, and coming to a clearing we found a fire had been lit and that a ceremony was in progress.

We stopped, and as we did so the central figure in the ceremony got up, waved his hand, and came running towards us. There was very little light from the nearly eclipsed moon, but we could see that it was the witch-doctor from the hill with three peaks.

"I thought you were at the central village," said the Swami, after the witch-doctor had welcomed him with delight.

"I meant to be there for the eclipse. Usually we hold our ceremony there, and it must be a lucky place. The ceremony has never failed. The moon has always come out quite bright again. But this time there was a stranger there and I did not think . . ."

"I understand. That's why I'm leaving Limbo," said the Swami.

"Tell me," said Bay, "about the miracle."

The witch-doctor peered at Bay and then, with a most friendly smile, said, "You must be the man who worked so hard to release the unhappy person who is in prison."

"I wanted to set him free, yes. But what about the miracles that the Swami did? Tell me."

"We are all very grateful to you for trying to convince the Judge. We heard about your plans."

"Did you . . . help . . . my plans in any way?"

"We were all very anxious to see the man free. He is such a good man and none of us lives very long in jail. We thought your plans were very kind, but miracles are so very rare and little boys who are fond of acting so very common, at least in Limbo. Yes, we thought it our duty to help your plans . . ." The witch-doctor paused, and avoided Bay's eyes. "It is such a pity," he said, "that the stranger should come and spoil all our plans."

iii

The witch-doctor looked at the moon. The drummers had stopped when he had left the circle, and now he threw up his hands in dismay.

"Oh dear, Oh dear, just look at what a mess I've left the moon in." He clapped his hands, turning away to the drummers. "Come along, come along, beat up, beat up, or the moon will be dark all night." He walked rapidly back to his place.

Bay said, "Wait here a moment," and went after him. The witch-doctor sat down and Bay sat beside him. The moon was blood-red, and a breeze blew the flames of the fire here and there, so that it was difficult to see what was happening. It seemed that Bay was talking earnestly to the witch-doctor, and once or twice the wizard nodded his head.

Then Bay got up and came over to where we were standing. "You wait here," he said to me, "until the truck arrives. It won't be long now. When it comes take it back to the central village and take the witch-doctor with you. He will explain on the way."

"What are you and the Swami going to do?"

"Finish our walk. I'm told it's only four miles to the border."

"Well, goodbye, Swami. Goodbye, Bay. I shall miss you."

"Not, I think," said Bay, "for a day or two." He shook hands, lifting his black hat, while the drums roared behind him and some men began a frantic caper.

He and the Swami moved off down the ash-grey road. The Swami made a remark and I heard Bay answering him. Then they were too far away for me to distinguish them in the shadows, because the moon had reached its full eclipse.

iv

" 'We only got the moon clear by the skin of our teeth,' the witch-doctor said to me, 'and if that doesn't prove she's a witch, what does. To say nothing of the tiger.' Oh, he was a very angry man," said Catullus with a happy grin.

He had come to my bungalow in a state of great excitement. A deputation of Limbodians had waited on him in the
morning, all armed with bows and arrows and headed by
the witch-doctor.

"They kept on testing their bows and arrows while the
witch-doctor was talking, and one of them shot down a
bird that was flying overhead, just casually, as a sort of
underlining to what the witch-doctor was saying about
Winifred. He had it all very nearly laid out. Item: the
eclipse of the moon was almost disastrously long; item:
she had caused a man to be wounded by a tiger; item: she
had deliberately annoyed the tiger by unnecessarily shooting at it and missing, so that it had come back to the village
that night and, ignoring the goat they had tied up for it,
stolen away a baby; item: she had matched her witchcraft
with our local witch and stolen away the Swami. Then she
had bound him by spells so that to save his life he had had
to run away from Limbo; item: she had pulled to pieces a
garland so as to dissipate the good magic of a kindly gift;
item the last: she had used for domestic purposes a jar
dedicated to holding food for the tiger-god, and clearly
marked on the outside with tigers to show what it was
used for. The witch-doctor said he could hold the Limbodians back just so far, but he couldn't say what they
would do if provoked. When he said this one or two of the
men began feeling the points of their arrows in an absent-
minded way."

"What did you say?"

"As I explained later to Winifred behind closed shutters
(I insisted that she hide herself) I had to take official
cognizance of it. Once trouble like that starts, you don't
know where it will end. Open rebellion, I shouldn't
wonder," said Catullus with satisfaction.

"Is she going?"

"Yes. Today. She argued a little, but I said it was a
question of my career. I couldn't have twenty years of
service blotted by a Court of Inquiry, especially on the topic

of my wife being a witch. That seemed to convince her."
Catullus heaved a great sigh. Then he said, "It was a very
dark night last night, wasn't it? You were out on the road.
Was it *very* dark?"

"Very. Did you give the man the key?"

"Yes. He'd gone when they brought breakfast to him
this morning. The warders reported it to me immediately,
but I was having a bath. It was rather late by the time I got
to the office and sent out a search party." He paused. "You
saw Bay go?"

"Yes."

"Do you think he'll come back? I'm writing to him to
thank him for this morning. Do you think he'll come back?"

"Well, yes, from what I overheard him saying as he
went away."

"Tell me," said Catullus.

v

When they had said goodbye to me (I told Catullus)
they went off together down the road. I heard the Swami
say to Bay, "Well, we've made history in Limbo."

"Contemporary history," answered Bay in a dissatisfied
voice. "Now what is needed is for us to give a past history
to Limbo. I have been thinking it over. I have been making
some notes. Of course, I shall need to do more research before they are complete. I must now tell you of the first and
rather eccentric King of the Limbodians that I have invented . . ."

He went on talking, but he was too far away for me to
hear what he said.